Compromised for Christmas

The Jennings Family Book One

Lizzie C Koz

Contents

Content Warnings

Compromised for Christmas is a steamy historical romantic comedy, but I want to share a few content warnings that some readers might want to be aware of. If you do not wish to read the content warnings please skip ahead to the start of the book.

*

*

*

*

*

CONTENT WARNINGS:

This book contains adult content and explicit language. It contains detailed sex scenes between two consensual adults that include elements of BDSM such as but not limited to: voyeurism, exhibitionism, toy use, rough/primal play, choking, degradation, and cum play.

It also contains themes that may be distressing to readers including pet loss (prior to book, but discussed on page), harassment/bullying by secondary characters (minimal mentions), mental health struggles around negative self-perception and loneliness, and using sexual encounters as a coping mechanism.

Author's Note

A NOTE TO MY READERS

Hi there, I'm Lizzie! Before you dive into my book, there are a few things I'd like to share:

First and foremost, I write stories that are meant to be enjoyable and relatable to the modern reader. I do an endless amount of research to create a historical backdrop for these stories and you'll find some of that fun research at the end of this book.

BUT. I'll be upfront—my writing has a modern tone, and sometimes I throw in a bit of playful wordplay that isn't fully historically accurate, all for the sake of humor. For example, in this book, I make a subtle play on the word head...as in giving head. That phrase was not something coined until the mid-1900s. But the thing is, sex jokes are funny. I realize this style isn't for everyone and I want you to know what to expect before you begin so there are no surprises.

Historical romance is a place where we can find many types of stories—it is a fantasy where we can highlight certain persons or movements that hold meaning to us. In my world, you won't find heroes with missing teeth, gout, or infested with the pox. My characters have all their teeth and they bathe (regularly, believe it or not!). They smell nice, because, let's be honest, the only thing that should stink is cheese.

My heroines have fire in their veins, and the men they fall for appreciate their intelligence and desire for autonomy. You'll find a diverse cast, where love triumphs no matter who the characters are—whether they're neurodivergent, LGBTQ+, or BIPOC. Love has always found a way, even in the face of obstacles, and in my stories, those barriers are always broken.

If this is not how you take your tea, this book is probably not for you. It is a lovely world we live in that we have a plethora of options out there to suit each and every one of our preferences.

So, dear reader, if my style sounds like something you'd enjoy, I invite you to step into this fantasy world with me and indulge in a little escape. Grab your wine (or drink of choice) and let's have some fun!

Xoxo,

Lizzie

1

Fitz

Thornfield Hall,
Jennings Family Country Seat
Kent, England
Christmastide Ball
December 1816

THE HONORABLE FITZWILLIAM JENNINGS, younger brother to the Earl of Bentley and next in line for the earldom, nearly always had his nose buried in a book. Which was why, when he entered his drawing room at his family's country estate, he failed to notice something was different in his domain.

Breasts.

Naked breasts.

Glorious breasts.

Dear Lord. This was the correct drawing room, was it not? The one he had repurposed as his study for working on his Italian translations? Yes, there was his desk. And there was his settee. With breasts on it.

His eyes stretched wide, so wide the room grew blurry. He attempted to rub his vision clear and was immediately met with glass and metal. Right. Spectacles—which he wore for reading, not distance.

He hastily removed them. But the breasts were still there.

"I've been waiting for you," the breasts said in a low, husky voice.

Wait. No. That couldn't be correct. Those words, and now a curse, came from *the woman* the breasts belonged to.

Oh my God, there is a bare-bosomed woman in your study, Fitz.

And what did a man do when presented with a bare bosom? He fled, of course.

Fitz dropped his spectacles and book, slapped a hand over his eyes, and spun toward the exit of his study. "My a-apologies, my lady. Miss. Ma'am." He rushed to the door, or at least what he was fairly certain was the—

Crack!

Bloody fuck.

His skull rang and throbbed like a gong. He sucked in a sharp breath and clutched his aching head, stumbling backwards. Holy buggering ballocks, that bloody hurt. His heel connected with something and—

Fitz's back collided with the floor. *Oomph.* The air shot from his lungs, and his eyes slammed shut as pain ricocheted through his head. Now the back of his skull screamed in pain, too. Along with his back. And his arse.

"Oh my God!" a feminine voice squealed. "Are you hurt?" The rustle of skirts interrupted the incessant throbbing in his head, and then small hands prodded his chest, then patted his cheeks. "My lord? Are you well? Can you speak?"

He hesitantly opened his eyes. And the answer was, in fact, no. No, he wasn't well. And no, he couldn't speak. Because breasts. There were so many breasts. Well. Not so many. There were only two, he supposed. But dear God. Breasts. In his face. Breasts. Did he say breasts?

He went to speak, but all he managed was a groan. The woman's slim blonde eyebrows pinched, her gaze darting over him as though looking for the source of his pain. Too bad the pain was everywhere. From his pride to his posterior.

Heat seared his cheeks, and his all-too-familiar embarrassment caught up with him. As did his nervous sweating. Someone shouldn't be able to sweat this much when it was as frigid as tits outside.

Urghh. Why did you think of tits, Fitz?

It wasn't enough he had just run into a pair of breasts—which was nerve-inducing all in itself—but the bosom belonged to the loveliest flaxen-haired, rosy-cheeked woman he'd ever seen.

Fitz was tongue-tied and tactless by default, but when he was around a beautiful woman? Let's just say there was a reason he rarely attended balls or soirées or supper parties or places where there were people. Hence why he was about to hide in his study while a ball went on at his country estate.

"My lord?" the woman said again, concern coating her words.

And then she slapped him.

His gaze shot to hers, and his mouth popped open. "Did you just slap me?"

Well, would you look at that, Fitzy. You found some words!

A breath exploded from her, and her body slumped. Egads, now her breasts dangled tantalizingly close to his face. He gulped. Audibly. Which only had him inhaling her cinnamon-sweet scent. Sodding hell. She *would* smell like the very essence of Christmas.

His gaze darted between her all-too pouty pink lips and her all-too perky pink nipples. Did she taste like Christmas, too...

"Oh, thank goodness," she was saying, blessedly interrupting *that* train of thought. "I feared you had done irreparable damage or some such when you seemed unable to speak."

He frowned. Was the woman unaware that her bosom was exposed? She was leaning over him, chattering away about—well, he wasn't actually certain. The combination of diddies in his face and knocks to the dome had made him deaf and dumb.

"Would you cover yourself?" he finally managed tersely. Before he did something outrageous. Like lick a stranger's nipples.

She tensed, and he winced. That had come out a touch boorish. But damnation, the woman seemed to have no compunction about waggling her wobblers in his face.

"I beg your pardon, my lord," she said stiffly. "How terribly thoughtless of me to come rushing to your aid and not cover myself beforehand. I hope I have not offended your delicate sensibilities."

Sweat trickled down the nape of his neck. He was botching this. If that was even possible. If something started out botched, was there even room for further botching?

Fitz botched it even further.

"Urrrgung..."

Lovely, Fitz. What in the bloody hell was that supposed to be?

She cocked her head. "Pardon?" She blinked down at him through thick, blonde lashes. Blonde lashes that framed vibrant green irises currently clouded in confusion. "Maybe I should ring for help." She drew out the words. "I fear you did damage your brain."

No, he really hadn't. This was actually quite normal for Fitz. Unfortunately.

2

Georgiana

This wasn't normal.

Miss Georgiana Hartley peered down at the amber-haired, red-faced, perspiring man beneath her. He wasn't even forming words. It wasn't typical for men to sweat that much, was it? Or turn the exact shade of cooked lobster. Come to think of it, with the sweating…he did somewhat resemble a buttered lobster.

"Maybe I should ring for help," she said slowly. "I fear you did damage your brain."

He shook his head vigorously, her body shaking atop him. The adamant gesture would have reassured her if the man hadn't immediately frozen, his wide-eyed gaze falling to her chest. A choked noise left him before his gaze began playing a rigorous game of shuttlecock around the room.

She blew out a sigh and glanced around the chamber that would have been just right for her attempted assignation: cozy and intimate, with its dark-wood walls and earth-toned furnishings. It *felt* seductive. Perfect. Or so she had thought.

She had been so excited to find an empty room; the first few she'd tested out had been occupied. One of which had been Lord Wessex with a woman who was very much *not* his fiancé. His fiancé...whose family was currently hosting this ball. Goodness, the nerve of the man, sleeping with other women in Lady Felicity's own home. She grimaced—both at that thought and the wheeze that just came from the man beneath her. Perhaps if she gave the startled clam a moment, he'd collect himself.

Georgiana soothingly rubbed his chest—his surprisingly *hard* chest. And not because of bones, which one would expect from the tall, thin, bespectacled stranger who had been buried in a book when he'd entered the room. No, that smooth, solid feeling beneath her fingertips was flesh, *muscle*. Who could he be? She definitely hadn't seen him in the ballroom.

But her soothing strokes, which had possibly, potentially—fine, definitely—turned exploratory, had the opposite effect she was hoping for. More wheezing. Disappointment settled heavily in her belly. Her fingers twitched with desire to discover. But this was undoubtedly not the man to do that with. If she tried to fondle him, he would probably have an apoplexy. What a waste.

Goodness, this had gone completely arse-backwards. Tits-sideways. She had been fishing for a savage shark and ended up with a crimson crustacean.

Georgiana had been positioning herself for optimal seduction as she awaited the Duke of Ironcrest. To be honest, she hadn't been certain the Duke would accept the invitation she'd murmured to him, but he rarely attended these events, and she wasn't going to give up on a chance to *experience*. Unfortunately, Georgiana's mother had a horrible habit of throwing Georgiana—quite literally—into the path of unmarried gentlemen. So the Duke had probably thought this a scheme to trap him into marriage. It wasn't, though.

What it was...

...was curiosity.

Georgiana had realized fairly young that she possessed...urm...particular proclivities. It may have been influenced by the fact that she had gotten her hands on *Fanny Hill: Memoirs of a Woman of Pleasure* when she had been just fourteen. Or when she had stumbled upon a secret stash of lewd publications beneath her older brother's bed after he'd left for America. Pamphlets that were full of illustrations of naughty, naughty things. Naughty things like women having their bottoms spanked, their hands bound, being watched, and watching as these naughty things were performed.

She fingered the man's cravat and then frowned. He was distressingly still besides an odd, gurgling noise emanating from him. This awkward man under her—who might have since expired—definitely did *not* partake in such things. But the Duke of Ironcrest supposedly did. Hence her attempt at an assignation.

She let out a sigh. Failed attempt.

Said bumbling man fumbled beneath her—he was alive!—and procured a handkerchief from his trousers. He lifted it to his head, the back of his hand skimming her nipple. She sucked in a breath. He froze. Again. His eyes went comically wide, and his face went even *more* crimson. Tingles. That had given her tingles. Why couldn't she have successfully rendezvoused with the Duke? She wanted tingles, blast it. She wanted to feel *something*. Something would be better than the empty, invisible existence she currently lived. Or the future that loomed—

"Gurrg," the man said, interrupting her maudlin thoughts.

Goodness, she was always getting lost in her thoughts. That's what happened when one's only company was oneself and one's dog. An anvil landed on her heart. Just oneself now. Now that her beloved Bernie had passed.

She shook her head, shoving away her heartache before she turned into a blubbering, bare-breasted mess. Her gaze tracked a bead of sweat slipping into the man's curls. Whatever could *gurrg* mean?

He cleared his throat and dabbed his forehead, looking everywhere but at her. "I meant to say, my apologies," he said hoarsely.

Ah, yes. *Gurrg* clearly meant apologies. How could she have misinterpreted that? The poor thing sounded like he hadn't had a drink of water in days, a man stranded in a desert. She should probably show him some mercy, get off him, and cover herself. But she felt oddly content here, making this flustered man even more flustered. Was it unusual that she felt more comfortable leaning on a stranger, bubbies on full display, than she did anywhere else?

"It is quite all right," she said with a smile, giving his chest a little pat.

But nothing was all right. Which was how Georgiana found herself here in the first place. She was tired of being the tempting carrot dangled before a *ton* of braying donkeys. That wasn't the kindest comparison, she knew. But it was oddly fitting, given the last man she danced with back in the ballroom. The one it seemed frighteningly possible she could end up marrying.

Georgiana didn't exist for any other purpose. She was useless as a woman to her father, and in her mother's eyes, the only way to fix that was to use Georgiana's beauty and their family's wealth to snatch a titled lord. Georgiana didn't give a fig about titles. She did give a fig about titillation. So, her rebellious self had thought, why not seek out said titillation with the depraved lords her mother wanted so desperately to marry her to? Well, the scandalous, handsome ones. She could do without the donkeys.

But instead, she had ended up with the one man—who now appeared to be struggling for air—in all of Christendom, who apparently couldn't partake in such activities. Perhaps he was a virgin. He had run *from* her instead of *to* her when he had accidentally stumbled upon her half-naked. That was typical of virgins, wasn't it? She snorted at the irony, considering she was a virgin.

Enough, Georgiana. You've tortured the poor lobster long enough. She pressed her hands on his chest and pushed herself up.

"Meep," he squeaked. A look of horror promptly washed over his face.

She tried her damnedest to hide her smile, but his horrified gaping—and yes, even more gurgling—was too much for her. Georgiana ran a finger down the bridge of his sharp, straight nose, a giggle slipping free. He was such an adorable little freckled lobster. She leaned down, letting her finger trail over his freckled, rosy cheek, pausing at his prominent cheekbone. Her heart did a little flip.

Their gazes clashed, and the flipping started up in her stomach. Lord, the lobster's *eyes*. They were a smoky, deep whisky—amber with dark mahogany striations. And just like the amber liquid, they were intoxicating. Her gaze fell to his lips, and her tongue slipped out, coasting over her own. Little girls were told of stories of enchanted frogs that transformed into princes with a kiss. She hovered lower, one hand resting on the floor beside his head.

What would happen if one kissed a lobster?

His gaze flicked to her mouth and back to her eyes. His pupils flared. Oh, God. What was happening? Her body buzzed. Her skin hummed. His lips parted, and he didn't just draw in air on that small breath, he drew her in as well. Her fingernails dug into the carpet as she tried desperately to ground herself. But she was helpless against the mystical pull of those amber irises.

The scent of ink and parchment and leather drifted to her. He smelled as inviting as the pages of a beloved book. Perhaps it wasn't so unfortunate he'd stumbled into the room instead of the Duke. What was contained in this intriguing man's pages—

The door to the drawing room swung open, and reality hit her like a slap in the face with said intriguing book.

Oh, my bloody God. No, no, no. No!

She scrambled off the gentleman and yanked her bodice up. Why had she dithered so thoughtlessly? Why was she always so careless and reckless? *Because really, who cares if you are?* Fortunately, that depressing thought didn't last long. The crustacean beneath her flew up to sitting, and his head collided with hers. Or maybe unfortunately. She fell backward on her bottom, clutching her forehead. Ouch, ouch, *ouch.* Of course, the clumsy crawfish would crash into her.

"Fitz?" a deep, alarmed voice boomed through the room.

"...Georgina?" And that low voice was oh-so-much worse.

Because she recognized that voice. Her eyes slammed shut. That voice was her father's: Mr. Thomas Hartley of Hartley Textiles. A man in trade, but richer than the majority of the ton. Hence why the Hartleys were invited to a country ball at an earl's estate. A man who was trying to get in the Jennings family's good graces.

Georgiana grimaced, a grimace so deep she was sure it would be permanently etched on her face. She slowly lifted her gaze to her father, whose mouth was opening and closing in what would have been a hilarious fashion if it had been happening during literally *any* other moment but this one. And that was when she recognized the second man. The owner of said estate, the head of the Jennings family—the Earl of Bentley.

"Fitz, I demand you explain yourself at once," Lord Bentley said.

A shiver traveled down Georgiana's spine. She discreetly studied the Earl. Broad, solid—his muscles straining against the protesting seams of his tailcoat—and incredibly handsome. No. Handsome wasn't quite right. Pretty was more apt. His features were beautiful. Now that was a man. One in charge.

But...who was Fitz? Her brows scrunched and then immediately shot to her hairline. Mr. Fitzwilliam Jennings, the Earl's younger brother.

She glanced at the man next to her, who currently looked like he was trying to disappear inside his cravat like a turtle. *He* was Mr. Fitzwilliam Jennings? She looked back at the Earl. *The Earl's* younger brother? This confident, commanding, composed man's younger brother? If she looked beyond the flushed, sweaty complexion and the disheveled amber curls, she supposed she did see the resemblance. Matching amber eyes, matching amber shade of locks.

"I. Urm. Ope. You see. Muromph."

She frowned. Truly? They were related?

Lord Bentley crossed his arms over his chest and waited for his brother to start forming actual words. Apparently, Mr. Jennings's odd behavior *was* normal. At least she no longer needed to fear for his brain. Just his future. Her future. Which was going to become *their* future without some quick thinking.

"I don't think an explanation is required, my lord," Georgiana's father said, his voice rising. Clearly Father had gotten over his shock. "It is obvious your brother has taken advantage of my daughter! He has defiled her!"

If only. She deflated with a sigh. If she was going to be caught in a compromising position, was it too much to ask that she had *actually* experienced a thorough defiling? Also, since when did her father care? Oh, right. Male pride. How dare *his* daughter be defiled... The daughter in question didn't matter so much, just that she belonged to him. The lobster could have defiled her father's boot, and he would have been just as offended.

"Father," she said soothingly. "There has been no defiling. It was all an accident." Yes, an accident. That was perfect. She could work her way out of this. "Mr. Jennings had been reading his book and walking"—she pointed to said book on the floor. *Ha! Evidence!*—"And we collided and tumbled to the ground. His foot got tangled in my skirts, which tore down my bodice." She spread her arms wide and smiled encouragingly at her father. "You see, it was all a most unfortunate accident." And a most perfect lie. "No one need ever know."

"Whose bodice was torn down?" a loud, female voice asked.

Her smile fled. Fled fast and far away. Because that was a familiar female voice.

Georgiana's shoulders slumped, and she wished she could turtle like the man next to her and disappear. Because Georgiana's grasping mama glided into the room, Lady Billingsworth—known for her wagging tongue—at her side. Getting out of this had been slim before, but now? Now that a calculating glint flared in Mother's eyes, and a look of pure glee lit up Lady Billingsworth's wine-flushed face?

Now Georgiana Hartley was most definitely *fucked*.

3

Fitzwilliam Jennings was fucked.

He didn't often wander from the safety of his London town house, but even he had heard of Mrs. Thomas Hartley's wild attempts at securing her daughter a husband. Just last year, she had accidentally shoved her daughter directly into the Serpentine. Her aim had been throwing the young woman into the Marquess of Dunmore. And if rumors were true, she had nearly succeeded, but the Marquess had given Miss Georgiana a discreet nudge to avoid her.

Miss Georgiana, meet Serpentine.

Fitz followed his brother, Felix, to his brother's study, the Hartleys in tow. There was no way out of this one. Not when Lady Billingsworth was a witness. Besides pistols at dawn, of course. And as much as marriage frightened the wits out of Fitz, it was preferable to a duel. Barely. But at six-and-twenty he'd like to keep living. He swallowed repeatedly, trying to gain some sort of moisture in his dry-as-sand mouth.

The problem was, Fitz struggled with social interactions until he got to know someone. And then he was *less* awkward. When it came to women, he very rarely got to that less-awkward point, like to the point where he could breathe properly. And the more attractive he found a woman, the longer it took for his awkwardness to abate.

So where Miss Georgiana Hartley was concerned? There was zero chance of abating, zero chance of breathing. Because she was stupidly beautiful. Annoyingly beautiful. Why did she have to be beautiful? Better yet—why did she have to attack him with her breasts?

He ground his teeth, hot frustration building in his chest. He was quite happy with his current life. His blissful solitude. He had his translations, and he had his mistress—a woman he *finally* had gotten comfortable with. *Safe*. His current life was safe.

And now he was going to lose all of that peace. He wasn't sure who he was angrier with: the young woman who had launched the bosom assault, or himself for not having the wherewithal to extricate himself from the situation before it turned calamitous.

Calamity, meet Fitz.

They settled themselves in Felix's study, and Fitz did his best to avoid eye contact with everyone. He curled his toes in his shoes and willed his lungs to continue to breathe air, in and out. *In and out.*

Thankfully, Felix's study was full of interesting—and more importantly, distracting—bric-a-brac. His brother had this fascinating clock that had come from Germany. Every hour on the hour, a small door opened at the top from which a bird appeared and made a "cuckoo" noise. Fitz was most definitely not avoiding the conversation at hand and focusing on the neat little clock.

"They must be married without delay," Mrs. Hartley said. "A week's time, no later."

That distracted Fitz from the clock. His gaze shot to the woman. She was blonde like her daughter, but much more generous of figure. A figure that was wrapped in luxurious fabrics covered in an overabundance of gold embellishments and glittering speckles. Goodness, had she had her seamstress throw an entire jewelry shop onto her dress?

Fitz fidgeted in his seat. Everyone was looking at him. Was he meant to respond? Oh God. *Words, Fitz.*

But whatever it was in his throat that was supposed to form words was currently being strangled by the cloying air in the room and the shrewd stare the woman was sending his way. She was a hunter who had found her mark. Her eyes may have been light in color, but there was a darkness to them that had nothing to do with their hue.

Fortunately, Fitz's brother spoke up. Unfortunately, Fitz had no idea what Felix was saying because a loud buzzing had drowned out all sound. But the vulture had turned her gaze onto Felix, and Fitz could take in an almost-normal breath.

Her daughter, on the other hand, didn't seem to possess any vulture-like qualities. Maybe it was the large, green eyes that had blinked down so innocently at him. There was a puzzling comfort in those irises, like lying in the lush grass beneath a tree's verdant leafy canopy, surrounded by every shade of green nature could conjure. When their gazes had met—clashed—egad, for a moment there, he had forgotten to be anxious.

That and when Miss Georgiana had been atop him, she had appeared nothing but worried for his welfare. Perhaps slightly amused by him, given the twinkling those enchanting eyes had been doing. But oddly, it hadn't seemed malicious. More like she found his inability to people properly...endearing?

But even with that slight positive note, if the way her fingers were currently trying to tear a hole in her ivory dress was any indication, she didn't want to marry him, either.

Of course, she doesn't want to marry you, you bloody dolt. Who would want to marry the bumbling, fumbling Mr. Fitzwilliam Jennings? He had found out the harsh truth of that statement at eighteen.

Then his head jerked back as he realized something. Something that should not have taken this long to figure out. She had clearly been in his study for an assignation. Which meant she not only didn't want to wed Fitz, but she *wanted to wed someone else*. An overflowing stream of relief flooded his veins. Perhaps there was someone else who could marry the young woman.

"Is there no alternative?" he blurted, hope taking over his tongue. How did one ask nicely if he could substitute himself with the man the maiden had been *trying* to ruin herself with?

"Alternative?" Mr. Hartley frowned at Fitz, and Fitz tugged at his cravat.

"Urm. Ah. Alternative person? For marriage p-purposes."

Oh dear. Mr. Hartley didn't like that. Fitz found it surprising steam wasn't emitting from the man's reddening ears. Goodness, that over-flowing stream appeared to be turning into a rampant river.

"Are you trying to pawn my daughter off on another gentleman? Do you have no honor?"

"No, no, no." Fitz gulped. Dear Lord, could he just drown in this river of his own making? "I just thought... Perhaps there was someone

Miss Georgiana had set her sights on." He looked at Miss Georgiana and gestured to his chest. "This was truly a misunderstanding."

Her brows pinched, little charming lines creasing her forehead. He huffed out a breath. How did he make her understand?

He flapped both hands in front of his chest in circular motions. Her eyes widened, clearly now comprehending he was referring to finding her in his study, breasts exposed—waiting for *someone else*. She shook her head violently, her delicate nostrils flaring.

Oh dear. Now he had her panicking. Why was she panicking? He was panicking. Again.

Breaths go in and out.

"Am I misunderstanding that my daughter was found atop you with her bosom in your face, sir?" Mrs. Hartley looked down her nose at him.

Yes, that was true. But that had been all Miss Georgiana's doing. Fitz couldn't be blamed for that. He inhaled on a count of three and then exhaled on the same count, trying to calm his overactive heart and create some sort of moisture in his chalky mouth.

He *had* asked the young miss to cover herself. He chewed his lip. Fitz was fairly certain he shouldn't mention that. He opened his mouth to say it anyway—

"My brother will, of course, do right by her," Felix said calmly.

Probably best his brother had stopped him. Felix's cool, authoritative tone seemed to placate the Hartleys. Well, all but one Hartley.

Miss Georgiana's features were drawn, lips turned down, eyes flat. Somber. Defeated. Resigned to her fate. Or...his brows furrowed. Not so much resigned as reverted—to somewhere else. He cocked his head. Where had she disappeared to? He was very familiar with disappearing inside one's head.

"And I don't see any reason for the rush," his brother said, throwing a sideways glance at Fitz.

There was so much in that glance. Brotherly concern and exasperation all tied together neatly in a bow. Fitz knew his brother—his family—loved him. But no one could deny that Fitz was *different*. The rest of the Jennings were free-spirited, confident, easy-going. Everything Fitz was not.

He didn't know why he was the way that he was. He had a great upbringing with a supportive family and wanted for nothing. The doctors always spoke of humors needing to be in balance for the body to function properly. Apparently, Fitz's humors were wonky.

He turned to his brother and gave a small shake of his head. He appreciated his brother's attempt at slowing down this carriage that was careening out of control. But the only way out of this mess was marriage. And if there was anything that made Fitz more nervous, it was anticipation. Weeks or months with an impending marriage hanging over his head? He wheezed as his lungs decided they wanted to stop working again. No, definitely not.

"Cuckoo!"

Fitz jolted at the sound of the clock. His time was up. No point in delaying.

"It is fine, Felix. I'll secure a license, and we will be married in a sennight." He was proud of how little his voice wavered. "The Hartleys can stay on after the ball is over, and we can have a quiet ceremony at the local chapel."

Miss Georgiana's gaze shot to his. He wasn't sure if her shock was because of his words or because he'd said so many of them. But either way, her wide eyes and parted lips spoke volumes. She didn't want this any more than he did. But it didn't matter what either of them wanted.

There was no hope.

4

"Fitzy, are you sure about this?" Felix asked, leaning his hip against his desk and staring down at Fitz. "I know you didn't truly compromise her. Honestly, it appeared much more like she was compromising you."

Fitz glanced at the closed door of his brother's study. The one the Hartley's had just exited through. He blew out a heavy breath with a resigned *pfffff*. He squeezed the cold leather arms of the chair he sat in and stared at his whitening knuckles.

"What other option is there, Felix? She'll be ruined otherwise."

Fitz liked his peace and quiet. The small slice of comfort he'd found. He was content to grow to a ripe old curmudgeon, donning his spectacles every morning and working on his Italian translations. But at the expense of a young woman's life? A ruined woman's life was bleak. And the Hartleys had no longstanding title to protect them, to fall back on. Blast and damn, Mr. Hartleys's business might even be affected. Fitz'd put them all in the poorhouse, in the slums of London, force that beautiful, kind-eyed woman into prostitution. He couldn't live with that on his conscience.

Felix studied him, arms crossed over his broad, deliberately honed chest, his identical amber eyes dissecting. Sometimes Fitz thought Felix was better at unraveling the peculiar puzzle that was Fitz than Fitz was himself.

"We could find a substitute," Felix finally said.

Fitz was already shaking his head. "Absolutely not." He drove a hand through his hair and winced when his fingers got caught in his wayward curls.

Bloody hell, he hated the dratted things. All three Jennings siblings had dark amber hair, but Felix and their sister Felicity were blessed with soft, wavy locks. Fitz, because apparently he was destined to be different in every way possible, had riotous curls. Annoying curls. Wish-he-could-shave-them-off exasperating curls.

"You know as well as I, Felix, that any substitute would be an absolute cretin, scraped up from the dredges of society."

Felix winced. "I'm not fond of the idea, either. I hate to sentence her to a life with a cruel, most-likely disease-infested man. But I could possibly find an especially old cuff, so it would at least be short-lived."

Something burned in Fitz's gut. His muscles locked tight, and he clenched his fists. He frowned down at his hands. He flexed his fingers and tried to relax, rid himself of the jarring resistance that had just overtaken him. Felix had a point. And with how lively the young woman appeared to be, she'd probably cause an old cove to slip the wind within days. So perhaps it wouldn't be horrible if they attempted to find a substitute.

Which made it that much more surprising when his mouth opened and he said, "No. I'll do it. I'll marry her."

5

Georgiana

Georgiana ambled down the hallway at Thornfield Hall toward her fiancé's study, a lightness bubbling in her chest. Because surely marrying Mr. Fitzwilliam Jennings was better than the man Mother had been pushing her towards at the ball—the feeble, donkey-toothed one who seemed a waltz away from the grave. She winced. *Not very nice, Georgiana.* But the gentleman had wanted her for breeding. He had *measured* her hips. She glanced at said hips and shuddered. Lords desperate for an heir took one look at her wide hips and instantly saw an advert with a large *womb for hire* splayed across the top.

Instead of that unsettling, albeit most-likely short future, she was looking at a long, uncomfortable one filled with painfully awkward moments. Yet, there was potential. Or she was determined to find some potential...somewhere. It had appeared as though Mr. Jennings had been doing his bloody damnedest to avoid her since the incident. He was either holed up in his study, working on his translations, or seeking out the farthest corner from where she stood in a room.

Georgiana had learned from Lady Felicity that Mr. Jennings worked on Italian translations. If her fiancé had deigned to speak with her at all over the past few days, he would have learned that Georgiana was fluent in Italian as well.

Mother was from Northern Italy. Not that Mama would *ever* let that fact get out. She had done everything in her power to eradicate any trace of her accent, and no one would assume her heritage based on her light features. But some of Mama's favorite artisans were Italian, so naturally when it served her, she broke out her Italian—including her doe-eyed daughter's Italian. It was amazing how much a price could be haggled down when you let a sweet little *bambina* loose in a fellow Italian's shop.

She trailed her fingers along the edge of one of the many hall tables, humming. Goodness, there were an incredible number of hall tables. Lord Bentley sure did love collecting bric-a-brac.

Georgiana couldn't help but think that perhaps she and her husband could bond over their shared linguistic proficiency. There was that potential. Common ground in a marriage was a good thing. At least, she thought it was. Georgiana didn't have any glowing examples of marriages, so what could she possibly know?

She thought conversation was typically a part of marriage, though, based on the short, stilted ones she grew up with. But in any moments she and Mr. Jennings were near enough to converse...he just didn't. Most likely couldn't. So she had taken it upon herself to study him. She had learned a couple of things about her soon-to-be husband in the past week during her observations.

She paused outside his study. Once again, her fiancé was sitting behind his desk, spectacles resting on his nose, quill scribbling frantically across parchment.

First observation: he was, in fact, dreadfully handsome. When he didn't resemble a tomato trying to cave in on itself. He had a habit of hunching his shoulders, almost like he wished he could make himself smaller and disappear. But when he stood tall? When there was a rare moment he wasn't consumed by nerves? Like now, unaware of her presence. He brushed back an amber curl that had just fallen over his brow. He was dashing.

She thought she might be developing an affinity for spectacles. Who would have thought? The woman who wanted a man to tie her up, bend her over, and tell her she was a whore—wanted said man to be wearing spectacles while he did it. She nearly groaned.

And then the other day, he had smiled when speaking with his sister. *Smiled.* Georgiana's legs had almost given out. Her knees had astonishingly vanished, departed on holiday. His grin was lop-sided and soft, like an uncertain puppy. Be still her heart. There was a hidden, handsome man inside her soon-to-be-husband. Which fueled her hope.

Mr. Jennings set his quill down and stretched his neck from side to side while rolling his shoulders. Oh dear. That jaw. Georgiana wanted to trace her tongue all over those hard edges. And then down the cord of muscle peeping just above his cravat. Yes, Georgiana most definitely was lusting after her fumbling fiancé.

And for her second observation: she made said fiancé *very* nervous. More-than-normal-for-him nervous. She had seen him interact with his siblings when no one was around. Shame on her for spying, but what was a woman to do when forced to marry a stranger? And said stranger couldn't even form sentences around her. She couldn't exactly get to know him if all he did was grunt and gurgle at her.

But he spoke like a normal human being with his siblings. Her parents made him flustered, but he still managed relatively well. Yet with her—Georgiana? She feared he was going to have a fit of the vapors. She had thought that was something that only pertained to females, but now she wasn't so sure. Perhaps she should start carrying smelling salts on her person to be safe. Just in case her future-husband fainted.

Georgiana squared her shoulders. Enough spying and sleuthing. They were going to have a conversation finally. With words. She was determined. She wouldn't take no—or whatever he managed to gurgle—for an answer. She put the friendliest, most approachable smile she could on her face, and entered his study.

"Hullo, Mr. Jennings." She stopped just inside the threshold, her lavender skirts fluttering around her, the familiar scent of ink and parchment...and something woodsy greeting her nose. "I was hoping we might become better acquainted."

She had chosen the lavender dress, despite her mother's objection because—*gasp*—how could one wear lavender in winter? But she thought it brought out her eyes, and it made her feel pretty. And one was supposed to look pretty for their husband, were they not? But with the way her fiancé was staring at her—like she had left off her dress altogether—perhaps that hadn't been the best tactic. Perhaps she should have donned a sack. Over her head.

"Divine," he breathed, his quill stilling, gaze roving over her.

She blinked. Then glanced around the room. Had that been directed toward her? She must have misheard, because it sounded like her fiancé just called her—

"Another time!" He abruptly jumped up, and she jumped back.

She opened and closed her mouth, but her mind couldn't even form words, let alone her mouth. What did one do when their betrothed unexpectedly shouted at them?

He cleared his throat. "A-apologies. I meant to say we can speak another time. I am quite pressing with occupied matters."

She cocked her head. His eyes widened briefly when what he said finally registered.

"Occupied with p-pressing matters," he said in a garbled voice. "Things of import." He waved flippantly and let out an awkward, strained laugh that ended in a wheeze. "Cannot afford to waste time on inconsequential chatter." He sent her a tense smile, one without teeth and without a touch of warmth. Then sat and picked back up his quill, effectively dismissing her.

She backed out of his study, jaw slack, his words ringing through her brain.

Things of import. Not her.

Inconsequential. Her.

When the loose-limbed shock finally faded, all that remained was an all-too-familiar hurt. She dragged her feet back to her room, tail between her legs. *Blast and damn.* Why did she think of *that* metaphor? Because it was only an aching reminder that there would be no wagging tail to greet her in her chamber. With Bernie gone, she was well and truly alone.

That hope bubbling in her chest earlier? Popped.

6

Georgiana

GEORGIANA'S CHEEKS ACHED FROM the strain of keeping the false smile she'd donned since she awoke that morning plastered on her face. But today was an especially hard day, and keeping up the facade of happiness while surrounded by Lady Bentley, Lady Felicity, and Mother in the Jennings family library was becoming an increasingly arduous task.

In general, Georgiana was a positive person. She always sought out the bright and shiny aspects of life. If she didn't—well, that was a dire spiral to spin down. Even in the darkest, dirtiest depths of London, the sun broke through the coal-laden haze, and flowers found a way to push their way through the cobblestones. So, she chose to bask in the sunshine and pick the scraggly flowers.

But some days the melancholy got the better of Georgiana. She feared today was to be one of those days. She desperately wanted to curl up in bed with her Bernie. He had made everything brighter, bearable. The band around her chest tightened.

Her mother set down her teacup with a soft clatter on the tea tray laid out before them and turned to Lady Bentley, seated opposite on a matching settee. "With all this thrilling marriage news, I must inquire: Is Lord Bentley seeking a bride for himself?"

Georgiana fought an eye roll. *Subtle, Mother.*

Lady Bentley smiled politely. "Not at the moment. I am sure if the right person comes along my Felix will decide to settle down."

Mother eased back, content as a cat who'd found the cream. Georgiana knew exactly what her mother was thinking. Opportunity. If Lord Bentley never took a wife, Mr. Jennings, who just so happened to be Georgiana's betrothed, was next in line. Which meant Georgiana could one day become the next Lady Bentley and birth the heir to the earldom. Mother would gain everything she'd so ruthlessly sought, had always prioritized over her own daughter's well-being. No wonder her mother had wasted no time insisting on a wedding.

Georgiana's stare landed on Lady Felicity. The young woman, near in age to Georgiana, absently traced the beveled edges of one of the diamond-paned windows, staring out at her family's snow-covered estate. She turned, her amber plait swinging over her shoulder, and their gazes collided.

Lady Felicity smiled warmly and beckoned Georgiana with a wave. "Miss Georgiana, would you join me?"

Georgiana smoothed her soft-blush skirts and stood, forcing her lips to tilt up. Perhaps getting to know her soon-to-be sister-in-law would be the perfect distraction from her glum mood. She usually would seek out some thrill, approach one of the young, eager dockworkers of her father's, perhaps the strapping lad of the meat pie costermonger—and get herself the most delicious kidney pie in all of London while she was at it. Those distractions wouldn't be an option for her now. And it didn't appear as though she'd be receiving any *distraction* from Mr. Jennings since he didn't want to waste any of his time with her.

"How are you fairing, Georgiana? You don't mind if I call you Georgiana, do you? We are to be sisters, after all. You seemed a bit forlorn. I know all about fake smiles. I'm quite adept at them, and yours was not very convincing, I'm sorry to say. You can call me Felicity."

Georgiana blinked. That had been quite a lot of words.

Lady Felicity laughed. "Apologies, I am just a bit overeager to have another woman in the family. *Brothers*." She rolled her eyes and groaned, but her amber eyes twinkled. Her smile softened, and she tilted her head. Her fingers fiddled with the bottom of her plait, fluffing the hair. "I imagine it isn't easy being thrown into a new family."

"It has been...dizzying. But you all have been exceptionally kind. And I'm looking forward to getting to know you all." If she was granted the opportunity at all with her husband. That seemed the most important of the lot—and the least likely.

Lady Felicity frowned. "There's that forlorn look again. Is there anything I can do to help?"

"I apologize, Lady Fel—"

"Ahem. *Felicity*." The young woman's amber brows shot up expectantly, and she batted her eyelashes patiently at Georgiana.

"Felicity," Georgiana amended with a faint twitch of her lips. "I assure you, your family has been nothing but gracious. The closeness between you all is...well, I only have an elder brother who has long since traveled to America, so, truly, I am excited to be a part of the Jennings fold. I have always wanted a family like that." *I have always wanted any semblance of family at all.*

Felicity's eyes sparkled, and she bounced once on her toes. "Oh, you will not be disappointed, I promise! We Jennings—we know how to have fun." She turned to gaze out the window. "We run wild over this estate. Even now, grown as we are." She glanced at Georgiana from the corner of her eye, cocking a brow. "As long as you enjoy a bit of wildness too, you'll fit right in."

Oh dear, if only the woman knew. Georgiana lived for reckless rivalry. It was her escape from her lonely existence. She had always known eventually she'd be granted an actual escape when she married—no longer a disappointment to her father and a pawn for her mother.

But she never fooled herself into thinking she'd be escaping into a better situation. Not with the sorry types her mother shoved her toward. The cloud of melancholy hovered over her, threatening to sink lower. Apparently, that hadn't stopped her naïve heart from hoping, from holding on to the fanciful notions of love and family and belonging.

There was no more dreaming, though. Because her future was now. And it depended on a stranger, a man she knew almost nothing about and who apparently had no desire to know anything about her.

"I do delight in a bit of devilry," she said, summoning cheer from God only knew where. "I'd love to hear stories of your escapades."

Felicity grinned, wide and impish. "Oh, do I have stories for you."

And so, Georgiana and Felicity chatted, the young woman's infectious exuberance gradually dispelling the gloom. They eventually joined Lady Jennings and Georgiana's mother for a fresh pot of tea and biscuits, only to be treated with more tales. Georgiana sipped on steaming hot tea and soaked in the stories of a childhood so much different from her own. She thought she was going to very much like the Jennings.

Smoky amber eyes and freckled cheeks, nearly hidden beneath a deep blush, flitted through her mind.

Why did that still leave her hollow inside?

7

Georgiana

GEORGIANA SHRUGGED INTO HER heavy wool coat, grabbed her muffs, and followed her mother from the drawing room to the carriages that awaited them on the front drive. She lifted her chin. Though this past week had done nothing to lift her hopes about her impending marriage, she was determined to give it her best try.

Because she was a fighter. She and Mr. Jennings were about to vow their lives to each other. For better or for worse. Right now, it seemed worse. In sickness and health. Right now, it seemed a bit like a sickness. But she would do her best to make this marriage tolerable for the both of them. She had a chance for a fresh start. Perhaps she would find a family who wanted to know her. Wasn't disappointed that she was born a woman and saw her as more than a pretty face to lure a lord.

So far, the Jennings had seemed welcoming and warm and simply...wonderful. A niggling feeling wormed its way into her gut. That same feeling she'd experienced when her fiancé had so blatantly dismissed her from his study. The one that said she was an inconvenience, a hindrance, a *bother*. A very familiar feeling.

She tried to remind herself that this could be much worse. She could have ended up with one of the balding, gout-suffering, elderly lords her mother had been pushing her toward. Like the donkey-man. Her soon-to-be husband was young. He had all his hair—and it was a lovely shade of amber. He did sweat quite a bit, especially for December, but the strong, square jaw and freckles dusting his face made up for it. The thought of bedding him didn't make her want to flee across the Atlantic.

Which had her mind drifting to their impending wedding night. She stepped out the front door, and her stomach dropped to the icy ground. She blew out a breath, and all her disappointment fogged the air in front of her. Georgiana supposed she could kiss her proclivities farewell. The nervous man walking ahead of her, who had just tripped and nearly landed face-first in a pile of fluffy snow, couldn't possibly entertain her desires. She wasn't sure he could entertain consummation at all.

A biting wind picked up, sharp against her cheeks and in her lungs.

"Dear heavens," her mother grumbled. "We are to have another severe winter. I am at a loss to understand this dratted weather. This year has been the wettest England has surely ever seen, and now the coldest."

Georgiana hummed in agreement; the unusual weather had caused a host of problems. Though mother complained because it meant she couldn't parade around with the fashionable set, showing off the expensive wares Father had purchased for her. Her mother didn't think about how the excessive amount of rain had caused a food shortage. How those who farmed were hurting because the harvest had been drastically hindered. How those who weren't sitting on a fortune from textiles had empty bellies. But that was Mama.

Georgiana settled in their carriage, her mother and father sinking into the seat opposite her. Her father sat back, unfolding his tall, lean form and rested an arm across the top of the squabs of the conveyance.

But her mother leaned toward Georgiana and patted her knee. "Do not fret, Georgiana."

Mother had clearly misunderstood Georgiana's silence as apprehension. It wasn't. Silence was just the best way to deal with her mother. It wasn't as though her mother heard anything Georgiana said anyhow. So why waste her breath?

"This isn't a terrible match," Mother continued. "Mr. Jennings is next in line to inherit. The current Earl isn't even married, and his mother—Lord knows why—isn't putting any pressure on him. If he were to die, your son would be heir!"

Georgiana blinked. As she had said, it was best to just stay silent. What on earth did someone say to such a morbid statement?

Her father's green eyes—identical to her own—lit with amusement. They were the one thing she'd inherited from him. Her blonde hair and porcelain skin came from Mother.

"Now, now, Augusta. Let us not wish ill health on the man." That was Papa, always with an amused expression on his face. He smiled at you without ever seeing you. People mistook it for joviality, but it was merely a superficial facade he put on for the world, family included. The only thing her father ever paid close attention to was his business. He was as shrewd and cutthroat in his dealings as her mother was with her marriage machinations.

Her mother flicked her hand in a careless wave. "Oh, I don't mean *right now*. But the Earl is past thirty now and has shown no signs of looking for a bride. Even if he were to live to a ripe old age, if he doesn't settle down and *produce*..." Her mother shrugged—she would become the mother of a countess, the grandmother of a future earl.

Georgiana struggled to understand the appeal. Wealth and title were so important to her parents. But if one took all that away, what would they be left with? If they all had to sit down at a table together, would they even have anything to say to one another?

Not to mention the man she was about to marry couldn't even look at her naked breasts, couldn't even look at *her*. How was he going to bed her? Georgiana feared for the Earldom of Bentley because it appeared neither brother was going to be *producing*.

She turned and stared out the window as the carriage rocked down the road. Thinking about producing just brought her mind back to her proclivities. She wished she had at least gotten to experiment a bit before her mother finally succeeded in saddling her with a husband. She had been kissed, fondled, and done her fair share of fondling. But never anything close to what she wanted to explore. Nothing *dark*. She had held tight to her virginity, as a good girl ought. Now she regretted that decision immensely. What she would have given to have just one experience with the brooding Duke of Ironcrest.

She let out a huff, clouding the window in front of her. She supposed it would just be her and Derek for the rest of her days, when it came to her pleasure. Derek being her trusty dildo. He was a beauty. Carved ivory. Quite expensive and difficult to locate. But Georgiana's curiosity had started at fourteen, and she was now twenty. She had *a lot* of time—years—to discover *things*. She had procured Derek two years ago.

The carriage rolled to a stop.

Apparently tonight she would finally see how a flesh-and-blood man compared to Derek. And she had to admit, she wasn't optimistic. At least if their interactions since the Christmastide ball were any indication. She hopped out of the carriage and shoved her hands in her muff as she and her parents made their way to the local chapel, Mr. Jennings and his family ahead of them.

They entered the chapel, her coat and muff were ripped from her, and then she was unceremoniously shoved to the altar by her mother. It appeared everyone wanted to hurry this along. Before the bride ran off or the groom's heart gave out.

And by his elevated breathing right now from where he stood in front of her, throat bobbing like apples at a country fair, it seemed likely. They really needed to get this over with. For Mr. Jennings's sake, more than anything.

She feared he wouldn't make it through the ceremony.

8

Fitz

Fitz had truly thought he wouldn't make it through the ceremony.

Miss Georgiana—no—Mrs. Fitzwilliam Jennings. Dear Lord. His *wife.* His wife was breathtaking, standing before him in a red velvet gown borrowed from his sister. Some sort of white puffiness lined the bodice and sleeves, and ivory buttons trailed down the front. And the fit. Dear Mary, Joseph, and the Holy Ghost, the *fit.* His willowy sister and Georgiana were most definitely *not* the same shape. Which meant his wife's abundance of bosom and tempting curves were on glorious display, even with the alterations done to the gown. The dress did things to her breasts that in turn did things to Fitz's anatomy that really shouldn't happen when in a chapel.

He should never have looked at her. He had avoided looking at his little wife all the way up until she had stepped in front of him at the altar. But then he had glanced down at her and promptly swallowed his tongue. Fitz appreciated a woman's figure. He liked breasts just fine. And bottoms. But Georgiana's figure? Let's just say he was only capable of inarticulate noises. What a surprise.

With her rich crimson gown and round, forest-green eyes, she was Christmastide incarnate. And he wanted to unwrap her like a Christmas present. Her hair was done up in some sort of elaborate hair-style-thing—whatever women called them—with a few curls trailing over her shoulders into the crevice of her bosom. A bosom he was already very familiar with. Tonight, he would get to touch those perfect breasts. His eyes flashed wide. Dear God, he would have to touch them. His breath sawed in and out.

As he had said. He hadn't thought he would make it through the ceremony.

Well, he made it through—somehow. He even made his mouth form the necessary words. But now he was stuck at the altar.

"Mr. Jennings..." Georgiana looked up at him from beneath furrowed, blonde brows. His gaze clashed with her evergreen one, and everything inside of him stopped. Stilled. Suspended in an endless, timeless void. His lungs no longer worked. The blood in his veins no longer flowed. Sound disappeared. All that was left was her. Was that verdant green gaze that had him trapped.

She was saying something. Her tempting lips were curling around syllables. *Work, blasted ears, work.*

"Mr. Jennings, are you well?"

He almost laughed. He almost cried. Instead, he said, "Pine."

She blinked twice.

Fitz cleared his throat. "I mean I'm ferfect."

His eyes slid shut. He was hopeless. This woman somehow managed to make a typically witless Fitz even more witless.

He opened his eyes and met his wife's kind gaze, her deep-pink lips tilted in a soft smile.

"Well, *ferfect* husband. Shall we make our way back to the estate?" She proffered her hand for him to tuck into the crook of his arm, like any gentlemen would do.

But Mr. Fitzwilliam Jennings? No, no, he couldn't possibly touch her. And still breathe. Especially when with every breath his lungs drew in her sweet scent. She smelled like freshly baked biscuits. Or a creamy, frothy, vanilla syllabub spiced with cinnamon. Which had his mind going places it decidedly shouldn't. Like burying his face between her thighs in search of other creamy delicious—

His eyes widened. "Y-you go on ahead," he stammered. He needed to get himself and his cock under control before everyone in the chapel was aware of where his thoughts had wandered.

A flash of hurt wrinkled her brow before she replaced it with a sad smile. Which really wasn't any better. Because now, as his wife walked away from him, he not only had enough anxiety tumbling about his insides to fill a circus tent with acrobats, he also felt bad for hurting his wife's feelings.

He longingly watched her retreating figure. "You smell too delightful," he said softly, sorrowfully.

She turned and tilted her head. "Pardon?"

Fuck. He snapped straight. Had she heard him? Oh God.

"Nrrumph."

Not better.

"I said you smell frightful!"

He winced. Dear Lord, that was most definitely *not* better. Why hadn't he just gone with the compliment? That would have been the totally normal option. But no, he went with *you smell frightful.* Welp, in for a penny, in for a pound.

"Urm. Yes. I'd recommend you request a bath upon your return. With haste."

Her eyes rounded and her cheeks grew pink. "O-of course, sir." She turned and hurried over to her family.

He groaned inwardly, mentally smacking himself over the head with a very large tome. *You bumbling idiot, Fitz.* This moment was like an incredibly painful repeat of their interaction in his study earlier in the week. If he were being honest, every interaction with her since the moment they met had been painful in its awkwardness.

But his very new wife continued to surprise him. She'd marched up to that altar, chin lifted high, determination glowing in her green eyes. A ferocious little warrior. Fitz had actually been a mite frightened. If she'd had a weapon, he probably would have fled. What must it be like to have such resolve? Assurance? And resilience—considering he had been nothing but a bumbling bear to her since they met. But she had not once wilted, not once given any indication she was anything but strong and fierce.

Her beauty was remarkable, but so it would seem was the woman beneath.

9

Georgiana

GEORGIANA FEARED FOR HER wedding night. And that had been before her husband had showed up at her chamber. Having one's husband
say *you smell frightful* wasn't exactly what one hoped for on their wedding day. Georgiana had done a discreet sniff of herself in the carriage,
and she didn't think she was particularly malodorous, but she had requested a bath, regardless.

She had said her quick goodbyes to her mother, which had included
an alarming number of reminders that Georgiana needed to copulate
with her husband with haste. Repeatedly. Her father had been typically
absent, so she hadn't even managed a goodbye to him. Apparently, he
had been dealing with some business matter with Lord Bentley. She
wondered if he would even care if he ever saw her again. She blew out a
breath. Not a time for those gloomy thoughts. Right now, she had bigger
problems.

Like the husband who was standing dead-center in her chamber, looking everywhere but at her, hands fisting and unfisting in the fabric of his loose-fitting gray trousers. His face was slowly turning his typical fifty shades of red, and his forehead was developing a sheen.

The sweating was starting.

Georgiana was a little heated herself. Because Fitzwilliam Jennings in a state of undress? *Buon Dio.* She fanned herself. The V of his shirt gaped open, exposing a dusting of amber chest hair, and his unruly mahogany curls were tight and wet from his bath—well, what she hoped was his bath and not sweat.

She giggled. He gulped. *Oops.* That wasn't going to help the poor clam.

She slowly approached him, her cotton night dress—nothing especially seductive, but she hadn't been planning on having a wedding night any time soon—swishing around her legs.

"Are you going to look at me, Mr. Jennings?"

"Urm, I...I... You know, I believe it m-might be for the best if I don't."

Well, she was going to look her fair share. He wasn't wearing stockings. Her gaze caressed his calves, flexing and unflexing. She supposed that was one benefit to his tension. His muscles were *tense*. Glorious. His biceps hardened and softened under his thin linen shirt with every fidget. There was surprising lean strength to the bookworm. If she could just get him past his bumbling, there might be some promise here. There was most definitely attraction on her end. She wasn't sure if there was attraction on his end. But the way she made him nervous had her hoping that just maybe...he was nervous *because* he was attracted to her?

She reached him and rested her palm on his chest—his gloriously hard, muscled chest—and he sucked in a breath. And never released it.

Her shoulders slumped. She should accept right now that this night was going to be torture for them both.

"Breathe, Mr. Jennings."

A breath burst from him, and he broke into a fit of coughing.

"Should I douse the lights? Perhaps if you cannot see me, if we leave our clothes on, we will be able to get through this." Her words came out with more bite to them than she had intended. But disappointment was wading its way up her body until it nearly consumed her whole. She was trying not to be frustrated with him, with her circumstances, especially since technically this was all *her* fault. But she was only human.

His gaze flew to hers. Finally. "Are you cross with me?"

"No, I'm not cross, sir. Just resigned." She tried to smile, but her lips refused to tug upward.

Her husband tugged at his cravat, only to realize too late he wasn't wearing one and instead just jabbed himself in the throat. "F-Fitz will do, or Fitzwilliam, if you prefer."

Oh! That seemed like progress. She opened her mouth to test his name on her tongue—

"Y-you don't need to be resigned. I promise I'll make it as painless as possible. There might be some pain, I've been told. I—I did some reading. And you see, there is something called a hymen..."

Her eyes nearly bugged out of her head. *Oh my God*. He was not speaking of her hymen, was he?

"...a pinch, or so I've heard," he was saying.

And then his rambling and his admission that he had done *some reading*, and all their prior interactions came rushing to the forefront of her mind.

"Have you never done this before?" she blurted. She'd had the thought before, but she hadn't believed it would actually hold any truth.

The incessant rambling stopped, and silence settled thick and suffocating over her chamber.

"No…" he said slowly.

Oh God, they going to be a pair of fumbling, stumbling virgins. Heaven, help her. She should just douse the lights, he could stick her with his prick, and have this done with.

He opened his mouth, but words didn't come. He closed it and tried again. "Or at least, I don't believe I have ever bedded a virgin before."

His shoulders sagged. *Phewf.* All right. He would at least know where to put it. "So, you have bedded a woman before?"

"I…had a m-mistress," he said carefully. "I know it is not something typically discussed between husbands and wives. I dismissed her upon our betrothal."

She pursed her lips and examined him. A confusing mix of gratitude and disbelief settled over her. That he dismissed his mistress was quite thoughtful and not very common amongst the ton, nor the wealthy. But also—he had a mistress?

"You. *You* had a mistress?"

Whoops, that had come out rather rude. But she couldn't see it.

He pursed his lips back at her. His lips looked soft.

"Is that hard to believe?" he asked her, but his eyes were somewhere in the evergreen canopy that hung over her four-poster bed. He looked adorably befuddled.

"Yes, I do find it hard to believe. You couldn't even bear to look at my breasts. You can't even look at me right now. And I'm to believe you had a kept woman. A woman *solely* for bedsport. Or did you not hire her for those kinds of services?"

His gaze found hers again, amber brows scrunched together. "You know of such things? And of course I had s-sexual congress with her."

Sexual congress. Sexual. Congress. A little part of her died inside. As did her fantasies. She wanted a man to tell her she was a bad wench. To discipline her. Perhaps throw in a few *good girl*s too. A delicate balance of punishment and praise. A man who said *sexual congress* would never.

His forehead lines deepened. "I'll have you know, she was very pleased with my performance," he said tightly. "It's not as if I need an instruction manual."

Interesting. There wasn't one stammer in that sentence. So, he was capable of conversing with her. Apparently, if he was distracted enough, he could speak. She noted that.

"Excellent. I'm glad you don't need a manual. Shall we get on with the consummation?"

She gripped his hand and walked backward toward her bed. He was back to gulping, and she had to tug him with more force than should ever be necessary when bringing a man to bed. But eventually her backside hit her bed, and she hopped up on the mattress.

His breaths came short and shallow, sharp mint and soft cedar wafting to her with each breath. His gaze flickered toward her, only to quickly dart away, like he wanted to look at her, but couldn't quite handle it. He wrenched his hand from her grip, and ran it through his curls, his lips moving in what looked like silent prayer.

"Is there anything I can do to make this easier for you?" She was fairly certain that was not the question the *bride* asked the *bridegroom* on their wedding night. But nothing about life this past week had come close to resembling something that could be deemed normal.

He was still praying.

She let out a frustrated huff through her nose. "Fitz?"

His gaze flew to her mouth, and his lips parted, his lids lowered. He liked that. Excitement thrummed through her veins. Progress!

"Unghy."

The excitement fizzled out.

"If you had a mistress, or so you said…"

His mouth flattened. "I did," he bit out.

"Then why could you bed her and not me?"

He blinked at her. "Well, I was paying her."

He said it like she was a simpleton. Maybe she was? Because she didn't think that made a lick of sense.

"Yes… And you get to bed me for free. You can do what you please with me. Shouldn't that make you the opposite of nervous?"

His lips quirked in a half-smile, and he let out a little huff-of-a-laugh, assaulting her senses with more of that tempting peppermint scent. "I was nervous at first with her, too."

Georgiana's gaze locked on that self-deprecating half-smile. Oh, if only this man could get past his nerves. She'd very much like to try a taste of her freshly tooth-powdered husband.

"But I became comfortable over time. And until I did…"

Silence.

"Until you did…what?" she prodded. These were the most words they had exchanged, probably even if one tallied up all their conversations over the past sennight. And they were very helpful words. Insight into the anxious mind of her husband.

"She was a mistress. She was well-versed in these matters. She took control, so I didn't have to."

Oh. An uncomfortable knot formed in her stomach. He wanted her to take control? Even if she had done this before, that wasn't very appealing to Georgiana. She wanted to *be* controlled. A tightness snaked around her chest. Oh dear. That might be overwhelm cinching around her.

Up until now, she had been doing very well, considering.

Considering she had just married a veritable stranger, been thrust to an altar, and then thrown into a new home with a new family. Not to mention that it was the Christmastide season. Christmas was in a few days. And she wasn't spending it with her family. She wasn't spending it with anyone remotely familiar. Granted, Christmas wasn't all that jolly a time in the Hartley's household. But she had always celebrated with Bernie. Until this year. Her first Christmas without him.

Her heart lodged itself in her throat, making it impossible to swallow. Christmas always fell flat, filled with material items that meant nothing, all for show. There was no laughter, no joy, no hope—like right now.

Oh dear, that was definitely overwhelm she was feeling, it was spiraling around her, tighter than the threads in a weaver's loom.

And now... Now she had a husband who *she* needed to take charge with. In all things. Conversation and copulation.

She took a steadying breath. One of them needed to breathe normally. And it was definitely not going to be her husband. She hadn't let life destroy her yet, she wouldn't now.

He needed her to take control. She would try.

"Why don't we start with a kiss?"

10

Why don't we start with a kiss?

It seemed the logical place to start. Even Fitz could admit that. And he wanted the press of her lush lips against his. Desperately. There was just one problem.

Him.

Fitz had been nervous about tonight. He kept telling himself that his natural instincts would take over. He had bedded women before. The number of which might only require one hand, but still the number wasn't *zero*. He couldn't speak for the others because they had been hurried, drunken, one-night encounters, but he knew with utmost certainty his mistress was very happy with his conjugal abilities. Adelaide had always been honest with him. When he did something she liked, she told him. When he did something she didn't like, she told him. He appreciated that about her. There was no guessing. Less anxiety that way.

He blew out a breath. He knew his way around a woman. He could do this. He could bed his wife.

But this was different from Adelaide. And that was ignoring the fact that there was some elusive element to his wife that had his heart heaving and his lungs beating a mile a minute. Wait. That wasn't quite right. He groaned. She made him a blundering, brainless, bottle-headed buffoon.

Besides *that* nonsense, this was different because there had been a comfort in knowing that if he took a wrong turn, his mistress would guide him back en route. What if he did something Georgiana didn't like? Virgins didn't know to voice concerns, did they? She would just endure. She wouldn't even know what felt good. Did she even know what an orgasm was? Goodness, what if he couldn't make her come? *Oh God.* He hadn't thought of that.

There went his breathing again.

He tried to reorient himself. A kiss. Start with a kiss, she said.

She was blinking her overlong blonde lashes at him.

Because you have been staring at her like a lobcock.

Right. Response required. "A most excellent proposal."

She gave him the same look she'd made when he had said 'sexual congress' earlier. And he didn't think it was a good look.

Just get it over with, Fitz. He was sure once they got this first kiss out of the way, things would get better. They couldn't possibly get worse.

He leaned forward and pressed his lips to hers.

She froze.

He froze.

They stood there, lips pressed together, frozen.

Frozen.

Oh God, this is bloody awkward.

Somewhere in the deep recesses of his mind, he knew he was supposed to move. Lips were supposed to pass over lips, hands were supposed to caress over curves. But instead sweat beaded up on his back, his hands grew damp, and his mouth grew dry. Now he was terrified to touch her with wet palms. His palms were not what was supposed to get wet.

His mind raced and the blasted thing wouldn't stop. Thoughts barreled forward that were doing little to help his current frozen predicament. The kinds of thoughts where he over-analyzed all of her reactions since he had entered her chamber. He had detected anger and frustration. Disappointment. That one had especially stung. Too familiar a reaction. And just before this kiss? He had detected panic. He thought her eyes might have even gotten a bit glossy. Which meant tears.

How long have we been standing here?

And then things got worse.

Her lips moved tentatively over his. Her small hand settled on his abdomen.

He squeaked and jumped away. Jumped away from the heat that seared his stomach at her touch. The only blessing in all of this was that he managed to break the most awkward kiss known to man.

If he wasn't the one in this situation, he'd be impressed by the amount of awkwardness. Award-worthy. Perhaps the King would bestow a title on him for it. The Earldom of Awkward. The Marquess of Muck. The Baronet of Bumblefuck.

He dared to peek at her. She sat there on her ivory bedding, large, green eyes blinking at him, little lines forming between her blonde brows.

Bloody hell. He had *squeaked*. His face flamed. He wished the flames would just consume him right then and there.

"I. Shurrr. Go. Shurrgoh." He stepped back, swallowed, and tried again. "I should go."

And then he fled, the taste of cinnamon and spice lingering on his lips.

11

Georgiana

Her husband had fled.

Last night. When they were supposed to consummate their marriage.

She tried to shove the thoughts aside and focused on the task at hand: kissing boughs. Georgiana snorted. The irony. Kissing this prickly pine would probably be more pleasant than the one from last night. But it didn't mean she didn't want to try again. Because the dining room was thick with the woodsy aroma of greenery, and all it did was remind Georgiana of how delicious her fleeing husband smelled.

Georgiana sat with her sister-in-law, Felicity, and mother-in-law, in the family's dining hall. Evergreens of every variety, of every shape and size, were sprawled out on the wood table before them while they each made their own kissing boughs to be hung around the manor. Lady Bentley had insisted Georgiana call her Lydia. Georgiana had stumbled over that the first few times. It was so familiar.

But she was coming to find that the Jennings family were a very close-knit bunch. They jested, they swore, they did things that were decidedly not done for members of the ton. And it was shocking because when the Jennings paraded about in society? One would never have guessed. Lord Bentley was so formal, so *lordly*. Not very descriptive, but everyone knew what a lordly lord was like. Lady Felicity was above reproach about town. At home? The woman swore like a knave. And Lady Bentley—Lydia, Georgiana corrected herself—smiled fondly at her children as they carried on in their coarse behavior.

Georgiana bloody loved it.

She snatched up another peppermint candy from the bowl between her and Felicity and popped it into her mouth. She rolled it over her tongue, the frosty flavor tingling over her senses. She might not be having the best of luck with her husband. But she couldn't be happier with the family that had welcomed her with open arms.

Speaking of her husband, who she hadn't seen since their abomination of a kiss last night—Georgiana had noticed, while he was comfortable with his family, something seemed a bit different about him. Almost like he appeared to be an outsider in his own family. He never relaxed like Felicity and Lord Bentley did. He jested, he swore, he smiled, but never to the same extent. It was something Georgiana was determined to find out more about. Why did he hold himself back—apart—even from his family?

Lydia stood in a flurry of ivory muslin skirts. "I don't think we have enough greenery. I'm going to find Mrs. Smith and have her send some footmen out for more boughs."

Georgiana frowned down at the long dining table, at least fifteen feet in length. Covered in holly and ivy and mistletoe. They needed *more*?

Felicity nodded vigorously. "Agreed. This isn't nearly as much as we had last year. We must out-do ourselves."

Oh, that was the other thing. The Jennings? They were a competitive lot. With each other and even with themselves.

Lydia clapped excitedly and sashayed from the room, humming some Christmas ditty. She had an impressive amount of energy. She must be well past fifty years if Lord Bentley was in his thirties, but one would never know with how she bounded about just like her four-and-twenty daughter.

The woman was also extraordinarily beautiful. The whole family was beautiful, really. But whereas Lady Bentley's children were all amber-haired and amber-eyed, Lydia had light, strawberry-blonde hair and glowing, blue eyes with laugh lines creasing the corners and around her lips. A family who smiled, who loved. Odd that.

Lydia's daughter, Felicity, was her exact replica besides coloring. As was Lord Bentley. Large eyes, slightly tilted in an almost feline variety, perfectly proportioned noses, full lips. They were all pretty, including Lord Bentley.

And then there was Georgiana's husband. Fitzwilliam Jennings. He was tall and broad-shouldered like Lord Bentley, though much leaner. But his features were sharper, squarer. Georgiana had learned that Fitz held a likeness to his father. Riotous curls included. She let out a dreamy sigh. He really was dashing. When he wasn't the same shade as the red ribbon she was tying to her bough. Even then, he was still handsome.

It was just...his awkwardness was a little cringe-inducing to observe. She desperately wished she could comfort him—sometimes this manifested itself into her wanting to shake him and yell, *relax, you lout!*—which she didn't do, of course. At least, not yet. So far, almost everything she had done had made it worse. So, she wasn't counting out the possibility.

"There!" Felicity exclaimed. She held up her kissing bough and examined it. She had managed a sphere double the size of her head, dotted with gold and red bows and dried oranges, and it was so thick with greenery there wasn't even a peep of empty space.

"Lovely, Felicity. I might need some of your assistance with mine." Georgiana's wasn't nearly as full. "I can't fill these bloody spaces," she muttered.

Her sister-in-law scooted closer with a chuckle, grabbing another peppermint for herself, and started helping Georgiana secure more greenery to the hoops making up her sphere.

Felicity dropped her voice. "Now that Mother is conveniently absent, you *must* tell me the details of the night you were caught with my brother."

Georgiana fumbled with the branch she was trying to secure to her sphere. "You want to know how your brother compromised me?"

A grin split Felicity's face. "I know some specifics. Like how you were found on top of my brother, breasts in his face." She sniggered. "I can only imagine Fitz's panic at *that*." Felicity leaned forward. "But I know for a fact that Fitz would never take part in an assignation. The only reason he was there was because you were unfortunate enough to choose his study for your location. I want *details*. Who were you intending to meet?" She waggled her eyebrows. "Come on now, we are friends—*sisters*—it's practically a rule you must share."

Georgiana's lips twitched. The woman was a dog with a bone. "I don't know..." Should she really admit to it?

"I guarantee nothing you say will shock me more than anything my best friend has told me. She is married and has taken full advantage of her freedom. *Trust* me."

Well, all right then. "I had been trying to meet the Duke of Ironcrest."

Felicity's eyes grew to nearly the size of her kissing bough. And then she started clapping as her eyes danced. "Oh, *that* is excellent. Goodness. You were aiming for the Duke and ended up with Fitz." She broke out in a fit of giggles. "They are soooo very different." She paused and eyed Georgiana curiously. "You do know the Duke is known for his unique...preferences, do you not?"

Warmth rushed to Georgiana's cheeks. "Yes," she mumbled. Which only had Felicity squealing with glee.

"Oh my, oh *my*. You like those sorts of things?" Her eyebrows bounced in a very suggestive fashion. "My best friend, Lady Camoys, has had a few romps with the Duke. He is *depraved*."

Georgiana ducked her chin, her face on fire.

Felicity squealed. "Oh my, oh my, oh my. You like depraved things!" She leaned forward and dropped her voice. "No judgment on my end. Just...urm...best to proceed with caution with Fitzy. Poor man will probably end up injuring himself."

Georgiana's eyes widened. Heavens, the woman was probably correct. But this was not a topic she wanted to discuss out in the open in the Jennings's dining room. Time to change the subject. She fingered a spare branch of pine on the table.

"You know...if you are looking to best your decorations from last year, I might have an idea."

"Yes?" Felicity sat straighter, a soldier awaiting command.

"We could put up a full tree."

Felicity's mouth dropped open, and she stared at Georgiana with awe. "That is bloody *brilliant!*"

"We are *not* putting up a tree," a male voice echoed through the dining room.

12

Put up a tree? That was an outrageous idea. Who did such a thing?

"Why ever not?" his wife asked, a pretty pink pout on her lips.

Fitz stopped on the opposite side of the table from his wife and sister. "Because it is not done. Next, we'll be bringing in the woodland creatures as well."

His sister crossed her arms over her chest and glared her identical amber eyes at him. Lovely. Two against one.

"It *is* done," his wife said pointedly. "Queen Charlotte did it." She arched an *I-have-you-there* brow.

And he supposed she did, because that was true. "But there is a crucial word in that sentence that you seem to be missing."

"And what is that?" Felicity asked with a saucy shake of her head. Clearly, his sister was going to fight for his new wife's inane idea.

"*Queen.* The Queen can do whatever she bloody wants. She also houses an elephant in her stables. Shall we procure one of those next?"

"We're getting an elephant? What a marvelous idea." Felix strode into the dining room and dropped into the chair next to where Fitz was standing.

Fitz's shoulders slumped. He had a feeling they were going to be putting up the tree. Lord, his wife seemed to radiate from within, apple-cheeks bunched from her excited smile as she and Felicity eagerly informed Felix of their eccentric plan.

It was almost comical that Fitz—the odd one in the family—was the one who *didn't* want to do something as odd as put up a tree for Christmas. It was also alarming how many words he had just spoken, sans-stutter, to his wife. He had been articulate! He gave himself a little imaginary pat on the back.

If only the reason why wasn't so depressing. It was because his brain was too busy digesting the fact that the man his wife had been waiting bare-breasted for in Fitz's study was, in fact, the depraved Duke of Ironcrest. Big and beastly, dark and sinister, and chock full of all the confidence that Fitz himself lacked.

And if what he had overheard was correct, his wife was interested in the sorts of wickedness the Duke was known for. It was said Ironcrest always bound his lovers. Sometimes gagged them. And yet women clambered for a spot on their knees in front of him. *Oh, to be used by the Duke,* they whispered behind fans. That was what his wife wanted?

Fitz knew how to please a woman. And he knew *eventually* he would be able to bed his wife. But he had no experience with that variety of intimate activities. He supposed sex with the Duke was like a trifle to the ladies: multi-layered with fruit and custard and sponge cake soaked in sherry, loaded with whipped cream. But Fitz...Fitz was plain vanilla custard.

"I think it's a brilliant idea," Felix said, regarding the tree.

Of course he did.

His sister grinned. An evil, Felicity-has-an-*idea* grin. "I think Felix and Fitz should be the ones to chop down the trees."

Trees? "When did it become plural?"

"Since there are two of you, there must be two trees. Whoever chops down the largest one wins!"

He glanced around at everyone in the room as though they'd lost their wits. Apparently, they had. Because no one else shared a mite of his incredulity.

Fitz crossed his arms over his chest and tapped his foot on the floor. "Yes, let us go swing axes *for fun*. That seems spectacularly safe."

"It's perfectly safe, Fitz," Felix said with a roll of his eyes. "We'll be swinging them *at trees*. Not at each other."

"Don't be a prat, Fitz," Felicity added.

His wife's gaze darted around the group, her eyes wide with a mixture of alarm and amusement.

Felicity leaned toward Georgiana, eyes never leaving Fitz's, and said the words that always made Fitz capitulate. "Fitz is only trying to dissuade us because he knows he'll *lose*."

Ha. He'd lose. His arse, he'd lose. Plus, after overhearing about his wife's desires and whom she had those desires about, it would probably be beneficial to heave an axe at something.

"Get me an axe," he growled.

13

Georgiana

GEORGIANA SCRAMBLED AFTER FITZ as he trudged through the nearly ankle-deep snow toward a copse of trees off to the side of the manor. Cold air stung her face and was sharp in her lungs. The blasted man was on a mission.

They had quickly changed into warmer attire and then met back in the entry, both Fitz and Lord Bentley's faces grim masks of determination. This family. She shook her head. Competitive was too tame a word. Lord Bentley and Felicity had gone left out of the front entry, and Georgiana and Fitz had gone right. The thing was, her husband had much longer legs than she did. And they had walked at least the distance of two large ballrooms already. She could barely keep up without huffing and puffing about like a portly pug.

Fitz reached the edge of the copse and halted. *Thank the bloody gods.* He spun on his heel to face her, axe resting over one shoulder, hatchet in the other hand, brows set in a hard line.

He opened his mouth and hesitated.

Georgiana hesitated.

He glanced away.

She glanced at the snow.

This was awkward.

She didn't know what to say to him. Not after last night. And the uncomfortable kissing and the fleeing. The tree debate had been a welcome distraction before.

"Shall we pick a tree, then?" she ventured, toeing the snow.

"Yes, I suppose that is our aim. Urm, since you are so familiar with the Queen's Christmas tree, perhaps you choose what makes a good tree?"

He spoke to a random patch of snow to the left of her. One day, she would get her husband to look at her. The more he struggled, the more determined she became. She had no idea why *she* made him nervous. She was a nobody. A nobody whom nobody wanted.

She inhaled a breath and blew that undesirable thought right out of her, gloomy white cloud and all. It was a beautiful December day, with clear skies and snow-covered countryside. An opportunity. This was going to be fun. Fun with her new husband.

With a new bound in her step, she strode toward the small wood, eying the evergreen options. "How big does it need to be?"

"The bigger the better."

She stifled a giggle. Yes, well, she supposed that was true of most things in life. She glanced back at her husband. He was a large man, taller than average, but lean. She liked that fact about him. She wanted to feel small. At a man's mercy. Her gaze dropped to his hips, hidden behind his large wool overcoat. *The bigger the better.* Would she ever find out?

She shook away her lascivious meanderings and continued her march. She paused before a towering evergreen, its branches stretching wide, the bottom ones easily spanning two of her wingspans. Generously spaced limbs, leaving about a half-foot of space between each tier, ascended the tree, creating the perfect canvas for draping ribbons and beads and whatever other festive adornments Felicity and Lady Bentley could conjure up.

"Do you think we will win with this one?" She scanned up the tree, her head tilting back.

It must be twenty feet. Granted, she was a horrible judge of such things. For all she knew, it was actually fifty feet tall. She turned to Fitz, who was sizing it up.

He gave a decisive nod. "I think the odds are good." He tossed the axe into the snow by the tree, dropped his hatchet at his feet, and shrugged out of his large wool coat. His gaze flicked to her, and he held out his coat.

"Would you mind holding this for me, please?"

She hurried forward. "Of course."

She shot him a smile, and his cheeks, already rosy from the cold, bloomed a deeper pink. She gathered his coat to her chest. He glanced away and began attacking his cravat until he pulled it free and handed it to her.

"This, too, please."

She blinked, staring at his exposed neck. He had a nice neck. Was that a thing? She hadn't realized it could be. But her husband most definitely did. Corded muscles led down to more muscles where his neck met his thick shoulders and disappeared into the collar of his linen shirt.

Fitz cleared his throat. "Urm... Georgiana?"

She shook herself out of her daze and quickly took his cravat. "Apologies."

She clutched his items to her and stepped back while he gathered his hatchet and set up at the base of the tree. He rolled up his sleeves, exposing even more tempting sinew and strength: firm, clearly delineated, muscled forearms dusted in amber hair. She sucked in a breath. And promptly found herself enveloped in the scent of parchment and ink and cedar. She brought his coat even closer to her nose. Her eyes fluttered shut. *Shite.* Her husband smelled delicious, like reading a book while wrapped in evergreens. And he looked delicious.

Georgiana hadn't thought of how torturous this tree competition would be. She hadn't realized there would be exposed necks, and rolled up sleeves, and—her eyes stretched wide on Fitz's first swing with the hatchet—bulging biceps. Oh heavens. How was there snow out here when it was this hot? Because Fitz with a hatchet? She fanned herself. Which only wafted more of her husband's scent into her nose. He was all bumbling and blushing and brawny. And she liked it. Very much.

The muscles in his arm and back pulled his white linen tight with every swing, his breath labored. He grunted. Georgiana's breath caught in her lungs. Another hack at the tree. He grunted again. And again. And Georgiana nearly expired on the spot. Expired from lust. Because each time that hatchet connected with the tree, her core throbbed. Lord, those were *sex* grunts. Or at least she could imagine them being sex grunts. And he was sweating—this time in a delicious way—sweat born from exertion, not anxiety. She wanted those muscles, those grunts, that sweaty exertion—all directed toward her.

"I'm close," he grunted out.

Oh, dear.

"Just a little harder," he panted out, his voice strained.

Heaven, help me.

She needed distraction. Now. Before she jumped on her husband and shagged him right here in the snow. Which probably wasn't advisable. Especially when her husband was holding a sharp object.

She glanced at the tree, its branches shaking in time with Fitz's grunts. It *was* awfully tall.

"Right there."

Yes, right there between my thighs, please and thank you.

Oh, God. Distraction. "I'm nervous it's not going to fit," she yelped out.

He paused in his sex-grunting and glanced back at her, his ragged breaths clouding the air in front of him. He peered at her through furrowing amber brows. "Won't fit?"

She let out a relieved breath, some of the lust tightening her muscles, fading away. She had been one grunt away from rucking up her skirts.

"Yes. I'm worried it'll be too big," she said, albeit a touch breathlessly.

He cocked his head at her. She cocked hers right back. What was he not understanding?

"We've never done this before, correct? Which means we have no idea if it'll fit." She gnawed on her lip. "I'm afraid we won't be able to get it inside."

Fitz gaped at her. "I-I-I assure you it will fit." His face was turning an alarming shade of red. Especially considering it was already a deep blush from his exertion. His gaze skittered across the snow, and his throat worked frantically. Why was he so nervous speaking of the size of trees?

"I suppose if you're sure... I wouldn't want it to get damaged in the process of forcing it inside, though."

A strangled sound escaped her husband. "I promise you that you're-you're-you're...*you're*"—he waved a hand in front of her—"won't damage it. These th-things are made to accommodate each other. Regardless of"—he swallowed—"s-size."

She blinked at him. What? And then it dawned. Her eyebrows shot to the top of her head. *Oh, oh, oh.* She choked down a laugh. He thought she was talking about penises? A breath burst through her lips, and she broke out in a grin. Oh, that was bloody fantastic. And potentially very *fun.*

She schooled her expression and tapped her chin thoughtfully. "That is good to know. I suppose if we had to, we could coat it with something and see if that helped us get it inside. Would that be odd? Perhaps we could cover it in cooking oil. And then give it a good ole shove."

He stared at her in horror, jaw nearly in the snow. A laugh bubbled up in her belly, and she clutched her stomach, pressing her lips together. *Phewf.* Almost let that one escape. But she had one more jest to torture her precious husband with.

"Though I suppose this will all be a moot point potentially. If Lord Bentley's is bigger."

"If-if Felix's is bigger?" he sputtered.

She bit her lip painfully hard to prevent the laugh creeping up her chest. "Yes," she said, her voice strangled from suppressed laughter. "If his is bigger, then his is the one we'll use, isn't it?"

"Why would you ever think that?" His face twisted in alarm, eyes growing wider by the second. "Y-you want to—Y-you want Felix's?"

Her laughter promptly faded. At the hurt filling his wide eyes and the despondency thick in his tone. She hurried toward him, dropping to her knees in front of him. "No! No, no, no, Fitz. I was talking about *trees,* Fitz. But I picked up fairly early that you had taken my words to mean something else entirely. I was merely jesting, teasing." Her words tumbled over one another. "I beg your pardon. I meant it in good fun, but I think I pushed the jest a tad too far."

Lord, she was bungling this. Georgiana saw how he and his siblings teased each other. She had just wanted to join in. She was out of her element—the one where there was banter and merriment and love.

He frowned, staring down at the hatchet he was turning over in his hands. "Trees..." He nodded and glanced up at her, then let out a long exhale before a sheepish smile slightly curved his lips. "I misunderstood—not unusual for me. Though, my blunders are not usually that bad."

She smiled softly, her heart melting a little at the sight of her bashful husband. "I'm happy you made the blunder. You should have seen the look of horror on your face when I—" She broke out in a fit of giggles.

Fitz huffed out a laughing breath, a lop-sided grin breaking out across his face, his gaze tracing over her. "I will admit I was a mite alarmed when you said you wanted to coat it in cooking oil."

Her giggles turned into full-blown, belly-racking laughs. "I knew that one"—she sucked in a breath—"was a stretch with a tree"—another gasp—"but I just had to."

She waved a hand in front of her face. *Get a hold of yourself, Georgiana.* Before her husband determined she was dicked in the nob. Which she probably was.

She gathered a bit of powdery snow with her gloved fingers, fluffing it. She had spent more of her time with her own thoughts or talking to her dog than actual people. Georgiana wasn't entirely certain what was considered normal. Though she knew laughing like this—and most definitely jests about penises—were not permissible in a ballroom. But were they with one's husband?

Georgiana glanced at Fitz from beneath her lashes and stilled. Her husband no longer smiled, the lop-sided grin from before gone, the twinkle in his amber eyes doused.

She squirmed, her skin prickling. He stared at her like she was an oddity—or maybe a curiosity. She finally had her husband's undivided attention, and she wasn't entirely sure she could handle the intensity of it, the weight of it almost too tangible to bear.

"What?" she whispered. "Is something amiss?"

"Nothing," he murmured. "Nothing at all." He shook his head, his gaze clearing, breaking the heady spell. His lips tilted up. "Shall we get back to it?"

Back to the sex grunts? God help her.

"Let's."

14

Fitz strode into the entry, Georgiana at his side, toward where his brother and sister waited for them, still bundled in their overcoats, gloves, and scarves.

Felicity arched an overconfident brow. "Here to congratulate us?"

"Not a chance, sister," Fitz said. "I'm confident once the servants are done measuring, that haughty grin will be wiped right off your face. My wife was set on choosing the biggest one she could find."

"Then why on earth did she choose you?" Felix threw back.

Felicity chortled. "Now, now, Fifi"—Felicity patted Felix's arm—"you know what they say; it's not the size that matters, but how you use it."

Whaaaat? Felix and Fitz spun to their sister in unison, Fitz's eyebrows vanishing somewhere in the two-story ceiling above him.

"Where on earth did you—"

"How would you-you-you—"

They sputtered together, staring aghast at their little sister. Which only had her doubling over in laughter. Small giggles floated to Fitz from his side. Georgiana's eyes, crinkled at the corners, danced with delight, her hand covering her mouth in a failed attempt to stifle her laughter.

His shock at his sister's exclamation faded, and a smile pulled at his lips. His wife was beautiful—no, that was too tame a word. There was something about her tinkling laughter, her twinkling green eyes, the way her rosy cheeks bunched as she smiled. She was joy, unabashed, untainted by the world they lived in. She was a glimmering, freshly fallen snow before the mud and muck of conveyances and everyday life disturbed it. And he would be content to sit in his study with his Italian translations, staring at such a scene for the rest of his days.

An odd warmth settled low in his stomach. He pressed his gloved hand there, as though that would settle the somewhat fizzy sensation. Perhaps what he'd had for breakfast hadn't agreed with him. But the longer he stared at her, at those large, genuine forest-of-green eyes, the worse it became. He prayed she truly was genuine. It wouldn't be the first time Fitz had been made a fool.

God, when she had jested about Felix earlier, when Fitz had thought she was implying she would rather bed his brother. It was like he was eighteen all over again. Every part of him had gone cold, like he'd shucked off all of his layers and buried himself in the snow he had been sitting in. Everything disappeared, and all he could see were soft brown eyes, matching glossy brown curls, furtive glances, secret smiles. Little did he know, the secret wasn't for him. The secret was he was just a pawn in a grasping young woman's attempt to get to his brother. He rubbed at the tightness in his chest, at the wound the dagger Miss Eloise Browning had thrown had left, a wound that hadn't ever fully healed.

A decisive clap rang through the entry, wresting him from his past.

"We have measured and have the winner," Mrs. Smith, their rosy-cheeked buxom housekeeper, announced.

The silence was deafening.

Fitz, Felix, and Felicity all leaned forward.

Mrs. Smith, the cruel bawd, drew out the announcement. The Jennings's competitiveness was no secret in this household, and the servants enjoyed the revelry just as much as Fitz and his siblings did.

"The winner is..."

Silence.

Dear God, woman!

Felicity growled.

The housekeeper's lips twitched, and she slowly lifted her eyebrows.

"...Mr. Fitzwilliam and his lovely new wife!" Mrs. Smith broke out in a smile.

Felicity's face fell, Georgiana squealed, and Fitz gave Felix a consolatory clap on the shoulder. The fizzy sensation in his stomach intensified. *They had won!*

"We won?" Georgiana exclaimed, hopping up and down. Her hands were clapping so fast they were nothing but a blur. "Oh my goodness, we won?"

Felicity's upset was short-lived, and she was grinning now, eyebrows lifted in a bemused expression as Fitz's wife did a victory lap on an imaginary horse around the entry.

"I've never won anything before! I think I see why you lot love competitions so much. Victory is thrilling," she said, her voice an excited squeak.

Good Lord—and were those?—yes, she was making *clip-clopping* noises. He snickered. Well, this proved it: His wife was adorable. How unapologetically she lived her life, not a single reservation about galloping around her new family's entry like—well, like a fool. What did it feel like to be so comfortable in one's own skin? To be surrounded by others and be free—from apprehension, unease, panic.

His wife halted her imaginary horse back at Fitz's side and beamed up at him. "Congratulations, husband. You did most of the work, after all."

He snaked an arm around her and pulled her tight to his side. "Congratulations, wife."

He gave her a small squeeze. His pulse thrummed, a lightness spreading through him. Something inside him shifted as he stared into her bright green irises, so open and honest. How could one pair of eyes contain so many shades of green?

Georgiana's smile faded. Her lips parted, and she blinked up at him, all signs of elation gone, replaced by flared pupils and a glossy, far-away look. Oh, God. He was touching her. And she was looking at him. And her lips looked so soft. And little puffs of peppermint drifted from them. He could almost taste the minty sweetness. His skin heated, and not just from a blush. Shite. Lust. A flood of lust surged through him at an alarming pace.

He dropped his arm as if stung and put a safe amount of space between them. Which for Fitz would have ideally been a wheat-field sized amount, but he'd have to settle for a foot.

"I-I realize I have left my translations unattended for far too long." He took a large step backward, nearly tripping over his feet. He glanced at his siblings. "Another splendid competition, brother, sister. Jolly-good fun." Their wide, side-eyed expressions spoke volumes: Fitz appeared to have lost his mind. "Must be going. No need to wait up for me." A strained laugh fled his lips. "Georgiana, I mean. That was meant for Georgiana. Since she might—It's typical for a husband..." He cleared his throat and addressed the ceiling as he started shuffling backward. "My work will keep me detained into the late hours of the night."

He hurried from the hallway.

Dear Lord, where was an axe when one needed to lop off one's head?

15

Georgiana

Georgiana splashed her face with cool water and then patted her face with a towel. The crisp water did nothing to chill her heated skin. Or her heated thoughts. Because Fitz with an axe? She fanned herself. Visions of his understated strength straining with every swing of his hatchet filled her mind, flooded her core with something hot and heady.

She snuffed out all but one candle and made her way to her bed. But she couldn't snuff out the images of her husband. When the tree had finally toppled, still partly attached to the remaining trunk, he had picked up the large axe, hefted it over his head and brought it down, splitting the trunk clean in two. The display of vigor—she didn't have words. Hand an anxious man an axe, and she was dead. She frowned. That probably could be taken the wrong way. Dead in a good way. *La petite mort* way. It was probably *not* advisable to give anxious men axes normally.

And the whipped cream on the trifle in this whole affair? They had won. Though Fitz deserved every ounce of credit, since all Georgiana had done was drool behind him as her nose-buried-in-books husband turned caveman on her. Not on her. If only. When they had found out they had won, Fitz had smiled. A face-splitting, teeth-glinting, and definitely heart-stopping smile. He had reached an arm around her and squeezed her to his person. He had *squeezed* her.

She let out a long, frustrated groan and set her candle on the nightstand. And stupid, feather-brained Georgiana had to go and ruin it. What had she done? She had frozen, blinking dumbly at her husband, her entire body thrumming. Something charged had streaked through her. Because he had been *touching* her. Grinning at her. A grin that had rapidly faded away. An arm that had quickly disappeared. A Fitz that had instantly turned back into his flushing, stumbling-over-his-words-and-feet self.

And now, here Georgiana was, very much in need of pillaging by a caveman, without a caveman in sight. She could still feel the weight of his arm around her, the press of his body against hers. Not once in her various encounters had she ever been so drawn to a man. Which didn't make the least bit of sense, since her husband was not the sort of man she typically favored.

She clambered onto the very tall, very large bed and stretched her arms out wide. She stared up into the fathomless evergreen canopy, nearly black in the low light of the lone candle flickering in her chamber. Her husband had said he wouldn't be visiting her tonight. She ignored the way her heart sank at the thought. Her fingers twitched against the bed linens. Her hands didn't reach the edge of the mattress on either side.

It was extra lonely to lie in a bed so large. Extra cold. And she was extra overheated from her tempting, tongue-tied, tactless husband.

That wouldn't do at all.

She quickly divested herself of her nightdress and rolled over to her nightstand. She tugged open the drawer, withdrew a leather-bound box, and flicked open the lid. If her husband wouldn't be visiting her, then...

"Hullo, Derek. It looks like it's you and me tonight, darling."

She pulled out her trusty dildo, the flickering flame of the candle reflecting off the glossy, white ivory surface. Derek was always so good to her. After a few discreetly placed inquiries, Georgiana had learned of a woman who possessed a stall at the local market selling *baked goods*. It wasn't loaves of bread women left with in their baskets, though.

The seller had exquisite options—wood, siltstone, ivory, some with intricate carvings—but Derek had caught Georgiana's attention from the start. The woman had warned Georgiana not to expect her actual lovers to be anywhere near the size of Derek. Now that Georgiana had a mite of experience, she could attest to the woman's warning. She wondered how her husband would compare. Her heart rate spiked.

Georgiana wrapped her fingers around the cool ivory, her fingertips not quite touching. Some nights, she warmed him with her hands before she used him. But tonight—tonight she was too heated. Too heated by thoughts of her husband's muscled form, naked before her, above her, on her. She had to get through to him, get past his anxious exterior. She wanted to experience Fitz. Desperately.

She slid Derek down her stomach until he rested on the apex of her thighs. She hissed at the contact of chilled ivory to burning skin. She slipped him lower, between her legs, stilled. She bit her lip. What she wouldn't give for her husband to be in Derek's place, his weight, his bare-heated skin, pressed against hers.

Georgiana rolled the dildo against where she throbbed, where she was already trembling with want from thoughts of her axe-wielding husband. Her breath hitched, and a moan fled her lips. After their disaster of a first kiss, she should be nervous for when they finally came together. But aching anticipation consumed her, drowning out apprehension. Because there was something charged, like an electrical storm, that raged between her and Fitz. And in her mind? Their joining was as cataclysmic as the lightning from one of those storms.

She coasted Derek between her legs, the ivory growing slicker, her core pulsing harder. She was on fire from thoughts of her husband. Legs clenched tight together, she teased herself, toes curling with every drag. Every drag was pure torment, her body shaking with need, demanding she sink her dildo deep inside. Her eyes fluttered shut, and in the backs of her lids, all she saw were visions of Fitz. Hovering over her, caging her in between his corded forearms, slowly thrusting between her thighs. Tantalizing her and never giving her what her body yearned for—something to fill the emptiness.

Her skin was so sensitive, so swollen. She pressed harder, clenched her thighs tighter, her hips canting up as she pushed down. She would grip tight to the biceps she saw so gloriously displayed today, use that solid strength for leverage. She'd fight him, try to force him to give her what she needed, craved. To be filled. But in her fantasy, he denied her. He would bring her to the edge, ready to fall, and then take it back.

God, how she wanted that. To be tortured. To have the pleasure withheld over and over again. Fuck it, she couldn't wait. She could only hope that one day her fantasies about her husband would come true. She had no restraint; she needed a man to restrain her—Fitz to restrain her.

Georgiana drew her knees up and let them fall open. Then she sank her dildo deep inside.

"Oh, God." Her words melded into a moan. Her core coiled tight. Tension radiated through her. Fast. Sharp. A promise of pleasure. Her hips thrust on their own accord as she fucked herself on her trusted toy, every part of her wishing he was flesh-and-blood Fitz. And she really wanted to know what her husband's looked like. Felt like. Tasted like. Was he thick and long? Straight or curved? Salt and musk and man?

Fuck.

A tremor shook her frame. Pleasure spiraled, coiling tight. Derek did an admirable job. She would give him that.

But she wanted her husband's cock sinking deep inside her.

16

Fitz was desperate to sink his cock inside his wife.

And he was going to do it. Tonight. He marched to her chamber, eyes narrowed in on his target. He would not fail. Fitz stopped in front of his wife's chamber door and rolled his shoulders. He had chopped down a bloody tree today. He could fuck his wife.

When he had tucked Georgiana to his side earlier, it had felt so *right*. She *fit* there. Not the most eloquent way of putting it, but he translated other people's words for a living; he didn't make up words himself. And then she had looked at him, plush lips parted, cheeks and the tip of her nose rosy from the cold, pupils blown wide in her round eyes. He was nearly as confident as he was in his ability to translate Italian that his wife's expression was one of lust. Lust. For *him*.

As usual, he had gone and ruined it. He had calmly removed his arm from her person. Well, jerked it away in a rather ungainly manner. Then muttered a polite excuse. He grimaced. More like stammered a stream of stupidity. And fled with dignity.

Yes, so much dignity, Fitz.

But she had lust shining in her eyes, and he had *panicked*. His body had reacted, blood racing south. He had almost kissed her. Right there in the middle of the entry, surrounded by his siblings, servants, and trees, of all things. Of course that would happen. He'd finally found the ability to kiss his wife—properly, because he would have done it quite thoroughly—and it was the exact worst time for it.

The only option had been to get as far away from her as possible. Before he rutted with his wife on the marble floor. He had never in all his life felt such a powerful pull toward a woman. He didn't understand it. He wasn't a stranger to lust, and he was usually quite adept at controlling those urges. Because he was Fitz. Doing anything without thinking led to disaster. But there had been something elemental about his need for her back in the entry. Like he needed her like he needed breath. Which was ironic—because often times around his wife, he struggled to breathe.

So, he had fled to his study, collected himself, and now he was ready. Prepared with as much confidence as a man like him could muster. He straightened his shoulders, drew in a deep draught of air, and lifted his hand to knock.

"Hullo, Derek. It looks like it's you and me tonight, darling," a muffled voice drifted from inside his wife's chamber.

His breath exploded from him, and his fist froze mid-air. *What?* Who was Derek? And what was he doing with Fitz's bloody wife!

A hand slapped down on Fitz's shoulder, and he jumped.

"Everything well with you, brother?" Felix asked. "You've been staring—and now scowling—at your wife's bedchamber door for quite some time now."

"I—I—" *Come on, Fitz. Form words.*

"You are working up the courage to bed your wife?" Felix arched a brow at him.

Fitz's gaze darted from the dark-wood chamber door to his brother's concerned visage, an understanding smile tilting Felix's lips. This wasn't exactly the best time for a supportive brotherly chat. Another *man* was in that chamber with his wife.

Felix squeezed his shoulder. "I know it is easier said than done but try not to worry overmuch. To be frank, first times are often awkward. But I've seen the way she looks at you. Most wives don't look at the husbands *they chose* like that. When someone looks at you like that? Regardless of if you hit some bumps along the way, you two will find your, ah...harmony."

Fitz cocked his head as his brother's words sank in. The way she looked at him? At *him*? He looked around the hallway. Him, Fitz? Inept, stilted, and clumsy Fitz?

His brother chuckled and cuffed him on the shoulder. "Yes, you, brother. Your wife must find your nervousness charming. I hated that you were forced into this predicament. But I think, perhaps, this was actually a blessing in disguise."

A blessing in disguise. Was his wife with *Derek* a blessing in disguise? *Shite, Derek. The man currently with your wife.*

"Do you know anyone named Derek? A servant, perhaps?"

Felix's chin jerked in, and he studied Fitz under scrunched amber brows. Yes, Fitz realized the timing of that question made him seem like he had gone mad. Which was exactly how Felix was looking at him.

"Not that I am aware of... The only Derek I know—and not well, I might add—is Roderick Blackwood, the Marquess of Dunmore."

"Roderick Blackwood," Fitz muttered, turning the name over in his mind. The Marquess of Dunmore.

"Are you sure you are well, brother?"

"Yes, yes," Fitz said, distracted. He shot his brother a smile. "I am fine." He inclined his head toward the door. "I should get to it."

Felix chuckled and started walking backwards. "Good luck, Fitzy." He turned and lifted a hand in farewell.

Fitz spun toward the door, hand reaching for the handle. Derek better be ready for a muzzler, because Fitz's fist was about to greet the man's face with a hearty *hullo*.

Oh God. Those were definitely moans coming from her chamber. Every muscle in his body went whipcord straight, and it wasn't nerves. It was searing. Savage. Fury. If he had more presence of mind, he'd wonder where this possessive, primal rage had come from. But if another man touched her? The man was dead. Deceased. A corpse. Food for the worms. A growl ripped from him. *Touch her, and I will strangle you with my bare hands.*

He burst through the door and kicked it shut behind him.

"What the fu—" His roar died a quick death.

His wife screamed. And then scrambled to cover herself. He slapped a hand over his eyes and bolted out the door. Well, that had been his aim.

Thwack!

Urghhhh.

Right, he had kicked the blasted thing closed. He really needed to stop doing that. He rested his throbbing head against the very hard, very solid door. At least he hadn't fallen on his arse this time.

Unfortunately, the pain distracted him for…well, not at all. Dear God. Dear Lord. Dear Almighty. Dear Mary, Joseph, Lazarus, and Barnabas. He swallowed and gulped and, blast and damn, he couldn't breathe. He had just walked in on his wife. She was—Georgiana was—

"Fitz?" His wife's small voice came from behind him.

"I must beg your pardon," he said to the door, his voice strangled. His neck burned, fire racing up it to cover his face. "I sh-should have knocked. I-I promise it won't happen again."

"Fitz…"

But he was already out the door. He raced to his room nearly as fast as his brain raced in his head. His cock was hard as stone. Because—bloody hell—he had just walked in on his wife fucking herself with-with-with—*with a sexual implement.* How had she even procured one of those things? Sodding hell, that was the most erotic thing he had ever witnessed. Granted, Fitz wasn't exactly a conjugal aficionado. He wanted to go back and ask her to continue, to let him watch. Until she came.

He groaned and slipped into his room, then walked up to his bed and fell flat on his face on the mattress.

Thwump.

His heart constricted, each beat painful and sharp. Yes, that had been a glorious sight. But Georgiana hadn't been thinking of him. She has been fucking herself thinking of a man named Derek. Apparently, Fitz was destined to end up with women who didn't want him.

He thought back to Felix's words. Roderick Blackwood, the Marquess of Dunmore. Fitz tried to think of what he knew about the man. Could Georgiana know him? He was thick as thieves with the Duke of Iron—Fitz froze. Dunmore and Ironcrest were best mates, nearly brothers. Both known for debauchery and dark desires. Like his wife. Like his wife, who had been trying to have an assignation with the Duke.

Apparently, Dunmore would do just as well. And Derek—his Christian name? Had she already been intimate with the man? Fitz didn't truly know much about his wife. Relatively typical when the first time you met your wife was the night you compromised her. He had assumed she was a virgin. Which probably made him beetle-headed, because what virgin arranged for assignations?

God, Fitz, you're a bloody idiot.

His cock was completely deflated now. As was his heart. He didn't even know why he cared. It wasn't like he held any sort of tendre for his wife like he had for Miss Browning. If anything, whenever he was around his wife, he experienced intestinal distress.

He would never be the man a woman preferred. He had thought he'd come to terms with that. Apparently, he had somehow let some hope slip into his heart.

Foolish Fitz.

He slammed his fists into his mattress. His marriage was like a curricle heading straight for a stone wall. And Fitz had never been adept at driving curricles.

Crash.

17

Crash!

Fitz started at the sound of a slamming door echoing through the hall. He was sluggish this morning—after a night of little sleep, a confusing mix of desire and disappointment over his wife plaguing him. But even that loud bang had made it through his exhaustion-fogged skull. That couldn't be good. It had come from up ahead, from the direction of his brother's study. Which meant—

"That bloody hog grubber! The nerve of the presumptuous prick." Expletives exploded from his sister as she stormed down the hall in Fitz's direction, amber hair flying about her face as her violent movements tore it from her chignon. "He deserves a swift kick to the tallywags. The *nerve.*"

She barreled past Fitz, mutiny written all over her face.

He shot an arm out and grabbed her wrist. "Flick, easy. What happened?"

Felicity looked at him, cheeks flushed in apparent rage, and the fire in her eye instantly doused, replaced by rapidly forming tears. A sob tore through her chest at the same time she brandished a scandal sheet in front of Fitz.

He knew what that meant. Her fiancé was at it again, then.

Fitz pulled Felicity into his chest, and she broke down. She shook against him, and he tightened his arms, his chest just as tight for his poor sister.

"I hate him." Her muffled, watery words drifted up from his waist-coat.

Despite the fact the scandal sheet she had just shaken publicized yet another amorous encounter of her fiancé's, he knew who her words were actually directed at: Felix.

"Yes, I know Flick. But you also love him," he said soothingly.

"N-no, I don't. He has lost my love. He is nothing but a pile of dung on a hot summer's day to me."

Well. That was a visual.

"Maybe I'll fill his boots again—"

"Why don't we indulge in a glass of whisky," he hastened to suggest and divert his sister from her vengeful thoughts. It wouldn't be the first time she had planted manure in Felix's boots. Or Fitz's. His little sister was a termagant. A hoyden. And hilarious and loyal and loving.

"Indulging in a bottle of whisky sounds just the thing," Flick mumbled against him.

He frowned. "I had said a *glass*..."

But she was already stepping away from him and grabbing his hand and dragging him to the library. She strode straight to the sideboard, snatched the decanter of whisky, popped off the top, and took a healthy swig.

Oh dear.

He hastily took it from her. "My turn," he said gruffly. Then proceeded to pour them each a finger of whisky and managed to herd his sister to the couch.

She snuggled into his side and drew in a wobbly breath. He rested his chin atop her head. "Do you want to talk about it?"

She slowly spun her whisky glass in her hands, and he gave her time. Finally, she drew in a large breath, steadier this time, her head lifting and falling under his chin.

"Felix is the most boorish boor to ever boor."

Her voice was soft and sad, and it twisted Fitz's insides. And just like his stomach was tied in knots, so were his hands. There was nothing he could do to help Felicity. He hummed in agreement with his sister's statement. Truthfully, Fitz sometimes struggled to understand Felix's adamancy that Felicity marry Lord Wessex. The man was to be a duke, but the man was constantly written about in the gossip columns cavorting with women of ill-repute, cuckolding husbands, gambling recklessly, drinking to excess—he was caught pissing in a potted fern at a ball once. In view of *everyone*.

"Felix believes he is doing what is best for you, Flick. Lord Wessex may be a prig—"

Felicity scoffed.

"Agreed. That is putting it lightly. But marrying him will give you security and immense influence. It is no secret within this family that we share progressive views, views that are looked down upon, shocking to many. With that sort of influence, you could conduct change."

If anyone could change the world, it was his little sister. Fumbling, stumbling, stuttering Fitz? Not so much.

"I suppose I just have to sacrifice myself in the process," she said sullenly and then downed the rest of her whisky.

He winced. Felicity had always had *dreams*. Fanciful dreams of a knight on a white steed coming to save her, a man slaying a beast for her—though in Fitz's eyes it would be much more likely that Felicity slew the beast.

Fitz had never understood it because he had never given a thought to marriage. *Lie.* He would have been happy never marrying. *Lie.*

He had wanted to marry once. Back when he was a foolish, even more awkward young man of eighteen. But Miss Eloise Browning had taken swift care of that. After that painful experience, marriage was the last thing Fitz wanted in his life. He hadn't been lonely. He hadn't secretly longed for a companion, someone to quietly share a space with in comfortable silence. Not at all.

But here he was, married anyhow. The disaster that was his marriage settled heavily over him. He supposed his sister was justified in her upset. A disaster of a marriage wasn't a minor quandary.

"Have you spoken with Lord Wessex? About your concerns, I mean."

She leaned back and cocked a brow at him. "Have I spoken to him about cramming his cock in every chit he saunters past?"

He choked on his spit. When he could finally breathe again, he said, "Yes, urm...that. Just with a modicum more tact."

She huffed out an amused snort.

"I mean it, though, Flick. Talk to him. Perhaps he will be faithful once you marry. Or perhaps he doesn't realize fidelity is something you desire. It is not exactly *en vogue*. You two are not a love match. Maybe he hasn't thought to even try at one. If that *is* what you want?" He glanced at his sister, but she gave nothing away, just contemplative. "Communication is important."

"Mmmm," she hummed.

She still sounded sad, but she wasn't crying, and he could practically hear the gears turning in that mischievous head of hers. His lips curved. He would consider that a success. He didn't always know how to handle his sister, but he thought he might have just done a fine job.

"I suppose that is sound advice." She looked up at him and grinned. "For a prat."

He rolled his eyes at her.

She gave him a playful shove. "You know you're my favorite prat."

"I'm not sure that makes me feel any better." But his smile and the warmth inside his chest said otherwise. He struggled to belong in this family, as different as he was from the confident, cool-and-collected Jennings. So, he'd bask in this small moment of belonging with his little sister.

"Speaking of marriage..." she said slowly. "How are things with Georgiana?"

Or perhaps he wouldn't bask in it. Because all warmth fled his body like water through a sieve.

How were things with Georgiana? Was there a word worse than horrible? Terrible? Catastrophic?

"I quite like her," Felicity added.

That was the problem. Fitz thought he might, too. But his wife quite clearly didn't like *him*. She liked *Derek*. He bristled, and a growl fled from his lips before he could stop it.

Felicity shot up and looked at him with eyes as wide as melons. She thrust a finger at him. "*What* was that? Did you just growl? Fitzwilliam Jennings?" A sly, knowing look that only a sister could make slid over her face. "Are you all growly over your wife, Fitz?" She bounced her eyebrows. "That can only be a good thing."

A sigh burst from him, and he threw back the rest of his whisky. "It is decidedly *not* good. The marriage is a mess, and I muck it up at every opportunity."

"But you don't want to muck it up," Felicity said, her eyes gentling. "You want to un-muck it."

He dipped his chin stiffly.

"I don't think she minds your awkwardness." She tipped her head back, studying him. "She is nothing like your Miss Browning," she added softly.

Heaven, he hoped that would hold true. But right now... Fitz wasn't so sure that was the case.

"I think you might have gotten lucky with this match," Felicity added thoughtfully.

Why did everyone keep saying that? "Is it lucky that my wife wanted someone like the Duke of Ironcrest and got saddled with me—a bumbling imbecile—instead?" he grumbled.

Felicity shrugged and bopped him on the nose. "Eventually you'll stop bumbling and babbling and blushing. Before you know it, you'll be just as comfortable with her as you are with us. It will just take time, Fitzy. I think you should heed your own advice. Communicate with your wife."

Yes, because that was so simple for Fitz.

His sister hopped off the sofa and bounded toward the door. She turned in a swirl of skirts at the threshold and arched a brow. "Perhaps you'll find it's not the Duke of Ironcrest she wants." With that cryptic statement, she left.

He highly doubted that. And even if Georgiana didn't want the Duke, she assuredly didn't want Fitz.

18

Georgiana

Georgiana stood just outside the door of her husband's study. He had requested her presence in his study whenever was convenient for her, so here she was. Delaying. Her skin prickled, nerves skittering over her like an army of insect legs. Most exchanges with her husband were uncomfortable, but the one they were about to have was sure to elevate that discomfort to a whole new degree.

She feared last night's incident had ruined everything. She wasn't sure what *everything* was because their marriage—their entire acquaintance—had been fraught with blunders. Yet, her husband seemed to possess some mysterious quality that had Georgiana longing for things she really had no right wanting. Wanting only led to disappointment. But, blast and damn, Georgiana wanted her husband badly.

She took a deep breath and glanced over herself—and winced. Crumbs dusted her bodice, and she hastily brushed at them. She tended to be a nervous eater, and the cook's spiced biscuits served as the perfect distraction. Satisfied with her appearance, she stepped into her husband's dark, earth-toned study and quietly closed the door. What she had once deemed a room perfect for seduction now loomed...ominous.

"Fitz..." she said, hating the uncertainty lacing that lone word. She was bold, damn it, not wilting.

He didn't respond, didn't look at her. Just continued to stare down at his hands, fingers drumming against the desk he stood behind. Warmth bloomed over her cheeks even though he wasn't looking at her. *Wouldn't* look at her.

Georgiana did not embarrass easily, but having someone walk in on her while she was...her eyes slid shut. The rapid tapping of his fingers roared through her head, like he was drumming inside her skull instead. She had never been more embarrassed and horrified in her life that someone had seen her while she was—well... she had been fucking herself. There was no delicate way to put it. She didn't have anything against being watched. The idea actually appealed. But when she was *fully aware* it was going to happen. Planned. That was a very important factor. Not barged in on unexpectedly by an anxious husband.

She drew in a deep breath and walked up to her husband's desk, infusing herself with a boldness she didn't feel in the slightest with each step. It wasn't much, but it kept her standing and not fleeing from the room.

"Fitz, please say something. Have I completely horrified you?"

God help her. Wives, *respectable ladies*, didn't do such things. There was a reason the woman she purchased her dildo from posed as a bread seller. Goodness, there was a poem—*Signior Dildo*—about how much men scorned women's use of dildos. Granted, that was back in the 1600s, but attitudes had changed little. Masturbation was considered a sin.

She thought women might have been committed for things like this. The blood in her veins froze. Did her husband fall in with that way of thinking?

"Horrified?" he croaked out. He finally looked at her, and he didn't look angry. He didn't look disgusted; he looked…broken. His jaw tensed; his throat worked. "The only th-thing I'm horrified about is the fact that I barged in and interrupted what was a-a-a"—he stumbled and flailed for a moment—"a very private moment. I'm so unbelievably sorry."

The light flush on his cheeks deepened. "I would never be horrified that you did such things. I don't adhere to that nonsense, that women shouldn't know… That s-s-elf"—he swallowed—"p-pleasure is a sin." He paused and took a breath so deep his chest and shoulders visibly lifted and fell. "I realize you wouldn't know that about me."

The uncomfortable dance her stomach was performing settled slightly. She *hadn't* known that about her husband. There was quite a bit she didn't know. She twisted her fingers in her skirts, and they stood in silence.

He let out a slow, careful breath, his shoulders relaxing, and extended a hand out to the side of him. "Would you come here?" he asked softly, his features just as soft, amber curls falling over his brow. And here was another moment where her husband's handsomeness ascended to harrowing heights.

She wound her way around his desk and took his hand. He didn't flinch; he didn't jerk back. He closed his fingers around hers and pulled her forward, pulled her heart right to him. Her stomach was dancing again, but it wasn't nerves. It was like her husband possessed some secret ability. He stumbled around under the facade that he was a walluping sort, an awkward, clumsy cove. But underneath it all, he was the most dangerous of rum dukes. That it wasn't something he flaunted made it that much more formidable.

He gently placed her between himself and his desk, drawing in measured, methodical breaths. If she wasn't mistaken, she thought she heard him counting on each inhale and exhale. She leaned against the desk behind her and gave her husband the time he clearly needed to keep his composure. She hadn't realized how much taller than her he was until this moment. Georgiana had always been on the shorter side, but her husband, who had at least a head on her, was very much on the taller side. He may be lean, especially compared to Georgiana's curves, but goodness he towered over her. She liked that. A lot.

And that was when his attire finally registered. She cocked her head and studied his waistcoat. It...it had *tassels* on it, large, curtain-sized tassels. And pompons. And was that *actual* greenery? "What in the world are you wearing?"

A bead of sweat dripped down his forehead, but he broke out in a semblance of a smile, the tension in his jaw easing. "This is my ugly waistcoat." He withdrew a handkerchief and mopped his forehead with an only slightly trembling hand.

"Your ugly...waistcoat?" She glanced back at the disaster. It was white and lumpy from the tassels and pompons. The pompons varied in size from berry-sized to—she wrinkled her nose—egg-sized. There were horribly executed snowflakes embroidered on it. And on each half of the garment was a half circle of—yes, it was the actual plant—holly, red berries and all. And when viewing the two halves together, well, her husband was wearing a lumpy snowflake waistcoat with a holly wreath on it.

"The Jennings family has an ugly waistcoat competition every year," Fitz said by way of explanation. "My father suggested we do it for fun one year and, well, we Jennings don't really need much of an excuse to turn something into a competition. So, each year, we make our ugly waistcoats and the most offending one wins."

Of course, they would have an ugly waistcoat competition. Only the Jennings. And her husband's attempt...well it looked as though a snowman had vomited all over it and decked a festive wreath on top. It was hideous.

"Urm, next year you are welcome to take part," he added belatedly. "We make them ourselves and it takes quite a bit of time, so there really wasn't much opportunity this year. And none of us were really expecting..." He looked over her shoulder and worried his lip.

Her.

This Christmas was much different from what she had been expecting, too. She reached out and ran her fingers over a lop-sided snowflake. He stilled.

"Does that mean you embroidered these yourself?"

The breath he had been holding burst from him. "Yesssss," he hissed out to the space over her shoulder. "That is the number one rule. You must make the entire thing yourself."

A silly, fluttery reel picked up in her breast. Why was it so charming to think of her awkward, blushing, Italian translator of a husband bent over a waistcoat, feverishly embroidering, all in a bid to win an ugly waistcoat competition amongst his siblings? Truly, could there be anything more heart-melting?

But they were not here for ugly waistcoats. They were here because he had walked in on her last night. The flutter in her chest turned into a rampant, agitated ticking.

"You asked to see me...Fitz."

His gaze finally shot to hers. He shifted on his feet, his throat bobbing frantically in time with his swallows. The nerves were back.

He cleared his voice, but even so, when he spoke, his words came out like he had a frog stuck in his throat. "So. Urm. I-I thought it was time we talked. Became acquainted. I realize I haven't made that easy—possible at all—this past week. But I was reminded how important communication is." He hadn't looked at her for any of what he just said, but his gaze latched onto hers now, sincere, vulnerable, beautiful. "And I *really* want to converse with you."

Georgiana's heart bloomed, bloomed like new life in spring. She really wanted to converse with her husband, too.

"I would like that, Fitz," she said, whisper-soft.

His gaze dipped to her lips and then back to her eyes. His amber gaze seemed tortured, those mahogany striations dark and stormy, and she didn't understand why.

"Perhaps we should start with what we want this marriage to be," he said, his voice choked. "D-do you want a marriage in truth or just in name?" His fists clenched, and her attention shot to the movement.

"In truth," she said instantly.

She hadn't even deigned to hope for such a thing under the circumstances. But if there was hope? Pardon a moment while she gathered her grit in one hand and determination in the other, because she was going to take that hope and turn it into reality. Georgiana was a fighter. She fought every. Blasted. Day. To smile, to maintain optimism, to find the beauty in a life that sometimes seemed determined to strip every bit of it away.

His shoulders relaxed an infinitesimal amount, and he blew out a small breath. "So you want to bed me? When I work up the nerve, that is." He glanced at her through thick amber lashes, that sheepish tilt she was coming to know and adore curving his lips.

Did she want to bed him? Good Lord, she had just fucked herself quite thoroughly imagining that exact thing.

She reached for his hand and squeezed. "Yes, I want to bed you." She shot him a gentle smile. "As you might have guessed after last night, I am not your typical blushing and ignorant virgin. If you'd prefer, we can start small and work up to a proper shag." She winked at him, and it earned her a quiet chuckle.

And somehow—that small chuckle?—was the most beautiful gift she'd ever been granted.

"So...urm...you are a virgin, then."

Her brows pinched. "Yes..." Though she supposed given what he saw last night, she couldn't blame him wondering. "I have never had...penetrative sex with a man."

Oh dear, now she was blushing again. Why was she blushing? She was always confident, flippant. But speaking so plainly about such matters, especially with a husband who just sucked in a sharp breath at the word penetrative, had her nerves jumbled.

He was nodding. And not saying anything. The nodding wasn't stopping. That was probably not good for his head. She reached up and gently cupped his cheek, stilling him. He opened and closed his mouth, but, as was to be expected, nothing came out. There was a question in his eyes—concern, doubt?

She searched his gaze. "Is there something you wish to ask me, Fitz?"

"Is Lord Dunmore your lover?" He blurted.

She dropped her hand and blinked at him. Her brain went silent. It stopped working. "Lord Dunmore…" She wrinkled her brow and stared at her nose. What on earth? Lord Dunmore? The Duke of Ironcrest's best mate? "I've barely spoken to the man." Let alone had any physical interactions with the man. Unless one counted when he nudged her into the Serpentine. But she didn't blame him. She had wanted to jump in herself after her mother's antics.

She looked up at her husband, who was wringing his hands in front of him. "Why would you think such a thing?"

"I-I overheard you last night speaking of a man. I assumed your lover. Urm. Derek."

Oh. *Oh.* She giggled. Oh, oh, ohhhh. That was actually quite hilarious. "Derek is my dildo, Fitz."

Fitz's face burst into flames. Red as hot coals and just as searing. She could practically feel the heat pouring off him.

"Purely named for alliterative purposes, I might add."

He was nodding again. "I see," he said in a garbled voice.

She bit her lip as he struggled to rein in his embarrassment. Apparently, she was the debaucher in this relationship. It wasn't her preference. When it came to amorous activities, she wanted to be ordered about, tossed around, dominated. But, staring at her husband—whose eye was twitching slightly—she found she didn't mind the thought of being the corrupter nearly as much as she originally thought. Because corrupting her husband held a potent appeal.

And perhaps... "If you ever want to, urm"—she took a steadying breath and lifted her chin—"if you ever want to watch me use him, like last night, I wouldn't be opposed..."

All right. So she needed a bit of work when it came to her sexual demands. But one didn't go from wanting to be controlled to confidently being the one in control in the span of a day.

His eyes widened and his breaths came faster. "You-gurrh-you-you."

Her lips twitched. Her poor husband.

He sucked in a breath. "You would want me to *watch*? Y-you would be all right with that?"

That sounded a tad like interest. "Yes. I..." Georgiana licked her lips. "I like the idea of watching and being watched," she managed.

Her husband's pupils flared, and he groaned. Oh dear. That groan was way too reminiscent of the other day. Visions of a grunting Fitz with an axe flooded her mind, and heat flooded her core.

He was much closer than before, his hands gripping his desk on either side of her, caging her in. When had that happened? His breath puffed over her lips, his eyes locked on them. The scent of whisky danced over her skin with each warm breath. Sharp, sweet, astringent. She could almost taste it.

"I'd like to kiss you again, wife." His voice dropped to a deep, rich velvet. "And this time I'd like to do it properly."

Georgiana trembled. Yes. Yes, yes, *yes*. She should probably say that out loud. "Yes."

"All right. I shall."

But he didn't. He rambled.

"I promise it'll be better than the last time—not that the last time really counts. I'm not sure that could even be considered a kiss. I panicked, you see. I don't think I'd ever been so nervous, and I'd never been with a virgin, and then I was worried, what if I couldn't make you orgasm? Did you even know what an orgasm was? Obviously, after last night, I know you know. I mean. You do. You *know*. Obvious—"

"Fitz?" Goodness, she couldn't get her husband to speak for the life of her, but now, *now,* when she wanted silence, she couldn't get him to *shut up.*

"Yes?" He swallowed audibly.

"Hush already and kiss me."

He nodded succinctly and finally, finally, her husband closed the distance. And unlike the last time, he didn't freeze. Soft, warm, sure lips passed over hers.

A hand slid up her back, guiding her flush against the solidness that was her husband. A soft rumble left her. Had she just purred? But who wouldn't purr when pressed into a hard, chiseled man.

Fitz's other hand nestled into her chignon and cradled her skull. He took full advantage of that leverage and slanted his mouth over hers. Over and over. Overwhelmed her with open-mouthed kisses.

And then he angled his head and sank inside her. She moaned at the contact, of the slick glide of tongue against tongue. There was no hesitancy this time. He filled her, devoured her with almost a feral need. Something had changed in her hesitant, apprehensive husband, and she was at a loss to know the reason why. Perhaps, like her, the need had stretched too taut and snapped. Allowing for pure, unadulterated hunger. Two people desperately hungry for each other, the barrier of discomfort and anxiety that usually existed between them gone. Blessedly gone.

And then he was gone.

No!

She chased him, but then froze. Large hands skimmed over her ankles. He was touching her. Up over her calves, knees, to settle above her winter wool stockings on bare skin.

There was a great chance she'd expire on the spot. If her lungs started working again, she'd be fine. *Come on, lungs, blast and damn.* She couldn't expire now. Not when her husband's fingertips were skimming lightly over her thighs. And thank all that was holy because she sucked in a blessed, life-saving breath.

He slid his hands up and down, each time closer to where she ached. His dark eyes bore into her, the bright amber gone, a murky mahogany left in its wake. His mouth was soft, lips parted, hovering close but not close enough. Heaven, help her, that stare. It gripped her like a hand wrapped around the nape of her neck. Helpless and completely at his whim. It was torture—his presence, his teasing touch—building a need in her core at a dizzying pace.

Up and down.

Closer.

Advance and retreat.

Closer.

So close to where she needed him. But always denying.

He slid back up and paused, his thumbs just below where she burned, throbbed for him. His fingers dug into her inner thighs.

"May I?" he asked hoarsely.

She whimpered at the coarse rumble of his tone, at the firm, possessive hold of his hands, her flesh only too happy to be at his will. It was delicious. Unexpected. Curious. A curiosity that was imperative she explore.

"Yes, anything. Just, yes."

His thumbs slipped over her center, and a soft cry left her. He watched her. And she watched him. Warm brown eyes nearly black, lips swollen, still wet from their kiss. A choked sound left him, almost like a half-sob. A desperate noise.

"Così bagnata. Così calda," he murmured against her lips. "So wet. So hot. For me?"

Oh, mio Dio. Did this man speak Italian in bed? Because if so, Georgiana was in very real danger of coming on the spot.

"For you, Fitz. It's all for you." The words were nothing but a whimper, barely coherent, because his thumb was destroying her.

He slid softly over her, spreading her wetness across swollen flesh. Gliding up and circling over where her body pulsed with a delirious want. Then he sank two fingers inside. Georgiana's hips bucked. Fitz groaned. She moaned. Apparently, her husband hadn't been lying when he had said he didn't require an instruction manual. Her body clenched around him, demanding. *More.* She needed more.

Their lips dragged over each other, neither able to muster an actual kiss, just a frantic skim of mouths, breathing each other in. And, as though he knew, he gave her more. He sank another finger inside, thrusting in a painfully sweet rhythm. He curled his fingers and swirled his thumb over her. The anticipation from the past few days had her blood heating to near unbearable extremes, fever hot. Every touch heightened, charged. Her mouth dropped open, small cries she couldn't control coming from deep in her throat. And each cry elicited a hitch in her husband's breathing. Like her pleasure gave *him* pleasure.

Lord, this man should write *his own* manual. Her husband knew exactly where all the right places were. Like that place deep inside that had even taken her a while to find. But Fitz knew. Oh, he *knew*. Another breathy cry left her.

"Micetta mia. Adoro come fai le fusa per me."

Her husband *definitely* didn't know she could speak Italian. Because—she whimpered—oh heavens. Fitz calling her his kitten? *I love how you purr for me.* He would never if he knew. And like hell was she going to tell him and have him stop. Her chest threatened to crack open. She was feeling too much, the pleasure pulsing through her veins too potent.

"Così bella, bellissima. Non ce la faccio più."

She couldn't take it either. She was so close. Just a little more pressure, just a little more—

Knock, knock, knock.

Click.

"Fitz, I need to speak to you."

And that was how Georgiana found herself unceremoniously shoved underneath her husband's desk.

19

FITZ HAD JUST SHOVED his wife under his desk. And now? Now Fitz was going to kill his brother. He was going to commit fratricide.

Because Fitz's fingers had been deep inside the tight, wet heat of his wife, and she had been moments from coming. He could feel the quiver, the hint of a flutter around his fingers.

Bloody fucking whoremongering ballocks!

"I don't know what to do about Flick," Felix said, his voice tired.

Fitz dropped into his seat, barely holding back his groan, hoping his brother hadn't seen his raging erection. He had no idea if he looked like he had been minutes from fucking his wife on his desk, but thus far, Felix wasn't looking at him strangely. He blew out a breath.

"Another talk regarding Lord Wessex go less than pleasantly?" he somehow managed, though his voice was noticeably deeper than usual.

There was a slight shuffling beneath his desk, and he hastily cleared his throat to cover the sound. And then hands slid up his thighs, and Fitz squeaked. He quickly broke out in a fit of coughing.

Felix eyed him but seemed to deem this normal for Fitz. For once Fitz was happy, he was a blundering buffoon.

"Flick spoke to you then. I am sure she had lovely things to say about me."

Were they really going to have this conversation now? There was a tugging at the placket of his trousers. His spine jolted straight in his chair. "I was able to convince her not to kill you." And now his voice was about fifty octaves higher than usual.

Felix cocked his head at him. "Thank you…" He scanned over Fitz, a slight question in his identical amber eyes. "I try to reason with her, but she cannot seem to get past the fact that Lord Wessex is fond of caterwauling."

Small hands dipped inside his trousers. And pulled out his cock. And stroked it.

"Nrrgh. Is that an un-unreasonable complaint?"

"Are you well, Fitz? You were acting odd last night and now you are again. Even for you."

Fitz sucked in a breath. Because his wife had just sucked his cock into her mouth. "Fine! Everything's fi-ine."

Felix paced the study, apparently too preoccupied to notice that Fitz's voice had just cracked like a green lad whose ballocks were dropping.

"I suppose it's not *unreasonable*," Felix said. "But it is *uncommon* to have a faithful husband. This match was exactly what Father worked so hard for. It is my duty as Earl to make it happen. I can't—won't—let him down." He yanked on his hair. "Not when I already have in so many ways," he grumbled.

Fitz opened his mouth to dispute *that*, but then promptly shut it to stave off his moan. Bloody fucking hell. The woman's tongue was criminal. He gripped the edge of his desk and started counting to one hundred. In Italian.

Uno, due, tre...

"The issue is they were betrothed young. Well, Lord Wessex was young. They were both one-and-twenty. Which is young for him and old for her," Felix rambled.

...Dieci, undici, dodici.

"Felicity will come around once they are married and Wessex settles down. I don't think it is all that shocking that he is out there"—Felix gave a toss of his hand—"frolicking about. It is what every young buck does."

It wasn't what Fitz had done. But that wasn't the point. He bit back a groan. The point was, his cock was now buried in his wife's throat. *She* was frolicking about quite fabulously with his erection right now. Dear Lord, how did she know how to suck a prick like that? Now was not the time for such a discovery. Not when his brother was turning and walking closer to Fitz's desk. Fitz ground his teeth. To sodding dust.

His blood thundered in his ears, pleasure streaking up his spine. Either his wife was the most talented wench to ever fellatio or Fitz was just now discovering he harbored a hidden desire for the thrill getting of caught. Perhaps both.

"Are you paying me any attention right now?"

Shite. Fitz hadn't been paying attention. How could he when Georgiana's tongue was swirling around his—

"Head!" He cleared his throat. "I-I am just in my head. T-Traaansla-tions."

Oh God. He was going to blow down his wife's throat any minute now. And *that* he wouldn't be able to hide from his brother. Not that he was doing an admirable job just now, as it were.

Fitz's hand shot to Georgiana's hair, and he jerked her head back. And his little kitten moaned. *Fuck.*

Felix's gaze shot to Fitz's desk and back up to Fitz's face.

Fitz's eyes widened.

Felix's eyes widened.

Bugger.

Felix started backing away. "I...I...think I'll come back later."

Georgiana, the little succubus, stroked his cock since she couldn't reach him with her mouth, still immobilized by his fist. She gave a little twist over his head, and Fitz hissed through his teeth, and Felix picked up his pace. Fitz couldn't answer his brother. Nothing articulate would come out. He was just trying to control his breathing, which wasn't easy when his lungs were slamming against his ribcage.

Felix stepped into the doorway and gripped the edge of the door. "En-joy your...head." He swung the door shut, his snigger echoing through the study.

Fitz's shoulders slumped, and he pushed his chair back. But he didn't let go of his *very* naughty wife. He glared at her. And what did the little minx do? She blinked at him, the picture of sodding innocence. Ha!

"You-you. *You!*" he sputtered.

More innocent blinking.

"You. Are," he gritted out.

"I am what, Mr. Jennings?" she asked demurely.

A shiver scurried down his spine. Her breathless words, her using his surname, her on her knees. *Fuck.*

"You are very, very bad. Incorrigible. Maddening."

Her eyes fluttered shut, and his mouth slackened. She liked him telling her she was bad?

"What are you going to do about it, husband?"

His gaze flickered over her face, her pleading eyes, her parted lips, her rosy cheeks. His wife had depraved desires. What exactly did she want from him?

He slipped his thumb over her bottom lip, coasting slowly.

She leaned forward, and his thumb disappeared into her mouth. Deep into her hot, wet mouth. His kitten purred again. He pressed down, and she gagged. Now that was a beautiful sight. His cock twitched, yearning for those throat muscles to contract around it.

"This?" he asked. She wanted him to be rough with her? To show her what happened to a bad wench? His blood thrummed, thick with lust.

She dipped her chin and pulled back, his thumb slipping free with a *pop.*

"Use me," she breathed. "Please, Fitz. I ache to be used."

His breath fled him in ragged bursts. Just as his heart beat ragged in his chest. He wasn't well-versed in this. He wasn't a man who had experience in any sort of darker desire. He wasn't the Duke, he wasn't Dunmore. He was vanilla syllabub. He wasn't who she wanted. The ragged breaths, the ragged beating, turned sharp and painful and choking.

He stood, his chair sliding back, but she followed him. Didn't let him retreat. Her hands latched onto his thighs, and she looked at him, sincerity shining in her green eyes.

"By you. I want—need—to be used by *you*, Fitz."

He didn't understand how she knew he needed to hear those words. But it was exactly what he needed. Sometimes when he was around her, he thought...she might be exactly what he needed. He shook off the terrifying thought and focused back on his flushed wife on her knees, begging him to use her.

And just for clarity's sake...

"You want me to f-fuck that pretty mouth of yours?" Lust pulsed in his cock. Just saying the words had him growing even thicker. "Hold you still, while I"—he paused, swallowed, trying to force the words out of his too-tight throat—"use you for my pleasure?"

"Please," she whined. Her gaze dropped to his cock, and she whimpered.

He could do that. God, could he do that. He just didn't want to hurt her.

"You...will tell me if it's too much?" He gave her hair a little shake, and her gaze left his cock to meet his eyes. This was important. "You will tell me if it's too much, Georgiana?"

"It won't be."

Bloody hell. She said it so quickly, with such surety. Fitz supposed he was going to fuck his wife's mouth now, then.

He tightened his grip on her hair and pulled her to sit tall on her knees. Her mouth parted, and her small pink tongue darted out to wet her lips. Readying herself for him. He groaned. She truly wanted this. *I am the luckiest man alive.*

He dragged her head back, stretching her neck to the side, delicate, elegant. He traced a finger down the soft column. She shivered. She was beautiful like this. Seductive. Supplicant. And for the second time in Fitz's life, a foreign, primitive impulse came over him. *His.*

He cupped her chin, turning her toward him. Then hooked his thumb on her bottom teeth and pulled her open for him. His free hand went to his cock, and he gave it a few slow pulls. He was painfully hard, his cock angry and weeping. The climb to orgasm with constant interruptions had him near exploding. With frustration. With want.

He eased into her mouth, and they groaned in unison. His eyes fell shut as he slid in and out of her. Shallow, but slowly slipping deeper, deeper as she coated him, made him slicker, wetter. She wrapped around him so tightly; it was otherworldly in its bliss.

His gaze collided with hers. She watched him, nostrils flaring, lids heavy. The sight was too much, watching his cock disappear between her slick, pink lips stretched wide around him. He thrust harder. And Georgiana didn't bat an eye. Lord, could she have truly meant it? *It won't be.* He snapped his hips forward, and the chit bloody swallowed.

Fuck. Fuck fuck *fuck.*

His shock must have shown on his face because her heavy lids lifted slightly, a seductive glint glowing in her eyes. If her mouth wasn't full of his cock, he knew she'd be smirking at him. *Saucy kitten.*

"Mia audace micetta," he murmured through pants.

Pleasure careened through him, settling heavily in his cock, every slide of her tight, warm mouth over his prick devastating. He leaned forward, bracing a hand on his desk while holding her securely by the hair with his other. Her hands had latched onto his hips.

He thrust into her again and again, building up to a rough, ragged rhythm. Dear God, this was paradise, heaven, ecstasy.

"Tu mi prendi così bene, micetta."

His kitten took him so well. So beautifully.

"Sei bellissima."

Georgiana moaned, the delicious vibrations shooting a streak of pleasure straight down his spine. He glanced at his wife, and a long, low groan left him. Because Georgiana had her skirts rucked up to her waist, and one of her hands had disappeared beneath the fabric. Her eyes were glazed, unfocused. She took him easily, each drive of his hips. And touched herself. Her own hips moving in tandem with his. And something about that fact blew his lust into a burning frenzy, flames of pleasure threatening to destroy him. Because him fucking her mouth? Sinking his cock deep past those pretty stretched lips? She liked it. She clearly loved it. Lusted for it.

"Dio, vorrei poter sentire quanto è bagnata quella bella fica."

I wish I could feel how wet that pretty cunt is.

It was so much easier for him to let the words fall, knowing she didn't understand. One day he'd work up the courage to say them. But for now, Italian would have to do.

Her moans grew louder, and his thrusts grew harder.

"Così. Prendimi fino in fondo, amore."

He sank deep, and she gagged. He nearly came. He nearly ended this bliss much too soon. But then she pulled off him, her fingers digging into his hips, and she cried out. Her body tensed, then convulsed, and she buried her face in the crook of his hip as shudder after shudder wracked her frame, the most beautiful moans fleeing her lips, sinking into his skin.

He barely had time to savor the sight of her, the sound of her, the soft sighs that seared him. Shattered him. Because she was back on him, swallowing him to the root. And she took control this time. He merely held onto his desk for the ride. A ride of wicked pleasure that filled every crevice, throbbed heavily in every muscle, pulsed violently in every vein.

The pressure peaked, lurched to an unbearable height. Fuck, it was too much. It was—It was ecstasy. Fitz's lungs heaved, and he gritted his teeth, but he was nothing against what was raging inside of him. His hand shot to Georgiana's head, and he sank to the back of her throat, held her there as his pleasure crested. The release shot through him, surge after surge of agonizing bliss. Everything disappeared except for soul-crushing pleasure and the incredible woman on her knees delivering it.

"God, Gigi," he groaned, low, guttural, undone.

He had never come so hard in his life.

And neither of them had been anywhere close to quiet. If anyone was even remotely near, it would be no secret what they had just done.

Fitz slumped back, falling into his chair, and she fell back on her bottom, both gasping for air. He quickly tucked himself away and yanked a handkerchief from his pocket. He leaned forward and gently took her chin.

And paused.

She was achingly lovely. His stomach twisted and tightened. Painfully lovely. A few tears had left tracks down her cheeks, her mouth glistened, and—by God—some of his cum had dribbled down her chin. Oh, how he wished he could commission a painting of this image. No. No one was to ever see her thus. Just him. That word floated through his mind again. *His.*

He softly dabbed away her tears. Then swiped away the evidence of his release off her chin. He folded the cloth over and used the fresh side of his handkerchief to carefully clean her lips.

Fitz dusted his knuckles over her flushed cheek, warm to the touch from her blush. She leaned into his touch like a contented kitten. His contented kitten.

"Did I please you, husband?"

Did she please him? He almost scoffed. He couldn't articulate how well she pleased him. The words didn't come. And for once it wasn't because he was nervous, it was just that there were no words to describe the enormity of it.

He just stared at her. His beautiful wife. Green eyes glowing, lips swollen, a stark-pink against her creamy skin. Creamy all but for the blush painted high on her cheekbones. And bloody hell, her chignon in tatters from his touch. Just as his heart was from hers.

"You did so well, bella," he finally murmured. "No one has ever, nor could ever, please me so well."

She preened under his regard. And his chest swelled to the point he was sure it would burst. She wanted to please him. This beautiful, confident woman wanted to please *him*. And he, bumbling Fitz, had clearly just pleased her.

He pulled her into his lap, and she nestled into his chest. Like she wished to be there. He pressed kiss after kiss to every part of her he could touch: her hair, her forehead, the delicate curve of her ear. And then he trailed a finger under her chin, gently tilted her up to him, and dusted kiss after kiss to her lips. She sighed, one that whispered hopes and dreams and promises against his skin.

His swollen heart skittered across his rib cage. And even though he was the one holding her, the one doing the holding, he fell into her. And he thought, just maybe, this sensation swirling in his chest could be everything falling into place. Did she feel it? Or, like so many other things in his life, was he alone in this, too?

20

Georgiana

Georgiana wondered if Fitz felt it, too. How something about what they had just done, something about being in his arms, was different. Right. She hadn't lied to her husband; she wasn't a blushing virgin. She had sucked a prick or two in her twenty years of life. But never had it been anything more than a physical act, slaking lust, fulfilling a desire, a sexual experiment. But with Fitz? She had almost gone and done something completely embarrassing like cry afterwards. She had been so utterly overcome. Still was.

Maybe it was the way he had called her Gigi, a pet name that only existed for her with him. Or maybe it was the way he had instantly reverted into caretaker afterwards. There had been no thought for himself. He'd reverently cleaned away her tears, the evidence of what they had just shared, and then she was in his arms. His lips dusted over her, and it was like all the pieces of her, the broken pieces she hid deep inside, fit perfectly in his arms.

She ran her hands over his upper chest, a small twinge of disappointment piercing through her. She wished she had gotten to explore more of him. She plucked at his linen shirt hiding what she was sure was a delectable physique.

"Is something amiss?" he murmured.

"No." She glanced up at him and the words on her lips, the thoughts in her brain, died a swift death. Nothing remained but gleaming sated eyes darkened to a rich mahogany—intoxicating, entrancing. And that was what this man seemed to have done to her—pulled her into a spellbinding trance one only read about in folklore. Their breaths mingled, warm whisky and sweet cinnamon overwhelming her senses. Fitz overwhelming her senses.

Her fingers twitched, crisp linen dragging over her fingertips, breaking the hold he had on her. She cleared her throat and cleared away the headiness of whatever had just passed between them.

"I was just wondering if your body is as delightful as my fingertips have determined it to be." She smiled cheekily at him. "That and, to be frank, holly is not very comfortable to cuddle with."

His cheeks, already flushed from orgasm, bloomed a deeper hue. "I'm happy to remove it and, urm, make you more comfortable and satisfy your curiosity."

Her gaze went to his, and she smiled. Her fingers found his cravat. "May I?" But she was already loosening the knot and pulling the neckcloth free. He chuckled, a low rumble reverberating into her. She stilled, her eyes flicking to his. "You have a lovely laugh." And now his ears matched his cheeks.

"Me?" His lips twitched. "My laugh is usually as strangled as my throat trying to form words."

She nearly had his waistcoat undone—not a simple task with the giant wreath of holly on it—and then moved up to the buttons that closed the V of his shirt. "You don't seem to be strangling overmuch right now." She pushed off him and stood. "There, now off with it."

He shrugged out of his waistcoat and then reached behind his head for his shirt. "I'm chocking it down to languidness and temporary insanity," came his muffled response inside his shirt as he pulled it over his head.

A shy grin peeped from under his hem. "I'm sure I'll be bumbling again soon. And I'm still blushing, so there is that."

But Georgiana barely heard his words. Because she was struck dumb. She stepped forward, hands trailing over each little square of muscle on his abdomen. "How do you look like this?" she whispered. "I thought you did Italian translations for a living." She looked up at him, but didn't stop touching him. Couldn't. His skin twitched and quivered under fingers, hot to the touch.

"I-I take it you approve?"

A slight stumble, but she wasn't sure if it was because her fingers were perhaps tickling him or if her bold exploration had brought his nerves back. She nodded, her gaze falling to the large, hard discs of his chest. Her fingers traced the delineated muscle, circled his nipple. He hissed in a breath between his teeth.

He was broad and all lean muscle. Not bulky, not like a blacksmith or a dock worker. But there wasn't an ounce of fat on him. She leaned side-to-side, searching for it. Poked and prodded. Not. One. Bloody. Ounce.

"I s-swim," he finally answered her earlier question. "We have a bathing pool here at Thornfield Hall, heated with numerous fireplaces so it can be used during all seasons." His breath caught when her hands traveled over the triangular muscles where his shoulders met his neck. "I find that it is somewhat thera-peutic." He cleared his throat. "For anxiety, when I get in my head."

She tilted her head and studied him, his amber eyes now avoiding hers. "It would appear you swim quite a lot," she murmured.

He rolled his lips in, his fingers tapping at his thighs, like he didn't know where to put them. "I'm in my head quite a lot."

Her palms coasted down his arms to his wrists. She slowly brought his hands to her hips and stepped closer to him. His chin dropped down, hers tilted up, their gazes locked. She gripped his biceps to keep herself from falling backwards. Falling for him.

"I don't mind," she said, her words barely audible.

His strong amber brows pinched.

"The nerves, the awkwardness, the stutters and stumbles," she clarified. "If you get lost in your head and need time to come back out... I'm a very patient person, Fitz." She had been patiently waiting her entire life to be free from her lonely existence. Being patient with her husband would be no task at all. And she found...she quite wanted to know what that patience would bring.

His lips coasted over hers. "How did we get here?" he asked, his voice soft with what sounded like awe.

She pulled away and sent him a cheeky smile. "I believe my breasts might be to blame for that."

He stiffened against her, and she blinked, unsure of what caused the instant tension. And it wasn't a good tension. He cleared his throat and stepped back, grabbing his shirt.

"I should probably get back to my work," he said, throwing his shirt back over his head.

She slowly backed away. Was that hurt in his eyes? But whatever for?

"I—" He shook his head and seemed to shake away whatever upset had overcome him. "Thank you for speaking with me, Gigi," he said softly.

And then he was sitting and picking up his quill, and she was leaving, wondering how, after experiencing something that had felt so right, she suddenly felt as though everything was wrong. But he had called her Gigi again. So she was going to hold on to that.

21

Georgiana

GEORGIANA HADN'T SEEN HER husband since she'd left his study ear-lier. Since their incendiary connection had been doused by a bucket of cold water, one that had come out of nowhere. Well, not nowhere. Apparently, Georgiana had been the one to throw it. But now he was here, with her and the rest of his family in their library. Yet, he wasn't.

Fitz sat in an over-sized, leather armchair before the low-burning fire, adorable spectacles resting on his perfectly straight nose, and a book in his lap. He had turned the monstrosity of a chair to face the rest of them, but he was still...apart from them. He had barely acknowledged her presence.

Georgiana, Felix, and Felicity were gathered around a coffee table in the middle of the library, the pair of settees pulled back to give them plenty of room to sit on the floor around the table. His mother, Lydia, sat on one such settee observing her children while she embroidered what looked like a handkerchief.

So yes, they were all together, celebrating Christmas Eve, but...not. Georgiana glanced discreetly at her husband, who was brushing back a temperamental curl that kept falling in front of his spectacles while he read. *Argh.* That man. Beautiful. Awkward. Unexpected. She wished he'd join them. Join her.

Gigi. Him groaning the pet name echoed through her mind, and she shivered. She had liked that a great deal. She'd liked the entire thing a great deal. Until she had ruined it. She was all too familiar with being dismissed, with walls. When she had brought up their initial encounter in his study, him finding her there bare-breasted, he had closed himself off to her, erected a barrier, pushing her back into the lonely tower she had inhabited her entire life. She didn't understand why.

But it also didn't seem like it was only her he pushed away. It wasn't the first time over the short duration she had been in his life that she had noticed he always seemed to separate himself. *I'm in my head quite a lot,* he'd said. Was there room for her in that anxious mind? She was starting to realize she really wanted to take up residence there.

Could two lonely souls find a shared home together? She was foolish to hope that, to risk what it meant if it couldn't be. Her heart. It didn't matter, though, because she was helpless against it. For the first time in Georgiana's life, she felt seen, and with every peek into the enigma that was Fitzwilliam Jennings, the more she craved to uncover.

The man was endearingly awkward and unforeseeably filthy. The things he had whispered in Italian—Georgiana fanned herself. Thinking about her husband's glorious cock and vulgar tongue when about to play a festive game on Christmas Eve with his family was decidedly not what she should be doing.

A cork popped, pulling her attention to the coffee table where Felicity poured a hearty measure of amber liquid into four snifters. Georgiana fought a grin. Felicity looked completely ridiculous. Her ensemble consisted of a skirt paired with a separate bodice—the bodice of which was covered in white, gray, and black feathers. And in the center of the bodice? An exceptionally crafted, stuffed goose head.

Felicity's ugly waistcoat: the Christmas goose.

Georgiana's grin won out and spread across her face. An ingenious idea. Felicity had won the competition, much to her bemoaning brothers' dismay. But honestly, the woman had a floppy goose head hanging from her bodice. She deserved the win.

A shallow dish filled with raisins sat in the middle of the table, and small bowls rested in front of her, Felicity, and Felix.

"Felicity, what are you doing?" Felix asked with a huff and a jingle, his voice thick with older brother exasperation. Yes, with a huff and a jingle. Because his gold waistcoat was covered in silver bells. And strings of gold beads. And a blinding number of metallic accents. It was a little hard to look at, if Georgiana was being honest.

Felicity looked up and frowned. "What does it look like?"

"The brandy was for snapdragon. Not to drink."

She blinked at Felix. "You expect me to stink my fingers in fire without imbibing?"

A snort came from the massive armchair.

"What was that, Fitzy? Did I hear something come from that quiet corner over there?" Felicity asked loudly.

"Just think it's funny you'd say you need liquor to do something reckless, sister," Fitz mumbled back to her.

Felicity shrugged. "True, but it does make it more fun if you're a bit bosky." She turned to Georgiana and winked.

Felicity was a joy, impish and fun and a little bit naughty. Georgiana loved her. She was like a best friend and sister, all wrapped up in one. A small twinge stirred in her heart. Something Georgiana had never had. No sister, nor best friend. She had friends growing up, but no one she was able to get close to. Her family lived in a strange in-between, above the middle-class, but below the elite *haute ton*. Her mother didn't want Georgiana associating with other girls whose families were in trade, and the young ladies of the ton didn't want to sully themselves with associating with her.

"Fitzy, will you be joining us?" Felicity called to her brother. Then she leaned toward Georgiana and whispered loudly, "Fitz never joins us. Too delicate. Too worried about burning his appendages."

Georgiana chuckled. She hoped once she and Fitz moved into his London town house, they'd still be able to visit with his family often. She would miss this camaraderie. The only other time she'd had such friendship was with her beloved Bernie. A sharp jolt went through her chest, and she let out a slow breath. Sometimes the grief came streaking back out of nowhere.

"I personally like my fingers. Thank you very much," Fitz said, sounding very much like a cantankerous old man.

"I don't think she was talking about your fingers, Fitz," Felix's deep baritone chimed in.

He caught Felicity's gaze, and they glanced at their brother and broke out in sniggers.

Georgiana frowned and turned to her husband—who was quickly turning an alarming, blotchy red.

"What—" Georgiana began.

"A few years back," Felicity said eagerly. "We were playing snapdragon and one of the raisins Fitz pulled out was especially hot, still burning with a flame. He'd dropped it right on the front of his breeches." She grinned, devilish delight dancing in her amber eyes. "Burned his co—"

"Felicity Mary Jennings!"

"I beg your pardon, Mother," Felicity said, not an ounce of contrition in her expression or tone. In fact, the young woman's grin only grew.

"It was *one* time," Fitz gritted out. Her poor husband was still bright red. "And it gets brought up every year."

"Only because you haven't played since," Felicity pouted. "I had *thought* you were competitive. Or did you burn off your whirlygigs as well?"

Georgiana's hand flew to her face to cover her snort.

But apparently, Felicity's taunting was all for naught.

"It's not going to woooork," a slowly-returning-to-normal-coloring Fitz sang. "Some things are more important than winning."

Georgiana smiled softly. The hint of the playful side to her husband? Another layer pulled back. Another dangerous layer. She wanted to pull them all back until she found the true man underneath. Nothing but raw and naked Fitzwilliam Jennings. *Mmmm, naked Fitz.* She growled at herself. *Stop, Georgiana!*

Felix chimed in, drowning out her growl, "I'd have to agree, protecting one's cock trumps winning."

"Children," Lydia reprimanded. But there was no bite in her tone, and she hadn't bothered to look up from her embroidery. A small smile even tugged at the corner of her lips. This was clearly all very normal behavior for the Jennings.

"That is beautiful embroidery," Georgiana murmured to Lydia, studying the cloth: a book with initials overlayed on it.

Lady Bentley glanced up at her and broke out in a full smile. "Thank you, dear. I like to embroider handkerchiefs for my children. I'm always needing to embroider new ones for Fitzwilliam. He goes through them like a child with sweetmeats. You know, with the poor dear's propensity for sweating."

Georgiana looked at her husband, who was gazing at her in wide-eyed terror—she swore his eyes were larger than his spectacles—his blush fully back in place.

"Oh, don't look so horrified, Fitzy," Felicity said. "We all know how you're nervous and jittery and anxious and sweaty and stuttery and awkward and—"

"We get it, Flick," Fitz bit out.

"—you know, we always wondered if perhaps Fitzy had a different father. Because where in all of Christendom did all those qualities come from?" Felicity continued, despite her brother gnashing his teeth at her. "If he wasn't the spitting image of Father, I'd have had my doubts."

Georgiana's chin jutted in, taken aback that Felicity would make such a declaration in front of her mother, even in jest. She glanced around the group, but no one else seemed to blink twice at the statement.

"Mama and Papa were the epitome of a perfect marriage," Felicity went on with a dreamy sigh. "It is what I have always aspired to have in a marriage."

Georgiana's gaze darted to Lydia, who had stiffened at her daughter's words—not at the jest of an affair, but at the declaration of a loving marriage. The woman's hand fluttered over her throat in a nervous gesture. But Georgiana blinked, and the tension, the panic, whatever it was, disappeared.

"Let us leave Fitzwilliam alone, children," Lady Bentley murmured, smile firmly back in place.

Odd. Perhaps Lady Bentley's marriage hadn't been as perfect as her daughter believed. Georgiana knew all about facades. A vision of her father's smiling, amused visage flitted through her mind. How deftly they could fool.

Georgiana discreetly glanced at Fitz, rolling her bottom lip in with her teeth. The teasing was loving, but—it was still teasing. Her heart stuttered, and she was sure it paused. Because she thought—that tight expression on her husband's face? That thick swallow, like he could barely get his throat to work?—she thought that looked a lot like pain.

She grabbed a snifter and slowly swayed over to her husband.

Sometimes she wondered if she and her husband faced similar demons, two kindred lonely hearts. If maybe they had been brought together for a reason. That just maybe, a man weighed down by anxiety and apprehension but could lower his guard under the guise of another language, was meant to end up with the lonely, love-starved Italian girl.

She stopped before him; his head bent down toward his book. "For you," she murmured, holding out the glass.

"Thank you," he said rigidly, gaze not meeting hers as he accepted the brandy.

"You are sure you won't join us?" Georgiana ventured.

Felix's baritone rang through the library. "You know, Flick, I think you would have benefited from a tad more apprehension. If you had a touch of Fitzy's anxiety"—Fitz stiffened—"I wouldn't have to worry that you would sneak off and snuff out Wessex while he was sleeping."

"What a marvelous idea, Fifi," Felicity said with altogether too much enthusiasm.

Felix groaned, and a weak smile played across Fitz's face.

He glanced at Georgiana and said quietly, "I'd prefer to read, if you don't mind."

"Of course," she said with a soft smile, carefully keeping the hollow sensation in her stomach from her words and expression.

She made her way back to the coffee table and quickly took a sip of her brandy, needing to fill the hollowness with something, anything. She stared blindly into the amber liquid. Perhaps she had been mistaken earlier. The way he had held her, kissed her so reverently, as though she were important to him.

It had made her feel things. Things that twisted her insides, made her head spin, and filled her chest with a warm buzzing. Things she had never felt before. She cocked her head at her brandy. Well, that wasn't quite right. It was relatively similar to being in one's cups if she really thought about it. And she had no idea what it meant.

She glanced at her husband and caught him staring at her over the rim of his spectacles. For the briefest of moments, their gazes locked—held—and fireworks erupted in her stomach. And it wasn't a measly shower of sparklers. No, it was Catherine Wheels. It was Roman Candles.

And then he hastily turned away, pushing the brim of his spectacles back up his nose, and busying himself back in his book. And just like a firework, the exploding lights inside fizzled and fell away.

She blinked, placing a hand over her belly. What on earth was wrong with her?

"All right, is everyone ready?" Felicity flopped to the ground, a very welcome distraction. "Felix, do the honors."

Felix lit the brandy, blue and yellow flames emerging from the dish.

Felicity turned to Georgiana. "Now, we play a touch differently in this house. Normally, you snatch and eat as many raisins as you can, avoiding getting burned. *But*"—her eyes narrowed, and her lips curved in a smirk—"you have no way of knowing who wins playing that way." She tapped the bowl in front of her. "Snatch 'em and fill your bowl. Whoever has the most when they're all gone wins!"

The yellow flames had dwindled, and now solely blue fire danced over the dish. Felix leaned over and sprinkled a pinch of little white crystals into the flickering fire. The flames popped and flared a brilliant gold just for a heartbeat. Georgiana's eyes widened, and her breath caught.

"What was that?" she asked, her gaze trained on the flame. She had never played this game before, and she thought she shouldn't be so excited to stick her fingers into fire. But...had she mentioned she lacked any sort of apprehension in life?

"Salt." Felix grinned. "Just a little added flare."

Georgiana was helpless but to grin back at his boyish excitement. She wasn't sure there was anything more shocking than seeing *the* Lord Bentley casually cross-legged on the floor, about to partake in a not-so-friendly game of snapdragon. Georgiana glanced back at her husband. That wasn't quite right. Her husband did his fair share of shocking her as well.

"Everyone ready?" Felicity's gaze bounced between Georgiana and Felix.

Georgiana had never seen the girl more serious. But given how competitive she was learning this family was, she shouldn't be surprised. Georgiana and Felix nodded.

"Douse the lights!" Felicity called, and a couple of servants scurried around the room.

Darkness engulfed them, nothing but the blue flames dancing between them and the soft glow of the slow-burning coals in the hearth behind them. It was eerie, haunted, nothing but flickering shadows illuminating their faces. To Georgiana, the atmosphere felt much more fitting for sharing ghost stories than engaging in raisin snatching.

But she didn't have long to get lost on that errant thought because Felicity was yelling, "Go!" and—blast and damn—Georgiana was shoving her hand in a dish full of fire.

She hoped she wouldn't get burned.

22

Georgiana

GEORGIANA THOUGHT SHE MIGHT prefer sticking her fingers in fire than this. She stood outside her husband's bedchamber door, willing herself to knock. She wasn't nervous per se, but her husband had her all turned around, like she'd donned her dress backwards, or inside out, or upside down, or perhaps forgot it altogether.

And oddly enough, she was feeling a bit glum after playing a raucous game of snapdragon with his siblings. That shouldn't make a smidgen of sense. But somehow the laughter, the sibling banter, and even the playful teasing had made Georgiana feel terribly *alone*. Because she had never had anything even remotely close to that. And she never would. Was it odd to feel sad when surrounded by happiness?

The bond the Jennings family shared, the one with snappy quips, knowing what the other was going to say before they even said it... That kind of relationship was something that came from years—decades—of having someone's love. So, even though the Jennings family had welcomed Georgiana without pause, accepted her into the warm embrace that was their family—an embrace that was sorely lacking in her own family—she was an outsider. She rubbed her chest.

Urgh, again with this bloody hollowness.

And on top of it all, a thick, heavy cloud was settling around her, threatening to choke her and fill her lungs. Because tonight was Christmas Eve. Tomorrow was Christmas. And it would be her first Christmas without Bernie. Her eyes burned, like they were being filled with blasted lemon juice. She closed her eyes and willed the pressure building behind them to go away. She planted her palm against the door and pushed. Pushed all that glumdrum away.

And pushed herself right into her husband's chamber.

"Whoooop!" She stumbled, arms flailing, and just managed to stay upright. She hadn't realized the door would be *unlatched*. She had merely been going for some solid support, hence leaning on a solid door.

Fitz stood frozen, standing just outside his dressing chamber.

Georgiana's mouth fell open.

Her husband turned toward her. Which only made things worse. Because her husband—whose head was currently covered by a towel he was clearly using to dry his hair—was stark naked. And facing her.

Her gaze shot to his groin.

The towel fell off his head.

Her husband's jaw dropped.

And then a blush spread rapidly over his cheeks and down his muscled chest. Naturally.

And though usually her husband struggled for air, this time it was Georgiana struggling. *Breathe.* Oh goodness, heaven, hell, God, Satan, just...someone, something. Because naked. Fitz. Naked.

Her heart rate kicked up so hard, so fast, she thought it might have leaped out of her chest, performing a jig around the chamber. She barely heard her husband's words.

"Gigi?" he squeaked. His hands flew to cup himself.

Georgiana bit her lip and leaned back casually against his door. "Whoops," she murmured, placing a hand over her racketing heart.

What a pleasant surprise. Her gaze slowly drank him in, drank in the surprisingly lean-muscled form she had just begun to discover back in his study. Yes, it was *very* clear now—her husband swam. A lot. Her eyes locked on his strong thighs, flexing and unflexing as he shifted back and forth on his feet. Her tongue coasted over her bottom lip because...yum. She wanted to lick every lean inch of him.

Her gaze finally made it back to his beautiful amber eyes—beautiful amber eyes and scrunched brows that oozed disbelief.

"Whoops?" Those skeptical brows lifted even further. "You barge into my chamber unannounced, and all you have to say for yourself is whoops?"

Was that a bit of bite in his tone? Reprimand? Visions of him yanking her head back in his study assaulted her. She dipped her chin and blinked at him demurely.

"My apologies. It hadn't been my intention to do such a thing."

He shot her an *I highly doubt that* look. Her face split into a grin. He rolled his eyes and mumbled something under his breath as he snatched his towel off the ground and—in the most disappointing of fashions—wrapped it around his waist.

"What are you doing here, Georgiana?"

Her smile faltered. That hadn't come out even remotely friendly. And it wasn't the good kind of cross. It was the *you are a bother* cross. Fitz headed to his dressing chamber, and Georgiana pushed off the door and followed him.

She needed to talk to her husband because he had disappeared after the game of snapdragon, saying he was retiring for the evening. And once again, Georgiana had the sense that her husband was isolating himself, that something was wrong. It was past ten o'clock, and he hadn't visited her. She thought, after what had occurred in his study, he'd be more inclined to visit her now.

But he hadn't.

Which only fueled her fear that she had been right in thinking her husband wanted nothing to do with her. So, here she was, taking charge, bursting into her husband's chamber—albeit accidentally—and doing what her husband had said he wanted in his study. They were going to converse. *And I really want to converse with you.*

She supposed she would find out how true that statement was soon enough.

"I wanted to speak with you, Fitz." She stopped and leaned against the door frame, unabashedly watching him as he pulled on a pair of smallclothes—his foot got stuck, and he nearly tumbled to the ground. He recovered with a curse and a deeper blush. He was so bloody adorable. And lovely to look at, even slightly covered as he was now. The smalls were loose-fitting, falling to about his knee, and hung low on his hips, dangerously low.

"Do you not have a valet to assist you?" She thought, for safety's sake, her husband could probably benefit from a valet.

He looked at her, his brows coming together and inching up his forehead in an incredulous climb. "Me? Have a valet? Do you really think someone as nervous and awkward as me would be able to have another person do something as personal as dress me?" He glanced away, but she still heard the softly muttered words. "It would be painful."

Her heart went soft. There had been so much self-disgust in those words. She thought she might know a way to help with that. When Georgiana needed distraction, fooling around, dalliances, had always worked to push away the melancholy. So, perhaps that was something she could do for him, something they could do for each other.

She tentatively approached Fitz, not because she was nervous, but because she didn't want him to flee. She stopped before him, her neck craning up to hold his gaze. The scent of soap and pure, unadulterated Fitzwilliam Jennings swirled around her. He was so tall, a few errant, tight curls falling over his brow as he looked down at her. He watched her. Wary. Uneasy. Breathing soft bursts of warm minty breath down to her. She rested her palms on his chest, and heat seared her skin. He flinched but didn't pull back.

She lifted on her toes and pressed a soft kiss to his lips before sinking back down. He did nothing more than stare at her, study her, jaw set and nostrils flaring. She was determined to ease him into bedding her tonight. Things had been so good between them after their encounter earlier. Maybe that was the secret to a happy marriage. There really should be pamphlets on these types of things—for those who didn't have any real-life examples to guide them.

His chest quivered beneath her palms, his heart softly beating into her skin. What was going on in that mind of his? What anxious storm was he brewing up in there? She opened her mouth to ask—

"Would you let me watch you fuck yourself?" Fitz blurted.

She blinked. So much for discussion.

23

Fitz's eyes shot so wide he could *feel* his lids expanding. His wife's eyes did much the same. *Oh, bloody lawks.* Had he really just said that? He had. He had just asked his wife to let him watch her... *Watch her.* One would think he'd be able to say it in his head since he had just blurted it out loud. But apparently, he had hit his quota for vulgar speech for the day.

"Yes." She nodded vigorously, a few loose blonde tendrils flying wildly around her face.

A sigh of relief flew from him. Wait. She said yes? She was saying yes? Oh, God. She was saying yes. He hadn't thought about what would happen if she said yes. Which was dim-witted. She was going to fuck herself. Obviously. Box the Jesuit. Mount a Corporal and four. Fetch mettle. He frowned. Did that same terminology work with a woman?

He shook his head, focusing back on her. She tilted her head, and her brows pinched. She probably thought he'd gone mad. Which he had. He must have. Because he had asked, and she had said yes, and she was going to, and he was going to, and... Dear Lord. Where did all the air go?

His lungs heaved as they finally remembered to work. It didn't last long though, because the soft pads of her fingertips were trailing down his chest, down his abdomen, settling at the waistline of his smalls. His cock gave a jolly jump, and Fitz made a strangled sound in his throat.

"I will be but a moment," Georgiana said. "I just have to run back to my chamber to get—"

"No, no. I'll get it," he said hastily. "You-you-you." He paused and sucked in a breath, trying to regain control of himself. "Why don't you get comfortable on my bed?" The least he could do was retrieve her, er, implement. She was already going to be doing all the work. "Where might I find your...ahh...your..."

She smiled softly up at him, her green eyes dancing. "My dildo? It is in a box in my nightstand."

He jerked his chin in a nod and took a bracing breath. All right. He would retrieve the dildo. He could do this. He bounced slightly on his feet, working up his resolve. Before he lost the small amount he'd just built up, he grabbed his wife's hand and dragged her into his chamber with purpose. He swung around to face her and pointed to his bed.

"You get on that bed. I want you naked when I return."

He almost smiled and gave a cheer at how clear and authoritative that had come out. *Well done, chap!*

His almost-smile died, though, because Georgiana's eyes went dark, and her sharp exhalation sliced through the room. She glanced to the floor and licked her tempting, parted, pink lips. "Yes, sir."

His cock pulsed, and he groaned. He really hoped he could get more comfortable with this. Because Georgiana's reaction to being told what to do? He glanced down. Shite. He couldn't run through the hall in nothing but his smalls and a raging cockstand to boot.

He shrugged into his banyan, ushered out a quick, "I'll return shortly," and was on his way to her chamber. Fortunately, it was quick to retrieve the box with her *item*. He worked to control his breathing during the journey there and back. That was about all that was within his ability. There was no hope for the clamoring in his chest. His heart was spinning around like an out-of-control top.

He shouldn't be nervous. She was the one about to be on display. Doing everything. He was merely the observer. So the nerves? It didn't make any sense. But he would fight through it. Because this was happening.

He burst through his door and flicked it shut with his heel. And then nearly dropped the box—but fortunately didn't—because his wife was naked on his bed, an absolute vision framed by the maroon curtains tied to the bedposts. Legs spread, with her fingers... He gulped, and a breath fled him, choppy and loud in the quiet of his chamber. Her beautiful fingers stilled and started to pull away.

"No!" The word burst from him. "Don't you *dare* stop," he growled.

He blinked. Where had that come from? His chest puffed out slightly. He had sounded quite beastly. He strode to the bed. Perhaps he could do this.

He tripped.

Or not.

The box flew onto the bed, dildo shooting out—thankfully landing on the soft bed linens and not the floor where it would have cracked into a million little pieces. Unfortunately, he couldn't say the same for his head. Because his head cracked right into his bedpost. And holy Mother Mary, Joseph, and all Three Wise Men. *Ouchhhhhh!*

"Ohmygod, Fitz! Are you all right?"

"Yes," he gritted out. He rested his forehead against the offending bed post, his shoulders sinking.

Why could he manage to do nothing even remotely well? Small, warm hands ran up his chest, his neck, coming to cup his face and pull it from where he was hiding behind the column of wood.

Georgiana brushed back his annoying curls, her gaze scanning his face. Her fingers brushed gently over his forehead, and he winced at the sharp throb, sucking in a breath. But then she coasted her thumb over his parted lips, and *bloody hell* her fingers smelled like woman. Like intimate woman. Like intimate *Gigi*. He couldn't stop himself—the hunger racing through his body too rampant, too uncontrolled. He pierced her with his gaze and sucked her thumb into his mouth. His eyes slid shut. He could taste her. *Intimate Gigi.*

His eyes opened, and he was greeted with lids falling heavy over pupils blown wide. Lust-filled green eyes. For him. She had undone her plait while he was gone, her blonde waves framing her rosy cheeks, cascading over her naked breasts, rose-pink nipples peeking out at him. She was lust kneeling before him in his bed. His for the taking.

And he was bloody damned well going to take it.

24

Georgiana

"On your back," her husband said. No. *Demanded*.

Georgiana could scarcely fathom where this commanding, confident man had come from, but...

She. Was. Reveling in it.

She wanted it all and then some. *Please, sir, may I have some more?*

She scrambled back on the bed until she collapsed, head on his pillows. He crawled over her, lean biceps flexing, jaw clenching. He looked *savage*. A wild dog crawling over his mate. Oh God, she was going to expire. Her core was liquid. Molten. She was nothing but melted wanting for this man. And she wanted to be spread all over her husband like butter. Bloody hell, she was cracked. But he was her adorable, blushing lobster, and one was supposed to butter a lobster. So...

He lowered to his forearms, and his heat surrounded her, banishing all quips of the crustacean variety. His head dipped to her neck, lips and tongue and teeth devoured her flesh, laving the hollow of her neck. She arched into him, her legs sliding up his thighs, desperate to find his cock, to have him sink deep inside her. But he lifted onto his knees, pulling what she wanted away from her.

"Touch yourself." Another demand.

Her hands shot between her legs, and she picked up where she had left off. She was swollen, aching, painfully so. Walking in on him naked, having the time to leisurely admire his form earlier, had her wound tight. When she had been touching herself a few moments ago and he had walked through his door, she had been going so slowly, so softly. Because she had already been *so* close. And she refused to come without him watching. She wasn't sure what it had taken him to make the request, but she was sure it hadn't been easy for him. She was determined to give him the fantasy. Give them both the fantasy.

Tension flooded her body, her muscles quivering in a dance of clench and release. She was rapidly reaching that point again, the point where she was thrown into the abyss, the achingly devastating abyss. Pleasure coiled tight with each quick circle she made over herself. Because of Fitz's tongue trailing up her neck. Because of his lips dancing over her ear. She moaned, purred, her hips thrusting into her fingers, completely out of her control.

"Oh God, Fitz," she breathed. "I-I'm not going to make it much longer. I'm too close."

He abruptly left her, and she cried out. But he was back just as quickly, his lips dragging over hers, cool ivory sliding down her stomach. She shivered, her breath shuddering against his lips.

"You," he growled. "Are absolutely not going to come without me watching you-you"—he paused, drawing in a deep breath—"fuck your-self."

Oh God.

He took her hand and brought it to her dildo, wrapping her fingers around it. He pushed off and sat back on his heels. He gripped her ankles and slid them up, so her knees bent and pointed to the ceiling. Her heart hammered a staccato rhythm in her chest. Because he moved her body like she was his puppet. And she wanted nothing more than to be his puppet. She was incredibly exposed like this. But where she should have felt embarrassment, there was nothing but exhilaration, adrenaline, coursing violently through her. Oh, she most definitely liked being watched.

He spread her thighs wide and glanced up at her. Waiting. Eyes black. Just as overcome by the moment as she was. His chest surged, and it was a beautiful sight.

She'd always wanted to be watched. She wanted the thrill. But the thrill was so much stronger with Fitz, so much stronger than she could have ever imagined. He wasn't some rakehell who had every woman lifting her skirts with a snap of his fingers. She was a private performance for her adorably befuddled husband, who had just stumbled over the word "fuck." Something rare and just for him.

She wrapped her fingers tight around the dildo and slid it down her belly, stopping at the apex of her thighs. Her breaths came rapidly now, but instead of dipping between her thighs, she slowed down. Drew out the anticipation, savored the dark desire slackening her husband's face. His gaze was transfixed between her legs, his entire body still, poised, as he waited for her to move. She thought he might even be holding his breath.

And she couldn't wait any longer.

She whimpered, nothing but a broken mewl. Then dipped her dildo between her legs, sliding it down and gently rolling it over her flesh. She gasped, and Fitz's hands flew to her thighs, his body lurching toward her as though he had no control over it. Like his body wanted hers and he could do nothing to stop it. He squeezed, massaged her flesh, and rough, ragged breaths flew past his lips. She drew her dildo back up, bringing with it her slick wetness, allowing for the most delicious glide as she rubbed and rotated the hard ivory over her pulsing flesh. A strangled groan came from Fitz, and her gaze shot up to his. He was locked on what her hand was doing, his jaw ticking, every muscle in his neck corded tight.

"Hai la fica più bella, micetta. Così rosa. Così perfetta. Guarda come luccichi per me."

Lord save her. More Italian. Her eyes fluttered shut at his words.

You have the prettiest cunt, kitten. So pink. So perfect. Look at how you glisten for me.

This man was like a jarring stop in a carriage, head whipping back and then forward. One moment he was bumbling and blushing, and the next he was self-assured and seductive, whispering the most deliciously dirty things to her with that multi-lingual tongue.

Deep inside, she ached, throbbed for him. She was empty, too empty. She drew her dildo down and notched it at her entrance. Fitz groaned, his hands squeezing painfully tight on her thighs. Pressing her open for his view. The pain felt so good. Apparently, her pause was too much for her husband.

"Inside, Gigi. Fuck yourself. Now."

A soft cry left her at his command, and she sank her dildo deep in one swift thrust. Her eyes rolled back. That glorious stretch, that glorious feeling of being *full*. Her muscles clenched around the dildo, and she was nothing but an incoherent mess of moans.

Her husband sucked in a sharp breath. "Oh god, oh god, ohgodohgod." His hands skimmed up and down her thighs, almost frantic, as he watched her. She slid her dildo in and out, picking up speed, playing with the angle until she found the spot, the spot that had her toes curling and her back arching.

And then Fitz's hands left her. The loss of his large hands had her cold, shivering. But oh, *oh*. The result was worth the loss. Because Fitz hovered over her, one hand pressed into the bed linens at her side, the other wrapped around his turgid cock. His gaze was glued to her core, just the top of his tousled curls visible to her, and he stroked himself in time to her thrusts. This was heaven, sweet, sweet heaven. He watched her while she was able to watch him in return.

Her husband looked like he was close to losing control, Italian flying from his mouth, his hand flying over his cock.

"Non vedo l'ora di affondare dentro di te."

I can't wait to sink deep inside you.

"Dio, ti dilaterò così bene, micetta."

God, I'm going to stretch you out so good, kitten.

"Mi abbraccerai così forte."

You'll hug me so tight.

Dear God, she loved the words falling from his lips. She loved how they carried a soft accent. She loved how he said them, like he was devastated by her. As if his desire and want of her were akin to pain.

His gaze flew to hers, his eyes glowing fire, heated with dark longing, lust. And it latched onto her, tangible, reaching deep inside her, the most intimate of caresses.

"Sono così disperato per te."

I'm so desperate for you.

She sucked in a breath, her eyes flaring wide. The passion in that gaze, the ferocity in that tone. Her heart scrambled in her chest, determined to get to him. Because when he said those words, delivered them like that, it sounded like he meant more than just sex.

She wasn't sure if it was his words or her thrusts, but her orgasm was veering toward her, much too fast. She almost didn't want to come without Fitz inside her. But her husband took away that option. He swung around to the side of her, knees next to her head, planting his hands on either side of her hips, then buried his face between her thighs. His mouth went straight for her clitoris, his tongue licking and then flattening, providing a pulsing pressure that echoed in her core.

Ohgod*ohgod.*

The man's tongue was deadly. His mouth fatal. She could barely fuck herself, her body so overwhelmed in sensation her hands couldn't remember what to do. She pressed her feet into the bed and ground against his face, chasing the spiraling ecstasy building inside her. So. Close.

And then he sucked on her clitoris. It was exactly what she needed. The crescendo of pleasure spiked, detonated over her, and she cried out, her body convulsing in uncontrollable shudders. Fitz gentled his pressure, staying with her, drawing out every surge of blissful ecstasy possible. And then she was wriggling away, her skin over-sensitive after her release, and sinking into his bedding, replete.

Fitz grabbed her wrist and gently pulled her dildo out of her. He took it from her and threw it to the side of the bed. Then he was back over her, surrounding her, caging her in again.

He hung above her, nose brushing hers, lips almost, *almost* on hers.

The tip of his cock pressed deliciously against her entrance.

"My turn, Gigi."

25

It was Fitz's turn. His cock was pressed against his wife, and he was finally going to sink into the gloriousness that was Gigi.

Gazes locked, he sank inside, inch by blissful inch. Her breath hitched with each one, her mouth parting further. And then hips met hips, and he was fully seated inside her. And he thought he might die. Because nothing would ever compare to this feeling of being completely enveloped by his wife.

His eyes widened. Shite. She was a virgin. "Gigi, are you well? I should have taken more care."

She snorted. *She snorted.*

He frowned at her.

A soft giggle burst from her, which had her intimate muscles doing delicious things to his cock. His body went taut.

"Fitz," she said, eyes dancing. "I just fucked myself with a dildo. Something I do relatively often, I might add. And he's bigger than you. You have no need to fear the typical...complaints that come with virgins with me."

Fitz's frown deepened. He slowly pulled nearly all the way out, just the tip of his cock inside her. His gaze flicked to hers before it latched back on where they were joined. A low growl fled him. "Your implement isn't *that* much bigger."

Her face split in a saucy grin. "Apparently, it's all in how you use it, anyway. Unless you're not up to the task—"

He drove into her.

The breath fled her on an *oomph*.

Not up to the task? His little wife had just thrown a gauntlet. And Fitz loved nothing more than a challenge. This was one he was determined to win.

Bracing himself on one elbow, he reached for her hip and slid his hand underneath to cup her arse. Fucking hell, the arse on this woman. His fingertips dug into the plush flesh, flexing. Absolutely magnificent.

He tilted her, tugged her toward him, and sank even further. They groaned. He moved slowly, not capable of anything more without completely embarrassing himself. He simply savored her in a smooth, relentless rhythm, rocking against her with each thrust, purposely pressing against where he knew her pleasure centered. He tortured them both, gradually dragging himself in and out of the heat of her, reveling in the breathy cries that escaped her, delving deeper with each drive.

Fitz chased after those sighs and met with soft, sweet lips, cinnamon and spice consuming his senses. His heart rate kicked up. There was that delicious scent he seemed to always find on her. He licked into her mouth and groaned. Not just scent. Taste.

"Why do you taste so delicious?" The words rumbled from him, and he nipped at her lips, punishing them for being so bloody tempting. Everything about this woman was too much, too perfect. "You taste like fucking Christmas." He punctuated his statement with a hard thrust, and she gasped.

Then her delectable lips curved against his and she nudged his nose with hers. "Your cook makes the most e-exceptional spiced biscuits," she said, breath hitching as he sank to the hilt in another thrust. "I've p-practically eaten my weight in them s-since I arrived."

Ah, that would do it. He went in for another taste, and she moaned deep in her throat. Bloody hell, he loved the taste of her. From this moment on, his wife would have an endless supply of spiced biscuits at her disposal. He would make sure of it.

He ground against her harder. Her cries grew louder. His heart and cock pulsed in tandem. His grasp tightened on her hip, pleasure streaking up his spine. Searing. Scorching. Staggering. She was climbing to that peak again. He would take her there. And he would hold her as they fell off together. God, this couldn't be happening.

"This can't be real, Gigi," he whispered. "You cannot possibly be real."

Her hands gripped his face, her gaze locked on his—unyielding. A grip, a gaze, that promised of never letting go. "I am real, Fitz. This is real. We are real."

Fuck.

He buried his head into the crook of her neck and drove into her, over and over, harder and harder. Needing to fulfill the wild, breathy cries fleeing her lips. The ones of *more,* of *harder,* of *please.*

His hand clutched her arse, lifting her into him. There was too much churning inside him, disordered and dangerous and damn near earth-shattering. The headboard rammed against the wall with the force of his thrusts, and it sounded disarmingly like they were on the verge of damaging the house.

He pulled up and planted his hands on either side of her head as he slowed the pace, brought himself back under control. He had to make this last, savor it, never let it end. Her arms were above her head now, breasts lifted and on perfect display, her hands pressed against the headboard—that she had slid up against, the top of her head hitting the wood with each thrust.

His eyes flew wide. "I'm sorry, Gigi. Your head." He hastily tried to slide them lower down the bed without leaving her, because he had to stay inside her. He never wanted to leave her.

She gripped his wrist and stilled him, his hand frozen on her hip. "No, Fitz. I like it. I want it as rough as you'll give me. As hard as you'll give me."

"You want me to h-hurt you?"

Her delicate fingers tightened around his wrists, and she nodded, her half-lidded gaze darkening. "I want to ache tomorrow, knowing I was thoroughly used by you. To see marks on my skin, knowing you made them, and be able to think of nothing but tonight."

His lungs tried to choke him, and his cock tried to unman him. There was absolutely no way this was real.

He slammed into her and—*holy fuck*—the angle change from when he tried to move them was. *Was...* He groaned, raw and primal. Her cunt was squeezing him like utter perfection at this angle. Apparently, she agreed, because a guttural cry burst from her as he drove to the hilt.

"There," she cried out. "Oh, God. There, Fitz."

Fuckfuckfuck. He wasn't long for this world. Not when she said things like that.

"I can't—I *need* you to come again, Gigi. And I—" He froze and gritted his teeth, clenching his eyes shut. His chest heaved as he did everything in his power to hold himself back from falling over the edge. Not without her.

Not. Without. Her.

Georgiana's hand slid between their bodies, and just her soft fingers brushing against his cock was almost too much.

"I'm almost—I need—" she gasped out. "Hard, Fitz. Now."

Her words ended in a cry, and he gave her what she needed. He laid into her, one hand gripping her hip so hard for leverage he was sure he would leave a bruise. Mark her. Like she wanted. Her head tipped back, eyes shut, mouth open on a silent scream.

Her cunt fluttered and then clamped down on him while broken cries fled her lips. And as her body spasmed beneath his, her face slackened in pleasure, he was thrown right over the edge. With her. He pounded into her and then held, chest falling flush with hers, his body jerking as his nerves lit on fire, all sound drowned out by the pure heaven buzzing in his ears and blackening his vision.

Fitz sank atop her, mouths resting together, neither possessing the ability to even move their lips in a kiss, just existing. Surviving on one another's shuddering sighs.

A slight tug pulled at his skin, and he had the briefest conscience of mind to lift so she could withdraw her hand from where he had crushed it between their heated bodies. When he'd regained his breath, he pushed up on his hands and studied her, admired her. Her eyes were still closed, her beautiful breasts rising and falling with her slowly leveling breaths.

He reached over her and tucked a dampened tendril of hair behind her ear. She was stunning with the deep flush to her cheeks, the glossiness shining on her sweat-slicked skin. Slicked from their lovemaking.

His heart stumbled. And then his earlier thought ran through his mind again. *This can't possibly be real.*

Her eyes fluttered open, and when their eyes met, her lips curved into a soft, contented smile. He sank forward and pressed the barest of kisses to her lips. He should probably get off her, allow her to breathe, instead of being crushed by him. He rolled to the side and fell heavily on his back.

And promptly jumped ten feet in the air, let out an extremely unmanly yelp, and tumbled to the floor.

"Fitz!" Bed linens rustled and then a scrambling Georgiana appeared, peeking over the edge of tousled maroon bed linens. "What happened! Are you all right?"

Her wide eyes scanned him frantically and...he burst out laughing. She froze, and her chin reared back.

He lifted a hand, trying to signal everything was fine. "I... I..." He gasped between laughs, but collapsed into even more uncontrollable mirth, arm curling around his stomach.

When he finally calmed himself enough that he could breathe properly and form words, he met his wife's gaze. A smile bunched up her cheeks in the loveliest manner, her green eyes bright, chin resting in her hands as she stared at him. Her quite clearly dicked-in-the-knob husband.

"What on earth has gotten into you, husband?" she said, and if a voice could smile, hers surely was.

He chuckled softly once more and shook his head. "Your dildo may have unexpectedly poked me in the arse. Without warning or permission, I might add."

She snorted, and she hung her head as her body gently rocked with giggles. "I must beg your pardon on his behalf. I will have a stern talking to him about poking things without consent."

He pushed to his feet and hurried to his washstand, grabbing three cloths and wetting them before hurrying back to Georgiana. They—dildo included—quickly cleaned themselves, and Fitz tossed the rags into his dressing chamber with the rest of his dirty linens.

He hurried back to the bed and paused at the bedside. Georgiana sat, twisting the bed linens in her fingers, avoiding his gaze. "Is ought amiss, Gigi?"

"Urm. No, not exactly. I just…" She glanced at him with a wince. "I have to use the chamber pot." Her cheeks bloomed a deep pink. "I never thought of the logistics of all of this before," she said hastily. "And well, I drank quite a bit of brandy earlier. And quite frankly, a vigorous romp doesn't do a bladder any favors."

He grinned stupidly at her. She was so bloody fetching and darling and winsome. "There is a water closet just through my dressing chamber you can use."

She sat up straighter, eyes rounding. "A water closet? I've heard of some homes in London having them, but I've never seen one before."

He frowned. She hadn't used one before? Then what was she—Oh, right, Felix had only had the family's rooms plumbed.

"Come with me. I'll show you how it works. But yes, Felix has an obsession with inventions," he said as he led them into his dressing chamber. "His study has some of the neatest things that he's acquired over the years. He's been following advancements in flushing toilets for a while now—and people think *I'm* the odd one—but as soon as he thought it worthwhile, he found a contractor who specialized in the trade and voila"—he opened the door of his water closet and pointed to the flushing toilet—"he had them installed in our chambers."

She glanced at the mahogany wood carved toilet and then back at Fitz. "It looks like a chest, like a lovely piece of furniture, not a place to…"

He stepped forward and flipped up the lid, revealing a wooden seat over a hole that led into a porcelain bowl, similar to a chamber pot. "I suppose for aesthetics." He shrugged. "After you've relieved yourself,"—his cheeks heated—"you pull on this chain up here and it will flush the toilet. And then you're all set."

Goodness, perhaps he should have rung for a maid to show her this. This wasn't something husbands and wives were supposed to discuss, was it? *Great, Fitz, now she's going to think you are leather-headed and never want to bed you—or be anywhere near you—again.*

"Fascinating," she said, her gaze glued to the toilet. "Where does it all go?"

He blinked. Apparently, he had thought wrong. "Blast if I know. I happily leave all that shite to Felix."

She giggled, her hand shooting to her mouth, rounded cheeks peeking out from behind.

A bit of his tension drained away. *Ha! Drained.* His lips twitched—at his horrible pun and his adorable wife. "What's so amusing?"

"Oh goodness, it's really not appropriate." Her green eyes danced as they met his. "You'd happily leave all that shite"—she snorted—"to Felix. Quite literally."

He broke out in a grin. Apparently, he was full of puns tonight, and not even realizing it. "Why, wife, you're worse than an adolescent boy."

Her giggles subsided, her eyebrows lifting sheepishly. "I hope I haven't horrified you."

"Not in the least. I think I might like you even more because of it." He walked to her and planted a kiss on her smiling lips. "I'll see you back in the bedchamber, Gigi."

He made his way back to his bed, a stupid satisfied smile on his face, shoulders square and proud. All of a sudden, he felt about ten feet tall. He settled himself into his massive four-poster, folding his arms back and tucking his hands beneath his head. His wife surprised him at every turn. He meant what he'd said. He liked her even more for her juvenile sense of humor. There was a solace in it that he couldn't quite explain. It somehow took away some of his anxiety. There were always so many rules. In how you were supposed to act. What you were supposed to say. What you weren't supposed to say.

Out in society, the anxiety quickly coiled around him like a too-tight cravat, the pressure of slipping up, of embarrassing himself or his family. He thought that pressure would be ten times worse with Gigi, considering how inept he was with women—and he so desperately didn't want to muck up his marriage, which usually lent itself to even bigger blunders.

The soft tread of footsteps broke him away from his thoughts. She stood in his dressing chamber doorway, naked and unabashed. Enchanting. Somehow, this woman had worked some sort of magic on him, conjuring comfort when he thought it impossible. He still blundered—and would continue to do so—but those blunders were a bit more bearable, knowing they were with Gigi. Because he thought, if there was one woman who could handle them, handle him and all his Fitz-ness, it might be her.

"What is the time?" she murmured.

He stilled. Was she planning on leaving soon? He didn't want her to leave. It wasn't necessarily the done thing for a wife to spend the night in her husband's bed...well, strictly for sleeping purposes. But blast it all, did he want her to stay.

"Just past midnight," he said softly. He managed to keep the fear that she'd leave, the telltale quiver from his words. But his heart quivered with nerves just the same.

He pulled back the covers, a Gigi-sized spot clearly waiting for her to fill. He looked back at her and hoped. Hoped she'd take the invitation. Hoped she wanted this just as much as he did.

And clearly, tonight was a night of miracles. Because she padded to the bed and slipped in next to him. And just like in his study, she snuggled into his side, skin to skin, head to toe.

She let out a sleepy sigh and pressed a soft kiss to his shoulder. Her body softened, and her barely audible whisper coasted over his skin. "Merry Christmas, Fitz."

Warmth spread through him like a sip of piping hot drinking chocolate after a snowball fight. It settled in his stomach, swirling, simmering. There was that sodding fizzing again. He stilled. His eyes widened.

Realization hit him like a snowball to the face.

All that intestinal upset around his wife? It wasn't indigestion.

He'd fallen in love with her.

Her breathing grew slower, deeper, even, and she faded to sleep in his arms.

His heart let out a sigh, and he pulled her even closer.

Yes, he loved her.

"Merry Christmas, Gigi."

26

Georgiana

Georgiana sipped on her steaming cup of chocolate, the warmth of the creamy, bitter drink, lightly sweetened with sugar, infusing her entire body. She smiled over her porcelain cup, taking in the merriment floating around her at the Jennings's breakfast table. Felicity and Felix were laughing at some obscene joke Felicity had just made, and Lydia was doing her best not to laugh at—and encourage—her raucous daughter. Fitz was quiet, as he usually was, but his lips were curved up as he cut into the cold ham on his dish. It was a lovely Christmas morning, infinitely better than the ones she had grown up with.

It would have been a tad better if she hadn't slowly floated to consciousness this morning, only to find herself alone in her husband's bed, his spot cold. She wished she could have woken up next to him. She imagined a sleepy Fitzwilliam was an adorable sight. Hair mussed, bleary-eyed, and freckled—probably blushing. Yes, adorable.

After she had hurried back to her chamber and readied herself for the day, she had found him, unsurprisingly, in his study. All disappointment had fled when he'd flashed a bashful smile her way and they had walked together to the breakfast room. It had been a silent walk. But a happy silence. Comfortable. Easy.

Everything inside her thrummed. Last night had been...she didn't have words. Who could have guessed that the flustered and stuttering Fitzwilliam Jennings was an amazingly talented lover? The man had dove between her thighs like a man dying of thirst. She squeezed her legs together. *Oh, mio Dio,* that man.

She hadn't experienced that particular act before, and it had been delicious. She had much more experience doing the fondling herself. Men seemed to have no qualms if a woman wanted to practice on *them* but were much more hesitant when asked to reciprocate. At least the cads she had dallied with had been that way.

That was another reason Georgiana had previously sought the Duke of Ironcrest. Yes, he had a reputation for doing dark, degrading things to his partners that spoke to the hidden urges that lived inside her. But more than that, his lovers didn't leave his bed—probably because they were tied to it—until they attained their pleasure.

Clearly, she had somehow ended up with a husband who was much the same. *I need you to come again, Gigi.* She smiled behind her cup. The emphasis in his words, the fervor—as though her pleasure was the sustenance he needed to live.

And the awe in his voice when he'd said, *this can't be real.* The way he had held her afterwards, like she was precious to him. She swore when she was lying with him, chest to chest, she felt a tug at her heartstrings. Swore one of those strings tied itself with his, joining them in a knot that couldn't be undone, irreversible. Goodness, look at her getting all disgustingly saccharine. It was like she—

"Georgiana?" Felicity waved a hand wildly in front of Georgiana's face from across the table.

"Apologies, Felicity. Woolgathering." Her cheeks heated, and she glanced discreetly at her husband, the subject of said woolgathering. "I am forever getting lost in my own thoughts."

A sly smile flitted across her sister-in-law's face, the young woman's gaze dropping to Georgiana's cheeks. "Goodness, the Queen's entire menagerie could have stampeded through the room, and you wouldn't have noticed. That must have been some daydream. Perhaps one that was a continuation of your Christmas Eve night." She shot Georgiana a wink.

Fitz's face went as red as the raspberry preserves he was spreading on his brioche, and he broke out into a coughing fit.

Georgiana's face went up in flames, too. Goodness, his *mother* was at the table.

"Felicity," Lydia chided, tucking a strawberry-blonde curl behind her ear. "Leave the poor newlyweds alone. What am I ever going to do with you?"

"Love me unconditionally." Felicity blinked sweetly at her mother, who shook her head in response.

Felicity turned back to Georgiana. "What I was trying to get your attention for was we have been invited to the Rutledge's supper party next week. They have one in London every year, the week between Christmas and New Year's. Their supper parties are always the best, such an interesting crowd. Even Fitzy enjoys them."

Georgiana set down her chocolate and leaned forward. "Oh, how fun!" She'd been to a few supper parties, but they had always been just another excuse for her mother to maneuver her toward some fortune-hunting lord. She'd never truly enjoyed one before. "Do we know who will be in attendance?"

"Obviously the Duke and Lord Dunmore," Felicity said, ticking off her fingers.

"Obviously?" Georgiana asked, looking curiously at Felicity.

A clatter of silverware had everyone's heads turning toward Georgiana's husband. "Apologies," Fitz managed with a stiff smile.

Felicity cleared her throat and looked back at Georgiana. "Anyhow"—her eyebrows twisted in a *whatever that was* look—"they always attend the Rutledge's supper parties." She gave a little nonchalant wave of her hand. "I believe they were all friends at Harrow. And they all sponsor a foundling home together now."

"Oh, really? How wonderful of them," Georgiana said absently, half her attention on Fitz. Who appeared to be trying to cut his brioche with his gaze if the way he was glaring daggers at it was any indication.

"Yes, they are such lovely boys," Lydia chimed in.

The breakfast room fell silent, and all heads turned toward Lady Bentley. Because truly, those were the last two words anyone would ever use to describe the two rogues.

"Lovely. Boys," Felix said with deliberate slowness, staring at his mother like she'd grown a third eye. "Those two scoundrels? I'd rather not get into specifics with you, Mother, but you have heard the rumors about them, have you not?"

"Not rumors," Felicity murmured quietly, shooting Georgiana a knowing look and mouthing, "Maribeth." And Felicity would know the truth. She had first-hand reports from her best friend, Maribeth, Lady Camoys.

"Yes, I know it's no secret they like to have a bit of fun"—Felix and Felicity cocked identical incredulous eyebrows at their mother at that comment, while Fitz remained staring at his plate—"but I am quite close with the dowager duchess, His Grace's grandmama. They do not just fund the foundling home but take an active part in the home. A large reason they are in London for Christmas is so they can celebrate with the children."

Georgiana's heart instantly went gooey soft. Goodness, spending Christmas with children in need? Who would have guessed? The twin devils had hearts hidden behind their blackened exteriors. She was fortunate, she knew, to have had a warm home, with plenty of food, and two parents. But Christmas had always been exceptionally lonely in her home, and she couldn't imagine what it must be like for children who didn't even have families, who wouldn't have a Christmas breakfast or dinner.

"That is unbelievably sweet," she said, wonderment coating her voice. "Perhaps we could visit the foundling home when we are back in London."

Fitz went whipcord straight next to her. She frowned at him, at his clenched jaw, the muscle ticking, teeth grinding. What on earth—

A violent slash drew her gaze away to her sister-in-law. Where Felicity was currently mutilating her cold ham with her fork. "Apparently, some rakes actually have hearts. Unlike certain spoiled ducal heirs who are probably too drunk off their arse to give back."

"Flick," Felix groaned. "Let us not get into this on Christmas."

Fitz abruptly shoved back from the table and stood, dish clattering. "I need to leave."

Georgiana glanced around the room, but everyone else seemed just as taken aback as she was. He was...announcing he must leave the table?

Fitz swallowed. "For London. Immediately."

What?

"I need to make sure the townhouse is ready for Georgiana. I hadn't informed the servants. Since I hadn't planned on bringing home a wife." He let out a forced chuckle. "But obviously, now I will be. Because"—he flicked his hand in Georgiana's direction. "And, of course, business. So, I best be off." He turned on his heel and left.

"Well, that was odd," Felix said slowly.

"Even for Fitzy," Felicity added, her amber brows pinched together.

Lydia was frowning after Fitz as well, her hands on the edge of the table as though she was about to get up and go after her son.

"I...suppose I should go up and pack as well, then?" Georgiana said to no one in particular. She had no idea what that had been about. As far as she was aware, they were to leave in two days for London. Not *on* Christmas day.

Felicity gave her a helpless shrug, no less confused than everyone else in the room. Lady Bentley sent her an encouraging nod, settling back in her own chair.

"If you'll excuse me." Georgiana pushed away from the table, shot everyone an uncertain smile, and left the breakfast room.

Once in the hallway, she quickened her pace and made her way to her husband's chamber. She was sure after speaking with her husband this—whatever his odd outburst was—would be cleared up. She first tried his bedchamber, only to find a flurry of servants packing trunks, but no husband.

Finally, she found him in his study, sitting behind his desk, scrawling hastily. He signed his note with a flourish, folded and sealed it, and then glanced up, startling at the sight of her.

"We are leaving for London? Today?" she asked, stepping just inside the threshold of the room.

He frowned at her, shaking his head. "No... I am leaving for London. Today."

She looked left and right. Answers, where were the answers to the litany of questions racketing through her brain? "Just you? Not me?"

"Correct. Is that not what I said? You shall travel with the rest of my family as originally planned." He held up his freshly sealed letter. "But I have urgent business." He tucked the letter into his coat pocket and patted it. "Must get to London today and have this delivered straight-away."

"Could I? Travel to London with you, that is."

Fitz's eyes widened, and he blinked, frozen there like a marble statue whose eyes had been carved too large. She took that to mean he did *not* want her to come with him. She swallowed repeatedly, her throat suddenly not working as it should. Her mind instantly went back to when she was a little girl, trailing after her father, desperately wanting to join him in whatever task he was doing, anything. Always met with a *no, poppet.* Always met with a closed door. Always met with rejection.

"Hmm. You see. No. It will be better if you don't."

There it was. Her stupid, foolish, hopeful heart flattened like it had just been passed through a carding machine at her father's textile factory.

"Yes, you will travel with the others," Fitz was saying over the buzzing in her ears. He sent her a strained smile and then blurted, "More time to ready the townhouse!"

He stood from his desk and wiped his palms on his trousers. He made his way to her and stopped, wringing his hands in front of him. "I suppose I will see you, then?" His gaze fell everywhere but on her own.

"In two days' time," she parroted, not truly capable of much else. Because his words stung. Like a hoard of bees.

He nodded decisively. "Urm. Thank you for a lovely evening." His cheeks bloomed a deep pink, and he squirmed before her.

He laughed nervously, leaned forward—

Was he going to kiss her?

—And stepped around her.

Apparently not.

"Ta-ta, then," he croaked, and he hurried from the room.

She slowly turned, jaw slack, catching a last glimpse of her husband's coat before he disappeared completely from view.

What in the blazes?

Her mind spun. Her deflated heart flopped weakly in her breast. Because he was leaving her. On Christmas. And clearly did not want her to go with him.

Thank you for a lovely evening. They spent a night of indescribable pleasure together. An evening where she vowed pieces inside of her were permanently rearranged to make room for *him*. That wasn't *lovely*. That was *life-altering*.

But not for him.

She gnawed on her lip. Had she completely misread, mis-*felt*, everything that had passed between them last night? She had heard men would declare anything in the heat of the moment. Dear God, had he not meant a word? *This can't be real.* Was that purely in reference to the shagging? She had thought he'd been speaking of whatever this new, indescribable feeling was that had surfaced last night. But perhaps he had just been talking about her vagina.

She tried to breathe through the rising panic flooding her, forcing her lungs to find air. This was fine. Everything was fine. Perhaps this was normal. He said he had urgent business.

Much like her father usually said.

Her father always had urgent business.

Her father was always gone.

Her gaze dropped to the ivory skirts she was hopelessly wrinkling with her twisting fingers. She squared her shoulders and brushed off her skirts. Brushed away the wrinkles. Brushed away the nerves and doubt trying to multiply like bunnies in her brain.

Everything was fine.

But God help her. What if she'd just married into the same life she'd had before?

27

Fitz

FITZ'S HEAD ROCKED AGAINST the squabs of his carriage like his neck muscles had deserted him as the conveyance rolled out of the drive of his family's country estate. He was to London. To win his wife's regard. Because it had been clear at breakfast that there were two other men who currently held it.

He slammed his head against the squab. *Stupid, stupid, stupid.* Why did he have to go and fall in love with her? Why did he have to do something so quintessentially Fitz-like and accidentally compromise a woman who desired men like Ironcrest and Dunmore? Men so unlike Fitz that he couldn't fathom ever attaining their standard of sensuality. Not in his wildest dreams. But he had to try. If he wanted to be in his wife's wildest dreams. And he did. A searing pain shot through the pathetic slab of muscle in his chest.

His eyes slid shut, and a woman's visage stared back at him. But it wasn't his blonde-haired, green-eyed wife. It wasn't kind. It was dark-brown eyes swimming with disgust. Mocking.

He let the words fall over him, each one a heavy iron link in the chain of inadequacy that hung over him. The words Miss Eloise Browning had hurled at him when he'd found her in a state of undress in his brother's study. The words that had been so sharp, so scathing, that they'd sliced right through his flesh. Straight to the heart. She'd been spitting mad, infuriated at his brother's rejection of her advances. She'd spoken, intending to maim, to wound. And she had succeeded.

He'd stood there, incapable of words. For once from shock and wretched pain, rather than nerves.

"I h-had thought," he wheezed. "We were courting. I was to sp-speak—To p-propose."

"Marry you?" She scoffed. "You cannot even speak. Why on earth do you think I would accept such an offer? Not that it truly is one, though, is it? You're a second son who stutters and sweats profusely." She grimaced, turning up her nose. "You never had anything to offer me other than access to your brother."

And Fitz had jerked back as if slapped. Because that was what the words had been. He probably should have seen the signs. How she had always seemed excessively friendly with Felix. But he never thought anything of it. Felix wasn't the least bit interested in her—considering she wasn't a man. Fitz had completely forgotten the rest of the ton wasn't aware of—couldn't be aware of—this fact about his brother, that women would still vie for Felix's hand. Like the woman Fitz had become completely enamored with. All a ruse. Use the oblivious, bumbling fool to get to the Earl.

She'd never been seen in London again. Felix had made sure of that. Lord, the fury on his brother's face during that catastrophe. Fitz had actually feared his brother would harm a woman. But Felix was always in control. And what he dealt her was far worse than any physical blow.

He'd made it abundantly clear within their circles what she had done. Abundantly clear in his first year as the new Earl, that the Earldom of Bentley was not a family to be crossed. Their father may have recently passed, and Felix may have only been four-and-twenty, but the Jennings stood by each other. Always. Through anything. Just as they had stood by Felix after his trauma.

Fitz may be different, even from the rest of his family, but that didn't lessen the strength of the Jennings's bond for him. He was inordinately grateful for his family, and leaning on them had been what had gotten him through Miss Browning's betrayal and disparagement.

But he hadn't loved Eloise.

Enamored, infatuated, besotted? Yes.

But not love.

Egads, how had this even happened? He'd known Georgiana for barely over a sennight. He was no expert on the subject—it wasn't Italian, after all—but wasn't falling in love supposed to take a touch more time than that?

The offending muscle residing in his chest said otherwise, thrumming in a soft undeniable rhythm: *Gi-gi, Gi-gi, Gi-gi.*

It no longer beat for him.

It beat for her.

Fitz couldn't lose Georgiana because of his ineptitude.

He rested his hand over the letter in his pocket. He would get to London and get this letter delivered.

He would make sure he was the only man his wife wanted.

171

28

Fitz

Adelaide,

I trust this letter finds you well. I know I dismissed you upon my betrothal. However, I was hoping you would be willing to see me again. I find myself in a situation where I am in need of guidance that I believe you are uniquely positioned to offer. My recent marriage has illuminated that there are some areas where I am woefully uneducated, things that are intimate in nature. You see, I require instruction, and, given your familiarity with my challenges with anxiety, there are few I would feel comfortable seeking this out with. I entrust myself to your capable hands. I eagerly await your response.

With deepest respect,
Mr. Fitzwilliam Jennings

29

Georgiana

A KNOCK SOUNDED ON Georgiana's bedroom door. She looked up from where she sat on her bed, a book she hadn't read a single word of in her lap. She had retired early after dinner and settled in with a gothic novel, hoping she could distract herself until she fell asleep. Fat lot of good that had done.

"Come in."

The door slowly opened, and Felicity's head popped out from behind it, amber hair piled atop her head. "Hullo, Georgiana." Her velvet, forest-green swathed form stepped into the room. She shut the door behind her and leaned against it. She studied Georgiana silently for a heartbeat. "I wanted to check on you," Felicity said at last. "Are you well? Given…"

Given her husband abandoned her on Christmas. Georgiana was trying so hard not to fall into her melancholy thoughts. But it felt just like his study before they had married. When he'd said quite plainly that conversing with her was inconsequential. That business matters came before her. Apparently, not even Christmas changed that. Apparently, not even—she wrinkled her nose—a *lovely* evening changed that. She was, as always, not enough, not a priority. An afterthought. Oh dear, there she went, becoming all broody.

"I'm going to take this silence and the fact that you look like someone kicked your puppy as a no."

Oh, God. Her heart twisted painfully tight. Her puppy. Bernie. Her eyes welled. Shite—

Felicity clapped her hands. "We are going to fix that. Come with me. Chop chop!"

"Wha—"

But Felicity was already exiting Georgiana's room. She blinked, confusion cutting through her grief. *Thank God.* Georgiana scrambled off her bed and scurried after Felicity. She quickly grabbed her wrapper on her way to the door, shrugging into it as she entered the hallway. Felicity's form was nearly at the end of the hall, marching with purpose.

Georgiana finally reached her sister-in-law, breaths puffing past her lips. "Goodness, Felicity. With how fast you're moving, you'd think a new shipment of French silks just came in. Or they're giving away free samples at the confectioners."

Felicity bounded down the stairs, barely turning to address Georgiana. "I don't give a fig about French silks. Now if it was French brandy…Well, I'd be moving much faster than this."

Georgiana let out a small huff of laughter. A woman after her own heart. Goodness, she could use a snifter of brandy. Or whisky. Or scotch. She wasn't picky.

They walked into Lord Bentley's study, and Felicity went straight to her brother's sideboard.

Georgiana slowed. "Are we supposed to be in here? Isn't this the Earl's private domain?"

Felicity, facing away from Georgiana at the sideboard, lifted her hand above her shoulder and gave a flippant wave. "No, there is no privacy in this family."

Bangs and clanks and the *glug-glug-glug* of pouring liquid came from the sideboard. Felicity shoved some things in the pockets of her wrapper, and then turned, two glasses with generous amounts of amber liquid and a cigar in her hands. She grinned, eyebrows lifting mischievously.

"Care for a snifter and a smoke?"

"Would I ever." Georgiana hurried forward and divested Felicity of one of the snifters, throwing back as much of the contents as she could in one gulp. She choked back the burn, not caring in the least that fire rushed down her throat. Her eyes burned, and her body shuddered as the astringent flavor of alcohol seeped through her. Bloody hell. She had needed that.

Felicity blinked at her. "Well, then. I knew I liked you. But goodness, I think I love you."

Georgiana giggled and stepped up to the sideboard to top off the whisky in her snifter.

Felicity went to a basket by the hearth and pulled out a large wool blanket. "We'll be needing this, even with the whisky warming us. It's cold as tits outside." She ambled over to the door that was on the wall of windows in Lord Bentley's study. "This leads to the terrace that spans the entire length of the manor. Come now, my dear nug, time for a smoke and some serious bosom chum chit-chat." She headed through the door. "Oh, and just bring the decanter. I don't know why I didn't think of that in the first place." Her words faded as she disappeared into the night.

The warmth in Georgiana's belly from the whisky spread all the way to her heart at the term of endearment her sister had just used for her. She stilled. Sister. She thought of Felicity as her sister. Not sister-in-law. Because after her brief time in this family, with Felicity, it felt more like her true family than her own flesh-and-blood ever had.

Smile curving her lips, she snatched the decanter by the neck and hurried after Felicity. They settled at the balustrade of the terrace, snifters and decanter resting on the large railing. Felicity rifled in her pocket, pulled out a cigar cutter, the engraved silver glinting in the lamplight of the terrace. She clipped the edge and took out a long match.

"Have you ever smoked a cigar?" she asked, striding over to a sconce and lighting the match from the flame.

Georgiana nodded. "Another one of my rebellious indulgences. Liquor, cigars, and assignations." She affected a superior tone. "I am truly the most virtuous of ladies."

Felicity toasted the outer binding of the cigar slowly over the match's flame. "Yes, very demure, very chaste." She glanced up from her task, her white teeth flashing from her grin. She put the cigar to her lips, rotating it as she took a slow draw. She released a puff of silver vapor into the night, a spicy aroma heavy with cloves and cinnamon filling the air around them. "Like myself, of course."

Georgiana shook her head with a soft chuckle. It was amazing that this woman in front of her was *the* Lady Felicity Jennings. The incomparable. The woman who was above reproach. The woman who was nothing but charm and grace, prim and proper. Georgiana snorted.

"What?" Felicity handed the cigar off to Georgiana.

Georgiana snatched it up. "It is just...amazing, really. The difference between who you portray to the ton compared to who you are within these walls."

A wicked smile spread over Felicity's face before instantly disappearing. She dipped into a slow curtsy, holding the fabric of her wrapper out wide, gaze downcast. She rose and peeked at Georgiana from beneath her lashes. "I am honored to be graced with your presence, my lord," she said, her voice breathy and quiet. Her expression was soft, her eyes swimming with innocence.

The sister Georgiana had come to know over the past fortnight was gone. In her place was the epitome of virginal, shy maiden. Goodness, no wonder men fell over sideways trying to get to her. No wonder Lord Wessex had claimed her—even if it was to put her on the side for years. The image she portrayed begged to be corrupted.

Georgiana had never understood the desire men had to claim a woman's virginity. Frankly, she found it insulting and hypocritical—that a man would find some sort of thrill in being the only touch a woman would ever know, especially when they went and touched everything in a skirt. But looking at Felicity right now...goodness, Georgiana thought *she* might want to corrupt the chit a bit after that impressive acting.

"Please tell me more about your impressive land holdings," Felicity murmured. "Pray, do share more about your extensive travels abroad. Please tell me about your magnificent collection of unique antiquities that no one else has seen the like of."

Georgiana snickered.

"I'm a bloody virtuoso, aren't I?" Felicity lifted her chin and met Georgiana's gaze head on, eyes sparkling. She waggled her brows. "I've mastered the art of pretense."

Georgiana toasted Felicity with the cigar. "That you have. I applaud you, dear sister." She brought the cigar to her lips, and her eyes sank closed as the flavor of earthy tobacco hit her senses, followed by a spicy-sweet after note. She shaped her mouth into a tight 'O' and pushed out the smoke, small circles of vapor forming in front of her before fading into the night.

"That's bloody brilliant," Felicity said, bouncing on her toes.

Georgiana grinned. A neat trick the workers at one of her father's textile warehouses had taught her.

Felicity bumped Georgiana with her shoulder and wrapped the blanket around their shoulders. "I like that. Dear sister. I always wanted a sister. Stuck with these exasperating brothers." She sighed wearily, one only a little sister with two older brothers could make. "I'm quite happy my brother accidentally ruined you. I couldn't have asked for a more perfect addition to our family."

A somber happiness swirled through Georgiana at Felicity's words. She couldn't agree more—she and Felicity were kindred spirits. She just wished her husband shared this woman's feelings. It was the most painful tease, to be presented with hints and glimmers of the family she had always dreamed of. Falling just short in the area of adoring husband.

"You do know I can practically hear the sullen thoughts spinning in that head of yours."

"I'm sorry. I don't mean to dampen the mood. I just wish…"

"Wish that my brother wasn't utterly fat-headed? Bottle-headed? Beetle-headed. A complete cod's head. Goodness, I never realized how many phrases for saying someone is stupid had head in it."

"Loggerhead." Georgiana added.

"Pudding-headed!"

"Totty-headed." Georgiana waggled her brows.

They dissolved into mirth, their breath fogging the frosty night air. Georgiana passed the cigar back to Felicity and reached for her whisky, the two of them falling into a companionable silence.

"I don't know why my brother left today," Felicity finally said. "Often times Fitz does things no one understands, or for reasons no one understands. But..." Felicity rolled her lips in and appeared to weigh her words. "Just try to be patient with him." She turned and met Georgiana's gaze. "He is not intentionally cruel. As horrible as I am sure it must feel to have him flee on Christmas, I am sure there was a good reason behind it. And by good, I mean good in Fitz's convoluted mind."

Georgiana hummed and sipped her whisky. It was hard to imagine what could possibly be a *good* reason to abruptly leave one's wife and family on Christmas. One's brand-new wife. Who one had known only for a little more than a week. Abandoned. Blatantly stating said wife's company was unwanted.

"I think he quite likes you," Felicity said softly.

Georgiana scoffed.

"It's not always easy to tell with Fitzy," Felicity conceded. She handed the cigar back to Georgiana. "I think you might quite like him, too."

Georgiana let out a heavy sigh before puffing on the cigar. Yes, she most definitely quite liked him. She was fairly certain she started *quite liking* him from the minute she'd rushed to the crimson crustacean's aide that first night in his study. Her adorable, awkward lobster.

"I'm not sure he believes that's possible," Felicity said.

Georgiana frowned. "What do you mean?"

Felicity placed her whisky back on the railing and stuck her hand out for the cigar. "The woman Fitz had intended to offer for—"

"Offer for?" Georgiana froze in her passing of the cigar. Her husband had a love interest? Oh God, is that where he went? She hadn't given a thought to the fact that there might be another woman.

"Stop spiraling." Felicity chuckled. "This was *years* ago."

Georgiana deflated, the fear expelling from her in a white whoosh of breath.

Which only had Felicity chuckling harder. "I knew you liked him. But anyhow. Years ago—goodness, I think it was eight years ago now—a lovely young woman started trailing after Fitzy. Miss Eloise Browning. She was beautiful, from a well-respected family. I think she might have been the first woman to show Fitzy any interest."

"He was an awkward—even more so than he is now—gangly eighteen-year-old with spots all over his face. Honestly, his age alone should have aroused suspicions, because how many women vie for a lad of eighteen? She was all smiles, fan flutters, subtle flirtations; a complete sham. She sniffed around his boot heels for months. He even asked her father for permission to court her. And then he found her half-naked with Felix in Felix's study."

Georgiana's gasp sliced through the quiet night. "No!" Pain pierced her heart for the young man. Goodness, to not only be deceived by the woman he wanted to marry, but his brother too? "Lord Bentley?" She could do nothing but gape. The two seemed to have such a close relationship.

"It wasn't how you are thinking. Felix wanted nothing to do with her," Felicity murmured. "And Fitz knew that without a doubt. But it was revealed then and there that the only reason she was pursuing Fitzy was to get to Felix. He had recently inherited, and everyone thought he'd take a bride and procure an heir with haste. Miss Browning thought to capitalize on that.

"My brother was crushed. I wasn't there, but Felix told me she made the cruelest, most cutting remarks to Fitz. I've never seen Felix more angry. I swear he looked like he was set to burn down London just because she resided there."

Georgiana thought she could understand. Even now, she wanted to find the woman and, quite frankly, slug her across the face.

"The bawd actually thought Felix would marry her when caught with him in his study. Do the *honorable* thing." Felicity sneered, contempt dripping from her tone. "Ironic she would think that when there wasn't an honorable bone in her deceiving body. Instead, he made it known exactly what she had done, thoroughly ruined her to the point she had to flee England."

Good. That made Georgiana exceptionally happy. She hoped the waspish wench got the pox. She grimaced. That was unkind. But frankly, Georgiana didn't care.

"Anyway, the entire point of rehashing that steaming pile of horse-shite from Fitzy's past was that I'm not sure he ever fully recovered from the insults the treacherous tart threw at him. I don't believe he thinks someone could ever like him for him. And it's not as though you chose to wed him of your own accord."

Georgiana's heart struggled to beat through the painful clenches it made on her husband's behalf. "I may not have had a choice, and I may not have dared to hope for anything but a marriage in name, but now..."

Felicity's eyes glimmered gently in the lantern's soft light as she studied Georgiana. "But now you do hope."

Georgiana did. Sometimes possibility shimmered before her, like snowflakes fluttering in the moonlight. But when she awoke the next morning, would she find herself blessed with a beautiful winter wonderland or a disappointing dusting?

Felicity's fingers tangled with Georgiana's, and she gave Georgiana a comforting squeeze. "Trust me, I fully understand having those hopes and dreams. And how it feels when it appears they're not going to come true."

Georgiana sucked in a shaky breath, unsure if it was the cold or the ache in her chest causing the sharpness in her lungs.

"Be patient with him, Georgiana. Give him a chance."

30

London

THIS WAS IT; this was Fitz's chance. Excitement vibrated through his veins as he rushed up the stairs to his mistress's rooms. Why was Fitz excited? Because Fitz had a plan. A plan in which he was going to surprise his wife. Because after his night with Georgiana, Fitz knew he would go to any lengths possible for that woman. His heart clenched. He—and no one else—would fulfill every last one of her desires.

Now, he didn't really know what those desires were, just that his wife had somewhat—urm—risqué preferences. Her response two nights prior to his question... *You want me to hurt you?* Well, he was fairly sure her answer meant yes. She wanted him to give her bruises. Nerves rattled his ribcage. How did one go about bruising one's wife in a pleasurable way?

It was infuriatingly clear that a certain pair of rogues probably knew exactly how. His chest filled with white-hot fire. The way she had spoken of them at Christmas breakfast two days prior. It was seared into his brain. There had been such awe in her voice. Not only could they fuck her in every way she ever dreamed, but apparently, they also saved children. How was Fitz supposed to compete with that?

He paused before his mistress's door and blew out a breath. He would start with becoming the man his wife longed for. Every last carnal craving she had—he would deliver. And he knew exactly who could help him learn how to do just that. He knocked on Adelaide's door.

A moment later, the door swung open, and an abundantly curved woman wrapped in deep-purple silk, brunette hair tumbling down in artfully arranged curls, greeted him. She smiled wide, her red-rouge lips curving, eyes glowing.

"Fitzwilliam! It's so lovely to see you again, darling."

He reached up and squeezed the back of his neck. "Greetings, Adelaide."

She giggled. "Greetings, puppy." She stepped back and turned away, sashaying toward the sitting area of her parlor.

Her flat was set up for seduction, with a plush ivory sofa covered in blankets of fur and velvet, the largest forest-green chaise he'd ever set eyes on, and a very sturdy desk, all right when one walked in. There was a door that led to her bedroom, if one got that far, and a short hall that led to a kitchen area toward the back. Fitz hastily followed her and settled on the sofa opposite where she had spread herself out over her chaise, head propped up on her hand. He took off his gloves and stiffly slapped them over his thigh.

She gestured to the table in front of her which had a glass of whisky, Fitz's drink of choice, ready and waiting. He quickly picked it up and gently passed it back and forth between his hands. He was usually so comfortable here. But being back here felt...different. Like he'd accidentally put on a wrong man's shoes.

"Now, first thing's first, sweetie. I know how you struggle with your words. Your letter indicated you are in need of tutelage. Tutelage that requires my capable hands. So will this be hands-on tutelage?"

Fitz's brow puckered. "What do you mean?"

Her smile grew, and she stared at him fondly. "Fitz, will we be doing these things you want to learn about? Together. Say, for the sake of practice."

His eyes spread wide. "Oh! No, no, no, no." He laughed, but it came out wheezy and gargled. "I-I require informarghamation." He winced. "*Information*. Perhaps detailed instructions. Discussion." He cleared his throat, his foot picking up a rapid tapping. "Not actual, urm, practice."

Why did he find such difficulty with something as simple as words? They always came out wrong, skewed. If he wasn't blabbering, he was saying things that apparently held a much different meaning than he intended.

"I must beg your pardon," he hastily added.

"Don't worry, darling," Adelaide reassured with an understanding smile. "I knew there was a very good chance that was not what you intended, which is why I asked. I cannot say I'm not disappointed, but I understand." She pushed up to sitting and clapped her hands. "So, what do you need help with, my sweet puppy?"

Something uncomfortable danced around in his stomach, a feeling that made his fingers twitch and his feet itch to run. *My sweet puppy*. The endearment had never bothered him before. That was what Fitz was, wasn't it? A bumbling puppy, always stumbling over his own feet and words. But his wife wanted a *man*. Confident and knowing.

You can do this, Fitz. You can learn to be that man for her.

He lifted his chin. "Do you know of the Duke of Ironcrest's proclivities?"

Her eyes flashed with surprise, but she quickly schooled it. Adelaide was exceptional at her job. She would never judge her clients for anything—whether that came in the form of an intimate request or an inarticulate response. Fitz usually fell in the latter.

"Yes, I am familiar. I do not have personal experience, but I am close with others who do." She studied him and picked up her glass of champagne, swirling the bubbly liquid. "He is known for restraining his lovers, everyone knows that."

Fitz swallowed. The rumors were true then. R-restraints. He blew out a breath. Lord, he was stuttering in his own mind. How was he ever going to do this? *Everything will be well.* It's why he went to Adelaide. She would assist him, inform him. What did one even use? Rope—

"But that's not all. It is common knowledge that he is a...rougher lover. Marking his women."

Fitz's heart went cold. Because it was eerily close to the words his wife said to him the other night. That was the man his wife truly wanted. The one she had meant to meet up with in his study back in Kent.

"And choking them," Adelaide continued.

Fitz choked.

"P-pardon. Did you say ch-choke?" Did his wife want him to choke her? Oh God. Shite. Ballocks. Bloody hell. Buggering—

A hand rested on his knee, and he flinched. "Easy, Fitzwilliam. Darling, breathe."

He drew in a shaky breath.

"Maybe we focus on these items for now. Unfortunately, these items are tame compared to other things I've heard. But I'm sure it will give you plenty to try out with your little wife. Do you know any details about what exactly she is seeking?"

"Sh-she admitted she wants me to h-hurt her." This was incredibly difficult to speak about. "During one encounter, she, urm...she asked me to use her. Roughly," he managed to scrape out, though it sounded like someone had gripped him by the ballocks.

Adelaide studied him thoughtfully. "Well, this is very interesting. I will help you, darling. We will show her this puppy has fangs. Don't fret." She leaned forward. "The most important part in all of this is communication. Understanding limits and safety."

She paused, and he nodded to indicate he followed.

"It is of my opinion that it is always best to slowly work up to one's limits. If she wants you to be rough with her, to mark her... You pull her hair; you use an unyielding grip—*bruising*—you bite her."

Visions of their encounter in his study filled his mind. How his wife had practically purred when he had fisted her hair, controlling her with that firm touch. Perhaps he had a chance at this.

"Let her guide you if she wants it harder, if she wants more pain. And often times it is good to soothe after inflicting the pain."

That sounded doable. And he could just confirm with her if he was doing it satisfactorily as they went along.

"Though do not continually ask her if what you are doing is to her liking. That will do nothing but kill the mood."

Oh.

"Just think what an animal would do," Adelaide said. "Rough intimacies are simply embracing your primal side. You need to become feral, puppy. I am sure you are capable of that."

Feral. Right. He could do that. His want for his wife certainly felt feral. He took a sip of whisky and nearly dropped the glass. Damn his sweaty palms! The Duke probably didn't have sweaty palms. The Duke was the epitome of feral, a beast. An ox of a man. Fitz? Fitz was a billy goat.

Lovely. He was a feral billy goat.

"Now," Adelaide said, regaining his attention. "Things like choking require specific knowledge. You cannot simply wrap your hands around a lover's neck."

Fitz's fingers tightened around the hard glass. Just the thought of wrapping his hands around Georgiana's neck... It scared the ever-living shite out of him. He shifted in his seat. Apparently other parts of his anatomy felt differently. Other parts of his anatomy were...curious.

"Hand placement is crucial," Adelaide was saying. "Grip and apply pressure on the side, like so." She demonstrated on herself. "You don't want to cut off her airway, you just want to give the semblance that you're choking her. That's what's so titillating about it, the threat, the hint of harm, but not actual harm."

Fitz stared, wide-eyed, at Adelaide. "That is titillating? F-feeling like you're going to be killed?" And again, his cock pulsed. Should Fitz be concerned that he liked the idea of pretending to harm his wife? *This cannot be normal.*

"Desires practiced between consenting adults with full comprehension of what will happen is normal."

It would seem Fitz had said that out loud. His ears burned.

She waved him over. "Come here, puppy, practice on me. I think you need to see the difference. There is a thrill in being completely in someone else's power—when you can trust them with that. And being the one with that power. I think that could be good for you."

Fitz put down his glass and slowly approached Adelaide. He sat next to her, leaving a generous amount of space between them. She showed him where to place his hands. He reached forward, his hand made contact with her flesh—

His body rebelled. He jerked back.

"I-I'm sorry, I can't. I can't touch you, Adelaide." He sucked in a not-nearly sufficient breath. "You're not her. I can't."

Adelaide's face softened. "Oh, puppy. You're in love with her, aren't you?"

He glanced away and fidgeted with his trousers. That was not a topic he wanted to discuss with Adelaide. He was having his own struggles with coming to terms with it. What he felt for his wife was overwhelming. Uncomfortable. Disconcerting. It made the ramifications of failure too daunting to even contemplate.

He cleared his throat roughly. "This discussion has been...eye-opening. Would you be able to procure some informative pamphlets or illustrations, perhaps? Directions? I need to be able to do this. For her. I need to be the man she wants."

That made Adelaide frown, her pretty, slim brows pinching. "Fitzwilliam... You don't need to change or be someone else to earn anyone's love or affection. If she is requiring you to do something you're not comfortable with, if she is pinning her happiness on you changing, frankly, she doesn't deserve you at all. You are a rare, genuine man in this world, Fitzwilliam."

"No one wants a genuine man who is nothing but vanilla custard in bed," he muttered.

"None of that," Adelaide said sharply, and Fitz's gaze snapped back to hers. "You may be more nervous than most—"

Fitz snorted

She rolled her eyes at him. "Fine, *much* more nervous than most. But you are a phenomenal lover. You care so much about your partner's pleasure, utterly selfless in bed. A rarity. You don't need to be the Duke. You don't need whips and knives—"

"Kn-knives," he squeaked.

She waved him off. "My point is, you don't need these things to satisfy your wife. Just because you don't partake in these proclivities, it doesn't make your lovemaking boring. Multiple orgasms that leave one brainless are not *boring*. Your cock being ready within minutes for another round is not *boring*."

He rested his elbows on his knees and dropped his head in his hands. He knew her words were true...but it didn't help. Because his wife wanted those things—Lord, he hoped she didn't want knives—and he wanted to give her those things.

Adelaide studied him, lips pursed. "I wish I could give you confidence, darling. So many men who don't deserve it have it. And you, you surely are worthy of it in spades."

He lifted his head and smiled weakly at her. "I wish it were only that easy."

"I am going to help you, darling. I will procure some things for you. Fortunately for you, I know all the right people for this. I should only require a day or two, and then I will deliver them. In the meantime, if you have a copy of *Fanny Hill,* I would recommend you start there. Specifically, *Letter XI* I think you will find most enlightening."

Fitz left his mistress's flat feeling slightly better. He had a plan; he had an assignment to focus on. Fitz enjoyed studying. He enjoyed books. This was perfect for him. He would treat it like any other subject taught at Oxford. This lecture just happened to be on *The Principles of Pleasure and Sexual Proclivities.*

He was determined to get top marks.

31

Georgiana

GEORGIANA WANDERED DOWN THE hallway of her husband's small London town house. It was brightly lit with gold wall sconces and cream wallcoverings. There was no artwork, no bric-a-brac, no portraits, no personal artifacts. No signs of life. The entire house seemed that way, actually. Except for her husband's study, one wouldn't have realized someone lived here.

Which she supposed wasn't surprising given what she'd learned about her husband in their short time together—goodness, it had almost been a fortnight, hadn't it? Fitz seemed to focus solely on his Italian translations. It looked like it would be up to her to make this town house feel like a home. What exactly that home life was going to look like...was still in question.

Because when she had arrived an hour earlier from Kent, her husband had been noticeably absent. The butler, Pemberton, and the housekeeper, Mrs. Hutchinson, had received her in his stead. Pemberton was a thin, middle-aged, refined gentleman with neatly cut brown hair. Very formal. Very butler. Mrs. Hutchinson, on the other hand, was the opposite of the butler in every way—hair frazzled, cheeks rosy, wearing an apron that appeared to be smudged with coal dust.

The housekeeper, who spoke almost too fast for Georgiana to catch what the woman was saying, provided her with a quick tour. They had a small staff: a cook, a footman, and a maid. The maid, whose name was Jane, or Elaine—or maybe it was Lorraine?—regardless, the young woman could assist Georgiana in any lady's maids duties Georgiana would require until she found a suitable one for hire. Despite the matron's harried demeanor, Mrs. Hutchinson was jovial and quick with a smile, and made Georgiana feel welcome.

Much more so than her absent husband.

Georgiana worried her lip and halted outside her husband's study. He was finally home. He hadn't sought her out, which she was trying not to be too hurt about. He had said he had urgent business, so was most likely busy. She understood what that meant from growing up with her father. It wasn't rare for her father to completely forget she and her mother existed. Honestly, some days she had rather hoped her mother would forget she existed.

Right now, her husband's nose was inches from a book, spectacles dangling dangerously. Fitz was so absorbed with his reading he appeared about to fall *into* the book, so it wasn't all that surprising he had forgotten about her. It didn't make it hurt any less. It actually hurt a great deal more. Because he had been all she could think about since their night together—goodness, since their betrothal, really. He'd wormed his way into her heart and her mind just like the curly-haired, freckled bookworm he was.

Felicity's words floated back to her. *Give him a chance.* Georgiana thought she might need to give her husband a whole bushel of chances.

She tipped up her chin, cleared her throat, and stepped into his study.

Her husband squeaked and flipped the book shut with a *thwack*. He hastily shoved the book in the top drawer of his desk, a blush rapidly spreading over his cheekbones.

He popped up, bashed something—his knee?—on his desk, cursed, and then blurted, "G-Georgiana. You've arrived, then."

What a greeting. Her heartbeat dwindled, but she forced a smile. "Yes, Fitz. An hour or so ago." She didn't know whether to feel relief that the only reason he hadn't come looking for was because he hadn't been aware of her arrival—or hurt that he had been completely oblivious to the fact. Hadn't been waiting in anticipation for her. Like she had for him.

"Did you have a pleasant journey?" His gaze darted around his study, apparently unable to find a place to land.

"Yes, smooth travels. We were fortunate the weather has cooperated, and we haven't received any snow lately. It was a quick, half-day journey."

"Excellent. Excellent."

They stood there awkwardly; him finding his ceiling fascinating and her twisting her skirts in her fingers. Evidently, he wasn't going to invite her inside. How had they reverted to this? They had seemed to be making such progress. She thought he was becoming more comfortable around her. But this? This was just as bad as her first week at his country estate in Kent.

"You look well." He said it to the ceiling.

She thought he might have meant it for her, though. And she was going to count that as a small victory.

She dared to approach him. Perhaps she could make him more comfortable. She had no idea how to navigate a relationship, romantic or otherwise. He was always more at ease after a bout of lovemaking. He seemed to like her then. She ignored the pang in her gut that thought caused. Plus, she'd always wanted to be tupped on a desk. Yes, that was probably the answer. A tupping. Lust had never failed to make her feel, to make her forget.

She stopped before him, ivory skirts swirling around his gray trousers. His amber gaze finally settled on hers, and a breath puffed from him, his entire face softening with what she really hoped was longing. A face going soft could only be a good thing, right? All she knew was the way he was looking at her, those rich, amber eyes swimming with indecipherable emotion, had her heart melting.

She reached out and took one of his clenched hands and slowly pried his fingers apart and ran her thumb over the back. Staring at him, she whispered, "I missed you, husband."

He nodded.

Her lips quirked. Not really an applicable response.

She went up on tiptoe and pressed a soft kiss to his lips before gently falling back down. He sucked in a breath and stilled. She waited, pleading with her eyes, pleading for him to kiss her back.

Pleading for him to want her.

Want me.

32

FITZ REALLY, REALLY, *REALLY* wanted his wife. She was standing there, blonde hair in a loosely woven plait, tendrils falling about her heart-shaped face, lips parted, pink and pleading. Pleading with him to kiss her back. He didn't always catch physical cues. But his wife's green eyes, dark with dilated pupils, lips glistening from where her tongue had just coasted over them? He didn't need any help to decipher that.

The problem was his wife had absconded with his wits with that soft brush of her lips. He couldn't think straight when she looked at him like that, when her thumb coasted over the back of his hand whisper-soft, when she'd left a hint of drinking chocolate on his mouth from her kiss. But now seemed like a moment better fit for not thinking. Honestly, Fitz was better off if he avoided thinking altogether.

He reached up to cup her face and tilted her chin up to him. Lord, she was small. He felt like he had clown hands, cradling her dainty face. He always felt like a clown—like Joseph Grimaldi, not just in performance, but in life. Yet his wife seemed to want this clown. Visions of white-painted faces and attire covered in colorful spots flashed in his mind. Lord, he hoped that wasn't another one of her desires.

She blinked up at him, soft puffs of chocolate-scented breath coasting over his skin. He should probably kiss her now. But he took delight in looking at her. She was so lovely.

He closed the distance, and his lips fell on hers. Her hands fell on his chest. Soft, comforting, familiar. He slid his tongue over her lips, and she opened instantly, allowing him inside. He basked in the warmth of her mouth, the flavor that was Georgiana. Except one thing was missing. That cinnamon-sweet taste he had grown so accustomed to. The one that tasted like comfort, like home. He made a mental note to inform Cook to prepare spiced biscuits. Every day.

He groaned, and her fingers dug into his waistcoat. Her tongue flicked against his, soft at first—hesitant—and he had no idea why. His wife wasn't ever hesitant.

Fitz didn't have to worry about that thought overlong. Her tentativeness quickly vanished, and her tongue grew bolder, harder. He turned them, pressing her into his desk, and she sighed greedily into his mouth. Her hips rocked against his, and her hands clawed up his neck to push into his hair.

This was escalating quickly. Just as quickly as his pulse. But there was something about this woman, about her presence, about the feel of her in his arms, about the taste of her on his tongue, that had all his well-laid-out plans fleeing out his study door. Because he hadn't planned on this. He hadn't planned on kissing her at all. He had planned on avoiding her, actually.

When he had returned from Adelaide's earlier, after securing a copy of *Fanny Hill,* he had set out reading, starting with *Letter XI.* And that was how his wife found him, engrossed in the part of the woman's memoir when she was taking a rod to her backside. It was while reading that, that Fitz decided it was best he wait until he received the information from Adelaide before he attempted anything with his wife. Because he was out of his element. Which wasn't saying much, since Fitz was out of his element much more often than he was in it. But he wanted to ensure he did this...flagellation properly. If that was what his wife desired.

One of Georgiana's hands fell to the front of his trousers, tracing the outline of him. God, he ached for her. It wasn't enough, the tease of her fingers over fabric. He needed fingers on flesh, *around* flesh. And his wife delivered, her hands already having his placket undone. His mouth dropped to her neck, and when her fingers wrapped around him and stroked, he bit down softly, groaning into her skin. Her touch was torture. Pleasurable, ecstasy-inducing torture.

Her breath caught, and she moaned, her fingers tightening. "Yes, Fitz." Her words were mere breath, and she arched her neck, giving him better access. "Bite me harder."

He moved down her neck, sucking and licking, relishing the taste of her skin. Then he sank his teeth into her shoulder, and she cried out, her hips jerking into his. Something snapped in his wife. She turned wild, rabid, frantic—rucking up her skirts in front of him.

She tugged on his wrist, pulling his hand between her thighs. Between her thighs where she was very much hot and wet. He growled softly. His fingers swirled over her, and his cock jumped. It wanted her—he wanted her—with a fierce, frenzied, deranged need.

He sank two fingers inside and—fuck—she tightened around him so sweetly. His thumb went to her clitoris, and she fluttered around his fingers. Lord, she was responsive. He swirled over her, gentling his pressure, and she tried to rock into him, seeking. This was something he could give her easily. Vanilla custard pleasure. But that wouldn't ever be enough for her. Fitz was all too familiar with what it meant to be lacking. He didn't want to be lacking for his wife. She wanted dark; she wanted rough; she wanted untamed.

He caught her chin in his free hand and forced her mouth to his. He wanted to be all those things for her. So badly. He glided his thumb over her faster. She trembled against him, her core tightening on his fingers, and as soft as her luscious curves were, her muscles tensed against him. He gave her more, more pressure, more skimming over where her pleasure centered. And that was all it took. Her body shuddered against his, and she clamped down on his fingers. She arched against him, sobs of pleasure fleeing her parted lips. And he stole every last one of those cries. God, she was stunning when she came.

He trailed kisses along her jaw and slowly let his fingers slide from her. A slide that was pure torture. His cock throbbed like the devil. His ballocks drawn tight. He ached. Needed. To be inside his wife. She would just have to settle for another bout of bland lovemaking. Blancmange flavored. Because he couldn't wait until he'd studied more, until he had more information.

And apparently his wife couldn't wait either. Georgiana spun in his arms and bent over, proffering her bare arse for him. His hands instantly went to her pale soft flesh, hot, smooth—he squeezed her arse—plush. A choked sound came from him. God, he loved her curves.

She fit perfectly with him, her small, luscious body against his lean, tall one. That didn't actually make any sense given their forms were opposite in nearly every way. But he wasn't so sure it needed to make sense.

They fit. That was all there was to it.

She backed into him, ground against him, her mewls desperate.

Micetta mia.

Good Lord, he was going to fuck his wife on his desk, wasn't he? And the door was wide open. "The d-door," he managed.

"Leave it," she breathed.

His heart hammered in his chest, and he stared at the entry to his study. The thrill, the appeal of getting caught, spurring adrenaline to surge through him, landing straight in his cock. Perhaps not so bland a bedding, then. Not the most flavorful of dishes. But it was a far cry from blancmange. He'd work his way up to Charlotte Russe.

He pushed her thighs wide and slid his cock between her legs. God, she was scorching, her flesh soaked and swollen from her release. He notched himself at her entrance, his body screaming to drive home.

And then his wife panted out two words that made the heat in his veins freeze over.

"Spank me."

He didn't move. He wasn't sure he even drew breath.

She wiggled against him. "Please, Fitz."

But he couldn't. Panic was rolling through him like a boulder down a mountain, picking up speed and spinning out of control. His mind flashed back to what he had just read. How hard did he hit her? Was he supposed to do it a certain way? In a certain place? Was it like the choking? The woman, Fanny, had *bled*. He needed more instruction. He needed more time.

So he did what Fitz did best.

"If you'll excuse me. I forgot about a prior obligation."

And he fled.

33

Georgiana

THIS WEEK WAS NOT going how Georgiana had hoped it would. She most certainly hadn't expected it to include herself abandoned, bent bare-arsed over her husband's desk.

If you'll excuse me. I forgot about a prior obligation.

She shook her head as she sifted through the correspondence at the escritoire in her bedchamber. Un-bloody-believable. Who said such a thing when their cock was pressed against one's quim?

Georgiana dropped her head to her desk with a *thud*. She had been near fanatic when he'd kissed her back, when he'd kissed her back *with need*. Need for her. Want for her. She so desperately wanted him to want her. To love her.

She froze. Oh, God. Was that what this overwhelming feeling was? The one where her heart was fit to explode at any moment. Where her entire body warmed like she was basking in sunshine even though it was the dead of winter. Where a simple smile, a huff of laughter, a soft amber gaze, was all it took for an ordinary day to turn into the best day of her life.

Her hand went to her stomach. *Stop!* She sat up and scowled down at her belly. The butterflies or grasshoppers or frogs or whatever they were would not stop hopping around in there. Bloody hell. She'd fallen in love with her husband. And she had no idea where she stood with him.

After their almost amazing encounter ended in disaster, she had barely seen him. He had taken a dinner tray in his room and—shocking—hadn't visited her chambers that night.

So, ever the strong, resilient woman, Georgiana had attempted to visit him instead. Her eyes closed on a groan. That had been a resounding failure.

Georgiana! Here. Something, isn't it? Surprise. He had laughed nervously and wiped the back of his hand over his brow. *I m-mean. Live here. Of course. Why wouldn't you? Business calls. Must get to it back. Burning the midnight oil.* And then he promptly shut the door in her face.

She had stood outside his room for a good five minutes, stunned. Partly trying to make sense of the words her husband had just blubbered and partly not believing he had just shut a door in her face.

She turned the letter she was holding over in her hands and unfolded it. A lovely note from Lady Rutledge, whose supper party was tomorrow evening.

Dear Mrs. Fitzwilliam Jennings,

First, please allow me to offer my warmest congratulations on your recent nuptials! Your husband and his family are cherished guests and have graced our table many times. We are truly delighted to have the opportunity to meet the newest addition to the Jennings family. I am sure we are going to get along fabulously!

Yours sincerely,

Lady Rutledge

A supper party sounded like an excellent distraction from the toils of her marriage. And she wanted to speak with Lady Rutledge about the foundling home. She'd like to help in some way. Perhaps there was some way she could convince her father to donate textiles to the home. More than anything, she'd like to visit with the children. She'd been so lonely as a child. All she'd ever longed for was company. Her heart vibrated happily in her chest at the thought of going to see the children.

At least she could have something that gave her purpose, brought her joy. She might desperately need that based on the current state of her marriage. No. She wouldn't think such things. Her marriage was new, two strangers forced together. The fact that they had had *any* positive moments together must be a good sign. She just had to avoid pushing their relationship in the wrong direction. Like scaring her husband off by asking him to spank her.

She groaned.

Perhaps she should let Fitz know she had no qualms if he didn't want to spank her. And she would be careful not to request anything else. Definitely not restraints. She blew out a breath, a tendril of hair in front of her face fluffing upwards. She could only imagine her husband would have run all the way back to Kent if she'd asked him to tie her up. But he had fulfilled her in so many ways thus far, and he did get rough with her—though she wouldn't complain with *rougher*—so overall she was quite satisfied. Extremely so.

She didn't want him to do anything he wasn't comfortable with. Her desires were just that—desires. They weren't needs. She thought all she really needed...was him. Her heart clenched.

Terrifying.

Georgiana fiddled with the letter. She craved the closeness, the conversation, the comfortable quiet moments that she had gotten small hints of with her husband...more than the carnal moments.

Terrifying.

She didn't think that was normal to want in a marriage. Or at least not normal to expect from one. For as long as she could remember, she was paraded around as a womb for sale to the destitute lords of London. That was the way of things. Women were for breeding. Her parents certainly hadn't displayed any signs of affection. They reminded her more of how her father acted with his business associates. Amicable. *Blech.*

And she was also fairly certain her father had a mistress. Georgiana knew *that* wasn't a good sign. If one's husband was sleeping with someone else, she highly doubted there was any closeness happening. Thank goodness her husband had dismissed his. She would hold on to that. A sign, a glimmer of hope, for a marriage in truth.

It was just...things were different since they arrived in London. Even before he'd abandoned her in his study. He couldn't even speak to her anymore. How did she get back to the man who had held her in his arms on Christmas Eve?

This marriage felt impossible to navigate. What did one do when a relationship appeared to be stumbling? She knew what her parents did. They put on fake smiles and filled dinner with empty conversation until they could curl up in separate bedrooms and forget the other existed. She had thought sex might be the answer, but she had clearly made it worse with that.

Georgiana stood and headed for her door. She would start with conversation. She didn't even care what about, she just wanted to speak with him. And for him to speak back. When they had been in Kent, he had said how badly he wanted to converse with her. She lifted her chin. Well, bugger and damn, she would make it happen!

With resolve flowing through her veins, she nearly bounded all the way to her husband's study. She stumbled to a stop just before his door and took a calming breath. Best not to fly into Fitz's study and frighten the poor man. He was as quick to startle as a skittish hare.

She casually stepped into his study. And froze. Fitz lounged in one of the armchairs in front of the low-burning hearth, one leg slung over the arm, a whisky dangling loosely in one hand. He had a book in his lap, spectacles perched on his nose, brow puckered softly in concentration. He looked so relaxed, so at ease. She glanced at his stockinged foot, toes wiggling as he read. Her lungs grew tight, and air was suddenly very hard to come by, scarce.

Her eyes burned. Dear God, were those tears forming? She hastily took a step back and pressed up against the wall. It was just...it was almost painful to see him that way—because it was how she so desperately wanted him to be *with her*. Curled up together while they both got lost in a book. Just each other's comforting presence enough. The longing—it *hurt*. She focused on drawing breath in and out until the burning behind her eyes receded. They would never get there if they didn't speak.

She shook out her arms, stepped back into the doorway, and knocked softly on the open door. He glanced up from his reading, and scrambled to standing, slamming the book shut. He tucked his hands, book and all, behind him and rocked on his heels.

"Georgiana." He managed it without stuttering, but a blush was growing on his cheeks.

She smiled at him, hopefully in a way that was encouraging and not startling. His gaze locked on her lips, and he ceased all movement. She thought that might be a good sign.

"May I come in?"

"Of-of course." He strode over to his desk, tucked his book and spectacles away, and then gestured back to his armchairs.

They settled into the leather chairs. She pushed off her slippers and folded her calves beneath her. The rapid tapping of Fitz's fingers against the arm of his chair filled the room. Perhaps speaking of a topic he enjoyed would be a good start.

"What are you reading?"

"Nurrghle." He glanced away and pulled at his cravat. "Urm, apologies. Nothing. I mean something. Maybe t-translations."

The poor man's ears were lobster red. All right. Different topic, then.

"I'm quite looking forward to the Rutledge's supper party."

He blinked dumbly at her. "A supper party... With the Rutledges. Yes. Of course. How could I forget? We go every year. I mean, my family does. Which now you are. My family. A part of. I mean." He let out a strangled laugh. "You are looking forward to attending?"

"Yes," she said softly, glancing at him from beneath her lashes.

He gifted her a half-smile. A glorious half-smile with a dimple popping in his cheek. He was almost a normal color again, too. "Their supper parties are nearly bearable. For me, I mean. I can usually find another awkward academic to blather on with, so it is never too bad."

She arched a brow at him. "Another academic? No one else?"

He blinked slowly at her, beautifully befuddled.

Her lips quirked, and she leaned forward, snatching his whisky off the side table between their chairs. "Did you know, Fitz, an advantage to having a wife is you can blather on with *her* during such parties?" She winked at him before taking a sip of his drink. She hummed appreciatively, her body giving a small shudder as the sharp burn of alcohol slid through her. That first sip always had the biggest bite.

His lips curved up in the softest semblance of a smile. "I think you are aware I don't always do so well blathering on with my wife."

She shrugged and took another sip. "Perhaps we need to converse more often. Practice." She paused and chewed her lip. "Back in Kent, you said you wanted to become better acquainted. I know you have been quite busy since we've returned..." She let out a long, slow breath, trying to calm her twisting stomach. "Would you perhaps have time now? To sit and talk with me for a while?"

There. She asked. Her fingers tightened around the whisky glass, and she threw the rest back. The worst that would happen is he said no. He didn't have time for her. And that would be fine. She would be fine. It would be—

"I'd like that."

Her gaze shot to his. And relief flooded her lungs like that first breath of country air after leaving the smog of London.

He extended his arm toward her, palm up. "Would you care for a refill of my drink?" His grin turned lop-sided, and Georgiana swore the floor beneath her did, too. Had her husband just teased her? And with that bloody lop-sided smile?

Now she might be thankful he was a bit awkward. Because he'd be fighting off petticoats left and right if he let that charm loose. And no other woman would lay a hand on her husband. This clumsy cove was hers.

She leaned forward and placed the glass—and her heart—in his hand. Time to get to know her husband. And for now, she wouldn't bring up any of her worries, bedroom related or not.

She didn't want to risk ruining this moment.

34

FITZ PRAYED HE WOULDN'T ruin the moment. He made his way back from the sideboard with two glasses in hand, a finger of amber liquid in each. He was conversing with his wife, who was snuggled up in the armchair next to his. He wasn't stuttering, he wasn't sweating, and he wasn't scared.

"So, I take it you enjoy whisky then?" he asked.

She accepted her glass with a smile. "Yes. You'll laugh, but I actually would filch my father's whisky when I was younger. I thought it was *so* rebellious. I'd sit there with Bernie, coughing and sputtering down the horrible stuff. But"—she dropped her voice low—"tough men drank whisky." She huffed out a laugh. "I wanted to prove I was tough. And now I've developed a liking for the stuff."

"Bernie?" Something hot and acidic turned over in his gut. Who was this man she was so familiar with? *Imbibing* with.

Her smile grew fond and sad and small. "Bernie was my Bloodhound," she said quietly. She took a small sip of her drink, rubbing a hand over her bare arm.

His stomach settled, and his heart clenched. A pet, not a man. He'd never had a pet, never lost one. But by how little and lost his wife looked just now, he could tell it had been—was—hard on her. "Will you tell me about him?"

She shivered and nodded. He reached into the basket below the side table and snatched up a blanket. He stood, shook it out, and settled it over her lap. "Here," he murmured. "I run as hot as the coals in the hearth, so I have the servants burn the fires low. I'll be sure to inform them to keep them hotter going forward."

He hadn't thought of that fact. He hadn't thought to have a tray sent to her last night for dinner. God, he was blundering terribly as a husband.

He leaned over her now, hands resting on the arms of her chair. Only about a head of space separated them, her green eyes glued to his. Her presence was so potent. It drew him in, pulled him in like a dangerous tide. Every. Bloody. Time.

He moved a touch closer. Her lips parted, and she sucked in the sweetest little breath. Just one kiss. And then he'd back away. He thought he might need to prove to himself he was capable of kissing his wife—without things escalating, without doing something humiliating. He wanted to be able to kiss her any time he wanted. Wanted the press of those soft lips on his randomly, scattered throughout the day.

He slid his hand over her jaw and tilted her face up. He hovered for a moment, their gazes never breaking, and then slowly, slowly, he closed the distance. Warm, supple lips greeted his, and it was the best welcome he'd ever received. His fingers tightened on her, and he gave himself just a bit more. Lips passing over lips. Her breath hitched, and he knew he needed to back away. Back away before she completely broke down his restraint. One more drag of his mouth over hers, then he retreated.

She stared at him, evergreen irises glassy and glimmering. He swiped his thumb over her bottom lip once and pushed off the chair. By the time he settled back in his, her eyes had cleared, and a twinge pulled in his chest, already missing the way the lust had clouded her gaze.

"Thank you," she said, plucking at the blanket on her lap. She tucked her chin to her chest and fidgeted with the material, her gaze avoiding his. She almost looked bashful. Her. Not him!

She cleared her throat. "I had Bernie for just over ten years."

Right. Conversation. Goodness, he was horrible at this.

"Bloodhounds...are quite large. What made you decide on one of those?" Bloodhounds are quite large? *Clever, Fitz, really bloody clever.* Lord, he wanted to smack himself in the face.

She huffed out a laugh and met his gaze. "It was one of the few breeds my father approved of. They're not the most common or popular any longer, but some exceptionally wealthy aristocrats, who have deer parks still, have them. The rarity, the notion of extreme wealth that the breed hinted at, was something my father liked immensely.

"For me..."—her smile turned wistful—"I saw Bernie's long floppy ears and smooshed, wrinkly nose, and had to have him. He came bounding up to me, jumping all over my skirts. Chose me, I think." She giggled softly, her gaze falling to her lap, faraway. "Goodness, his ears were so long, I had to tie them up. They were always falling in his water dish whenever he took a drink."

She looked at Fitz, her gaze watery. But her grin nearly split her face in two. And it was breathtaking and mesmerizing and impossible not to return. "He was the strangest dog. Every time he greeted me when I came home, he'd rub his face all over my slippers and stick his wiggly bum in the air, demanding scratches on his bottom. And he was obsessed with my stockings." She chuckled lightly. "But only clean ones. Wouldn't *dare* touch the dirty ones."

She let out a weighty sigh. "Normally he was so noble and dignified. I called him King Bernard. He truly was a beautiful dog. But sometimes his top lip would get stuck in his front teeth, and he'd just sit there grinning at you with his toothy smile like the biggest, lovable buffoon."

Her green eyes twinkled, and Fitz swore she appeared lit up from within while talking about her beloved hound. Fitz's own cheeks ached from smiling. He was glad she'd had her Bernie. From the little he'd garnered about his wife, he didn't think she'd had the warm and loving upbringing that Fitz'd had.

"He was also exceptionally snuggly," she was saying. "You'll probably think me odd, but he slept in my bed every night. He even had his own pillow, because Bernie *required* a pillow. I swear he was part human." A sad breath whooshed from her, her entire person deflating. "But he passed last Spring."

His smile faded away. "I'm sorry for your loss, Gigi."

"Thank you." She still smiled, but it was strained, and her voice was tight.

He didn't want her to be sad. New topic. New topic. New topic. "Whisky!"

She blinked at him.

He cleared his throat and grimaced. *Smooth, Fitz. As smooth as tree bark.* But at least his unexpected outburst had washed away the melancholy. "You had said you would partake in whisky, with Bernie by your side. Because you wanted to prove you were tough?"

"Ah, yes." She rolled the edge of the glass against her bottom lip. "It was no secret my father wished I had been a boy, especially after my brother left—"

"You have a brother?" How did he not know that? They were married. Known each other for a fortnight now. Seemed like something he should have known. Was he that horrible of a husband?

Her lips tilted up, her eyes dancing with mirth. "Yes, I have a brother. But he is ten years my senior and left for America in his early twenties. My father was beyond enraged when he left. Wanted Geoffry to take over the family business. And with me being a woman...well, I couldn't run it."

"Before that he hadn't seemed to mind me so much, but I think when Geoffry left, it frustrated Father that I had ruined all his well-laid plans. If I had been a boy, everything would have stayed in the family."

She shrugged. "For a while, I wanted to prove to my father I was just as worthwhile, just as tough as any man. So, I would sneak to the warehouse and help the workers, wear breeches, drink whisky, smoke cigars. Oh, how I plagued my mother—who, in stark contrast to my father, was determined to turn me into the perfect genteel lady to ensnare a lord." She leaned forward and whispered, "She failed." Then winked at him.

He chuckled, admiring the way her green iris shone in the fire's light, the way the flames cast flickering shadows over her soft, porcelain skin. What a wild young girl she must have been, and even now he saw traces of that wild woman in her. No wonder she got along so well with Felicity.

"I don't know if you needed the whisky to prove it. I think you quite tough, strong, without it."

She tilted her head questioningly. "What do you mean?"

"While I can't complain that it led you to enjoying whisky—I find I quite like sitting here partaking with you." He shot her a quick, shy smile. "But, urm... Well, I would argue you're one of the strongest women I've known. You exude confidence. You walk around proud and tall." Even as little as she was, he swore she held herself taller than he himself did.

"And goodness, you had no qualms having your b-breasts on display when we first met." He chuckled, and a ping of delight filled him when he realized his face wasn't growing hot—and he had just said *breasts*. "Came straight to my aid, not a hint of insecurity. And after we were caught, you boldly launched into an attempt to extricate us from the situation." He glanced down at his whisky. "I couldn't even form words."

He finally glanced at her and found her smiling at him, a blush tinging *her* cheeks.

"It was nothing," she said with a self-deprecating laugh. "Plus, you had just injured yourself, and I promptly smothered you with my bosom. No wonder you couldn't speak. It was the least I could do."

His brows pinched. Was she brushing it off? She wasn't grasping the magnitude of having such a quality. "No, Gigi. It wasn't just then," he argued. "You were uprooted from your family, from your life, and forced to marry a strange man—one who couldn't even converse with you. But you marched right up to that altar and spoke clearly and confidently. I feared my heart would give out throughout the entire ordeal. And I wasn't the one moving in with a new family *during Christmas*.

"But you jumped right in, without hesitation, finding your fit within our fold." He grinned, memories of the past sennight flitting through his mind. "Demanding we put up *a tree* for Christmas, and convincing everyone it was a good idea. I think you started a new Jennings's tradi-

216

tion." His smile slipped away, and he stared seriously at his wife. "You have been nothing but strong. And it's admirable. Enviable. You are not giving yourself enough credit."

She was everything he was not.

Her eyes were glassy again, and she hastily averted her gaze. She blinked rapidly and cleared her throat. *Egads.* His eyes widened. Was she going to cry? Had he just made his wife cry? Why did he always make a bloody muck of things?

"Gigi, are you well? I must apologize. I hadn't meant—"

"No," she interrupted, her voice thick. She cleared her throat again and let out a slow breath. She glanced at him with shimmering green eyes close to overflowing. "No one has ever said anything so kind to me before." Her lips trembled as they curved into the smallest of smiles. "Thank you, Fitzwilliam," she whispered.

Fitz deflated back into his armchair. He hadn't said the wrong thing. She was happy. And as they casually conversed, sharing stories of their childhood, exchanging their likes and dislikes from food to games to seasons, finding out there were no other secret siblings, Fitz's heart grew with every word.

For what felt like the first time, Fitz had said the right thing.

35

"Fitzwilliam Jennings!" A loud, boisterous voice rang through the entry. "Georgiana Jennings!"

Fitz smirked. Only his sister's yell would reach him all the way in his study from the front entry.

Georgiana popped out of the armchair where she had settled with a book after they'd concluded breaking their fast not too long before. "Felicity is here!" She flew out the door, blonde plait and pale-blue skirts whipping behind her.

Fitz chuckled and followed his excited wife. He reached the entry to find a beaming Felicity holding Georgiana's hands and speaking animatedly, waving Georgiana's hands in her grasp while she talked. Fitz shook his head, biting back a smile. His wife was grinning at his sister, and he stood back admiring the sight, her pale skin flushing with excitement, green eyes bright and sparkling.

She turned to him and bounced on her toes. "Felicity said we are going to St. James's Park!"

"She did, did she?" He cocked a brow at his sister and crossed his arms over his chest.

"Yes, you are. It snowed last night." Her amber eyes turned devious.

He knew that look, and he knew what a fresh snow meant.

"Felix is waiting for us in the carriage. Lord Wessex and Lady Camoys are meeting us there. It will be perfect, three on three." She grinned. "Women versus men, I think?"

Georgiana glanced between the two of them, brow puckering. "What do you mean? Are we taking part in some sort of competition?"

One could say that. Competition. War.

Felicity inclined her head, letting Fitz do the honors.

"We are having a snowball fight."

His wife's mouth formed a small moue, and she clapped fervently. "I've never had a snowball fight before. I've always wanted to."

"Well, you are in for a treat," Felicity said. "The Jennings have the *best* snowball fights."

Fitz snorted. Best. Dangerous. Same thing. But he had no qualms that his wife would take to this like she did everything else with his family.

"Flick, why don't you take Gigi up to her room and help her prepare for the outing? We'll reconvene back here and head to the park."

Felicity nodded, a soldier ready for battle. Which was exactly what this snowball fight would be. This was one activity Fitz excelled at. No need to worry over conversing—the whole aim was to hit targets that were *far away*. No need to worry about stumbling or tripping—if one didn't fall during a snowball fight, they weren't doing it right. No worry about blushing—the cold would already have everyone rosy-cheeked. No need to worry about sweating—everyone would be sweating by the end of this battle.

Felicity went to pass him, and he discreetly reached out to halt her. "Lord Wessex will be joining us?" he asked in a low voice, quirking a brow.

She nodded, stiffening.

"Will you be well with him there? Given…"

She huffed out a breath. "It was far from the first time, and it won't be the last time, Fitzy." She leaned into him and rested her head on his shoulder for a heartbeat. "But thank you, brother."

She pushed off and hurried to catch up with Georgiana, who was already halfway up the stairs. Felicity turned and looked back at him, one foot on the steps. "I figure this is the perfect opportunity to hurl as many balls full of ice at his head as I can." She smirked. "Feel free to join me."

She went to turn back but paused. She arched a brow. "Gigi, aye?" She winked and scurried after his wife.

His cheeks warmed, but he laughed and trailed after them, heading for his chambers. Perhaps he'd accidentally push his sister's cad of a fiancé face-first into the snow. His hands were tied in helping Felicity extricate herself from the marriage. But he could at least do that.

36

Georgiana

Georgiana hopped from the carriage, assisted by her husband, his strong, firm grip around her waist as he gently lowered her into the surprisingly deep snow. She glanced down, her boots disappearing from view. It seemed they'd received a fair bit of snow last night.

She looked up at him, her lips tilting upward. They locked gazes, and his cheeks tinted a dusty rose. He smiled bashfully at her, and her heart fell right out of her chest and *plopped* into the snow. Goodness, he was so bloody sweet. Irresistibly endearing. And finally, *finally*, things seemed to be looking up for them.

She turned her attention to the snow-covered St. James Park. She loved nothing more than a freshly fallen snow. A pristine white blanket surrounded them. Trees and shrubbery painted with snow. Even the pond was covered, completely out of view.

She sucked in an icy breath, reveling in the sharp chill akin to breathing in peppermint. Everything was better today, brighter. She and Fitz had finally talked. Last night had been lovely. Nothing but warming whisky and comfortable conversation. And maybe tonight... Maybe she would be able to convince him to bed her again. She wanted to be in his arms again.

Fitz trudged over to his brother, his face a mask of seriousness as he bent down to scoop up some snow on his way, testing out its suitability for snowball-making.

She had been surprised the roads were already cleared for travel; they'd never been cleared that fast where she resided in London with her family. It wasn't the most fashionable of areas, but still respectable. But apparently it still made all the difference. Because Felicity assured Georgiana that there was no way the streets surrounding Grosvenor Square would go uncleared for long. Apparently, the wealthy aristocrats would never tolerate such an inconvenience.

Despite the roads being traversable, the park was relatively empty. The Jennings and their entourage were of the few who decided to brave the cold and snow.

"I see Mare!" Felicity tugged at Georgiana's hand and dragged her toward a woman bundled up in an evergreen wool coat in the distance.

"Mare!" Felicity waved wildly, and the woman beamed, waving back.

She was average height, with ebony hair almost completely hidden beneath her white fur-trimmed bonnet that matched her fur tippet dangling over her shoulders. That was about all Georgiana could discern with the massive number of layers needed to brave the cold.

"Mare," Felicity huffed, out of breath from nearly running, Georgiana in tow, to her friend. "This is Georgiana, Fitzy's wife. Georgiana, this is Mare. My best friend."

"It's lovely to meet you, Lady Camoys." Georgiana attempted to dip a curtsy. Not the easiest thing to do with the number of layers Felicity had forced her into.

"Oh, none of that. You must call me Mare, too. Or Maribeth, if you prefer. But most definitely *not* Lady Camoys. There is no such thing as formality with friends."

Georgiana's heart warmed, warmed her more than the endless number of layers she'd donned ever could.

Mare turned to Felicity. "Are you ready, Fliss?" She sent up a saucy brow.

Georgiana glanced between the two women, her brow wrinkling. "Why do I get the feeling that we aren't talking about the snowball fight?"

Felicity turned to Georgiana. "Oh, we are."

Mare stepped forward. "But not *just* the snowball fight."

"There is a certain someone who deserves the majority of our snowballs." Felicity's grin was evil. Pure evil. And Georgiana loved it.

She clapped her gloves together. "Lord Wessex?" she asked eagerly. And then realized that probably was extremely insensitive. She hastily added, "I'm sorry, Felicity. I shouldn't be excited about such a thing. I can't imagine—"

"No," Felicity cut her off. "You are exactly right to be excited. I have been betrothed to the man near four years. I'm about as numb to his escapades as I'd be if I were buried in this here snow."

Georgiana thought the tightening of Felicity's features might give that statement away as a lie, but she didn't voice that.

"If you can't take the cad out of the man"—Felicity shrugged—"pelt him with snowballs."

Mare was nodding vigorously. "Exactly."

"Is your husband not joining us?" Georgiana asked politely.

She knew little about Lady Camoys. Except what Felicity had mentioned about the woman having had some...amorous encounters with the Duke of Ironcrest. Georgiana stilled. Whereas before she had felt a rush of jealousy hearing that, now...now she felt nothing. The thought of being with the Duke—she shook her head, trying to shake off the thought. Her stomach turned. There was only one man she wanted.

"My husband wants absolutely nothing to do with me," Mare said. "We were betrothed since birth. Neither of us wanted this marriage. He's off in France with his lover"—she waved her hand in a direction Georgiana was fairly certain wasn't France—"so we both do as we please. Honestly, the freedom is a Godsend."

Georgiana glanced at Felicity, who was studying her friend, scrutinizing. Georgiana could understand enjoying that sort of freedom. But she also thought it sounded a bit lonely. Empty.

She glanced over to where her husband stood, nose pink from the cold, speaking with his brother and a newly arrived Lord Wessex. It was so subjective. She had hope that her marriage was going to be a happy one. She wouldn't relish in the freedom Maribeth spoke of. But then there were Felicity and Lord Wessex, a fiancé who didn't give a second thought to splashing his exploits all over the gossip columns. Not to mention the number of cruel men that existed out there. So, she supposed, sometimes that freedom was a blessing.

All three women stared at the group of men. The three formed quite a dashing image. Fitz, comfortable and at ease, was striking, his square jaw and tousled curls peeking from beneath his topper. Lord Wessex was an extremely attractive man as well, tall, lean, a rectangular face with a sharp jaw. He was one of the most handsome men Georgiana had ever seen, actually. And it was said his father was even more so. The Devastating Duke, they called him. And then there was Lord Bentley—

"He's so pretty," Mare whined.

"No," Felicity said sharply.

"But, but, but. Pleaaaaaaase."

Felicity planted her hands on her hips. "No, Mare. He is off limits."

The woman let out a dramatic sigh and turned to Georgiana. "Felicity says I'm not allowed to bed her brother."

Georgiana's eyes shot wide, and she glanced at Felicity. She sure hoped the woman wasn't talking about—

"Oh! Lord Bentley, of course." Mare giggled. "Oh, dear. I see how that could have been misinterpreted." She looked back at the group and stared wistfully at the man. "He's just so pretty. I don't think I've ever seen a man so beautiful."

Georgiana could see the woman's dilemma. He was stunning. Where her husband had a strong jaw with sharp angles, Lord Bentley had softer features with prominent high cheekbones. He was just as tall and broad, slightly more burly, but he was more feline in nature, like a lion. A lion in looks and how he led his family.

"You know the rules, Mare. You can sleep with the entirety of the ton, I don't care. But my brothers are off limits." Felicity turned to Georgiana. "I don't know what to do with this woman. Biggest lightskirt I know," she said fondly.

Mare's blue eyes danced as she gave a self-deprecating shrug, and Georgiana giggled.

"Now"—Felicity clapped, her voice commanding—"we must come up with a battle plan for this snowball fight. Objective one. Win. Objective two. Hit Lord Wessex in the head as many times as possible. Objective three—"

"Accidentally-on-purpose fall on Lord Bentley," Mare said.

Felicity blinked at her best friend, her face pure exasperation. She shook her head and pointed to a small grouping of shrubbery. "Let us start building up our ammunition of snowballs behind there. That will be our protective barricade."

They made their way to the shrubbery, Maribeth shooting looks Lord Bentley's way, swaying her hips, which really only made her look like an evergreen bell swinging back and forth stuffed as she was in so many layers.

"Lord help me," Felicity said, looking heavenward. "The woman is incorrigible."

Felicity blew out a breath and hurried after Lady Camoys, muttering that Lord Bentley wasn't in the least interested in what Mare had to offer, anyway.

Georgiana followed the pair, a sense of belonging lighting up inside her, brighter than the sunlight reflecting off the fresh snow before her. And sunlight reflecting off fresh snow? It was blinding.

37

Fitz's gaze followed the scurrying women disappearing behind a large, snow-covered shrubbery. No more time for dithering.

"Shall we get to it, then?" Lord Wessex asked, and then turned to Fitz. "I know Felicity enjoys a rigorous snowball fight, and Lady Camoys always seems to go for my jugular—no idea why. I swear the woman dislikes me for some odd reason."

Fitz barely held back his snort. *No idea why.* That was rich. How about because the man stuck his prick in every woman who wasn't his fiancé. Lady Camoys was a protective best friend. It was a bummer, truly. Because Lord Wessex was a fun chap. But he wasn't going to make Felicity happy. And Fitz hated that.

"But, ah, your new wife," Lord Wessex was saying. "Should I avoid throwing snowballs at her? I know most ladies possess delicate constitutions."

Fitz discreetly studied his wife as the three men made their way to a gathering of trees. She stood with Flick, while Flick was miming throwing a snowball, adjusting Georgiana's arms and legs. His wife's lack of experience didn't fool him. She would embrace this competition with the same vigor she did all endeavors. Blood rushed to his cock. Shite. He should not think about Georgiana embracing anything with vigor right now.

"How about this, Wessex; focus your throws at Felicity and Lady Camoys. But if the opportunity presents itself, I won't stand in your way." He wasn't worried about his wife's welfare. If anything, he feared for Lord Wessex.

Once they'd piled up an enormous hoard of snowballs, they shed their large overcoats—they'd need freedom of movement for this, and they'd be overheated and sweating soon enough—and armed themselves with as many balls as they could carry.

"Ready?" Felix bellowed at the ladies.

"Ready!" Felicity called back.

Felix drew his index finger and thumb up to his mouth. A piercing whistle rent the park.

And the game was on.

They spread out, sprinting between trees and ducking behind. They had set up at one of the paths of the park that was lined with trees on either side, the men on one side, the women on the other.

Fitz peered out from behind the tree he had his back pressed flat against. A flash of deep blue darted between the trees. Fitz jumped out from behind his tree and hurled a snowball, two more following his from either side of him. None hit their mark, and he and his battle partners hastily darted back behind their trees.

He shook his head. Lady Camoys and her love for bold colors. The women had shucked their coats as well. He knew Felicity would be in white, and she would have instructed his wife to do the same. Blending in with her surroundings. A wise tactic. But Lady Camoys had chosen a midnight blue dress. She should know better.

He waited, scanning the trees for more movement, his breath puffing small white clouds in front of him. Another glimpse of blue from behind a tree. He poised to strike. And then Lady Camoys popped out again.

He rushed forward, Felix's boots crunching in the snow beside him, and tossed two snowballs, one after another, in the direction of Lady Camoys. She darted each one, but Felix covered him and started his own assault at the woman, who giggled, weaving and ducking.

"It's a trap!" Lord Wessex yelled. "Take cover!"

But it was too late. Frigid snow smacked into Fitz's neck from the right, and he sucked in a sharp breath, snow shavings slipping down his cravat. His skin twitched in protest, and he brushed away the snowy projectile. He backpedaled, heading for tree cover, when another snowball came from the other direction and hit Felix square in the face.

Fitz's gaze shot to the culprit—a grinning Flick. Felix let out a roaring battle cry and charged after their sister. She hopped up and down with glee and then took off, but she was no match for Felix's long strides. He took their sister to the ground, and they rolled and scrabbled. And that was where Felix was no match for Felicity. Fitz squinted. Yes, she had Felix in a headlock. He grinned stupidly at the pair.

Which was apt, because it was pretty stupid to stand and watch during a snowball fight. And that was how he found himself hit in the side of the head with a snowball. He wiped the snow from his face, a shiver stealing down his spine. Turning, he spotted his wife dropping the rest of the snowballs she had been holding and clapping excitedly.

"I did it!" she squealed. "That was *two* hits!"

God, she was disarmingly sweet. He bent down and scooped up some snow. He quickly formed a ball, already heading in her direction, and lobbed it at her, hitting her smack in the chest. Her jaw went slack, and she glanced down, as though she expected to see blood staining her white wool gown. Her brows slammed together, and her face screamed retribution.

She went for her snowballs at her feet, but Fitz was already sprinting toward her. She launched one snowball at him, and he ducked, the ball coasting over his hair where, if he had still been wearing it, the bullet would have shot his topper clean off his head.

And then he was on her, arms wrapping around her middle and bringing them to the ground. She let out an indignant squeak as they landed with a *poof* in the thick, powdery snow, only to dissolve into a fit of giggles. Her cheeks and nose were flushed a cinnamon-sweet red from the cold—or excitement, perhaps. Or both. Her green eyes, crinkled with laughter, were barely visible through her snowflake-dusted blonde lashes.

She looked like joy.

She felt like joy.

He'd like to kiss joy.

He leaned forward, and her laughter faded. He was inches from her lips, from joy. Her hands came up around him. He went to close the distance—

"Fuck!" he screeched.

Icy powder slithered down his neck and back. He pushed up to his knees, hastily scraping snow from his collar. The wench had shoved a snowball down the back of his coat!

"You," he growled, thrusting a finger at her.

Her lips pressed together, a weak attempt at preventing a smirk from curling upward. Oh, she was a saucy wench.

He caged her in. "You," he whispered. "Are a *very* bad wench."

She sucked in a breath, the smile in her eyes vanishing. Replaced with something exhilarating, intoxicating. Heated. So much so he was shocked the surrounding snow wasn't melting away. Lord, he wished they weren't in the middle of a park.

He nudged his nose alongside hers, and she arched beneath him. He captured her mouth with his, and she pressed back greedily. There was nothing soft, nothing slow, about this. Not being able to have his wife was killing him. God, where was his ex-mistress with those pamphlets?

A loud catcall and a whistle broke them from their highly inappropriate, highly public intimate embrace. He lifted off her, grinning at Georgiana.

"Apologies, wife. I lost all sense of propriety, along with my wits, for a moment there."

She smiled back at him, lips just as rosy as the tip of her sweet nose. "Apology accepted, husband. It is not as though you can ruin me all over again now, is it?"

"If I remember correctly," he said with mock affront. "You were the one who ruined me."

She chuckled, and though they laughed together, his wife had no idea how true that statement was.

She had ruined him. In the best way.

38

A KNOCK SOUNDED ON Fitz's study door. He put down the translation he was working on. "Come in."

Pemberton stepped in and tugged at his perfectly pressed black coat. "You have a caller, sir. A Mrs. Adelaide Tremayne."

Fitz's heart jumped to his throat at the same time he jumped to his feet. "Send her in," he said, his voice taking on a high pitch.

She must have the items he requested. Finally. Finally, he'd have the instruction he needed. And he could bed his delectable wife. And potentially spank her. Or choke her. Dear Lord. He wiped his palms on his black trousers and let out a breath. He checked the clock on his desk. He would need to make this visit quick. They needed to leave for the Rutledge supper party shortly.

Earlier during their snowball fight had been pure torture. Georgiana had melted in his arms when he'd called her a bad wench. It had made him feel things he'd never felt before. It had made him feel powerful.

He'd never in his life felt anything remotely close to powerful. And now, with the information the woman sauntering into his study was about to deliver, he'd be able to test out that power.

Adelaide paused before his desk, a black velvet coat wrapped around her shoulders.

"Mr. Jennings," she greeted with a secret smile. "You look quite dashing."

He hurried around his desk to her, stumbling in his haste. "Thank you. Supper Party. You have what I requested?" he asked.

"Easy, puppy," she whispered softly. She raised her voice and continued, "Yes, I have what you requested. I was able to acquire a few pamphlets, some of which even have illustrations for you. Along with a few letters two acquaintances who work in my trade wrote between each other...with details, examples, and advice on more exotic proclivities."

He blew out a breath. "Thank you, Adelaide. Truly." He took the bundle she'd retrieved from inside her cloak and slapped it down on the desk. He pulled open the top drawer and withdrew a purse. "I have your payment here."

She glided over, but didn't take the purse. "There was one other thing I wanted to mention, Mr. Jennings."

It was so odd to hear her call him that, but he realized it wasn't proper for her to call him anything but. He frowned. He probably shouldn't be calling her Adelaide in his own home, either. Fitz paused. Actually...he probably shouldn't have had her meet him here.

"Mr. Jennings?" she prodded.

He cleared his throat. "Apologies. What was it you wanted to say, Mrs. Tremayne?"

She tapped the bundle. "These have plenty of instruction, but I have also included the information of a brothel in the top note. The brothel does not just serve those seeking a wench. The Madame there also provides rooms for the use of couples."

Fitz's eyebrows lifted, and Adelaide chuckled. He couldn't deny the idea was intriguing.

"Regardless, she will have everything you need to partake in your wife's wildest desires. You can rent rooms there that are furnished with every prop you could ever need. Rooms where you can watch or be watched, can find others who would be willing to join you, whatever your heart, or *other parts* desire..."

Fitz swallowed audibly. Georgiana liked being watched. Would that be something she wanted? He pulled at his cravat.

"And I am sure the Madame would gladly answer any specific questions you have. She is extremely discreet. I thought it might be a good fit for you."

Perhaps someday he would be ready for that. For now, his bed would do just fine. He extended the coin purse and smiled. "Thank you so much for your services, Mrs. Tremayne. I don't know what I would do without you."

She smiled, but it looked sad. She reached for the purse, her fingers lingering. "Goodbye, puppy," she whispered. She took the payment and tucked it in her cloak.

A throat cleared softly in the doorway.

His gaze shot to the doorway. Georgiana stood there, resplendent in a shimmering, silver gown, blonde curls done up with brilliants and pearls. She looked like an ice princess. And her expression was just as glacial. Oh, dear.

He glanced at Adelaide. Alarm bells tolled in his brain.

"*Breathe*," Adelaide mouthed.

39

Georgiana

Georgiana froze in the doorway of her husband's study.

Her husband smiled fondly at the woman, and Georgiana's stomach flipped over.

"Thank you so much for your services, Mrs. Tremayne. I don't know what I would do without you."

What the bloody hell? Her heart pulsed maddeningly in her throat.

The woman reached forward and lingered—*lingered*. Georgiana ground her teeth. Which was unfortunate, because the woman just whispered something, and Georgiana couldn't hear it over the grinding of bone against bone.

She cleared her throat, lips pressed tight together.

Their gazes shot to her, and her husband's eyes lit up. And then promptly faded as his eyes grew wide. He glanced at the woman standing across from him. Fitz's eyes grew wider. Panic, clear as glass, written all over his face.

"I believe I will take my leave," the woman said, stepping back. She dipped a curtsy to Georgiana. "Mrs. Jennings," she murmured, her gaze downcast.

Georgiana stepped stiffly into her husband's study and allowed the woman to pass. She had the powerful urge to do something ridiculously childish like stick her foot out and trip the woman. She took a breath. But she would speak to her husband first. And then, if things were as dire as they appeared, she would trip him instead.

"G-Georgiana," Fitz stammered. "I-I-I..." He swallowed, a blush rapidly coloring his freckled cheeks.

Her heart sank. This could not be good. Her mind was spinning. Going to all the worst possible places. Places that made the assumption that this woman was his mistress. That he was thanking her for her—Georgiana's hand shot to her roiling stomach. She blew out a slow breath.

"Who was that, Mr. Jennings?"

His face fell. "Fitz, Georgiana. C-come now, we don't need to revert to f-formalities."

"Who?" she asked quietly.

He looked at the ceiling. "She—urm. Well, you see. I s-suppose"—he grimaced and met her gaze again—"she's my mistress."

And there went Georgiana's heart. *Thump* on the wooden floor of her husband's study.

He hurried from behind his desk to stand before Georgiana. "I realize now I shouldn't have asked her here." He wrung his hands in front of him. "I promise I won't ever have her visit here again." He smiled hesitantly at her.

Was that supposed to bring her some comfort? Because it felt like he just took his foot and stomped on her heart, the one lying on the study floor.

He frowned at her, his gaze darting between her eyes.

"Are you well, Georgiana?"

She blinked at him. "Am I well?"

He nodded slowly.

"Am I *well*?" Her voice rose to a painful pitch, and he jumped. "You-you were just with your mistress. Who you paid for her *services*. And the reassuring response you provide me with is that *you* will visit her instead of her visiting here." She stared at him incredulously. No, she wasn't bloody well.

His eyes widened. "Oh! *Oh*." He laughed nervously. "No, n-no, Gigi. I am horrible with w-words," he stammered and shifted side to side on his feet. "This is a misunderstanding. I was not paying her for *those* kinds of services. Not in the way you th-think." He stilled in his shifting and took a deep breath. "I enlisted her help." He glanced away, his blush running down his neck, stark against his snowy-white cravat. "Her, ah, tutelage. She has been teaching me some things in the bedroom, certain proclivities that I think you desire."

Georgiana went numb. Her brain stopped working. All she could hear was a dull buzzing.

"I was visiting her for you." He smiled widely at her and lifted his eyebrows expectantly.

As though those words fixed everything. He was practicing sex with his mistress...so that he could do those things with Georgiana. That was supposed to make her *feel better*. She gaped at him. Gawked. Gurgled, even. She had no idea how to respond to that. She was too busy watching her heart bleed out into the grains of wood on the floor.

She wasn't sure what hurt worse. The fact that her husband had slept with another woman. The fact that he was fool enough to think she would *appreciate* the fact. Or the fact that she had been dim-witted enough to have hoped their marriage would be one of fidelity and love.

Which only sent something searing and sharp shooting through her. Because she hadn't hoped for those things. Not until her stupid bloody husband had made it seem like it was what he wanted to. Not until her stupid bloody husband made her feel all these stupid bloody feelings for him.

"I thought you had dismissed her. I do not understand why you would go to her—" She swallowed and inhaled a shuddering breath. "Why couldn't you have come to me?"

"Because I realized on Christmas that—"

"On Christmas?" She cut him off, her voice sharp. "*She* was your urgent business? You left me on Christmas. To run to your mistress."

His smile dropped. "W-well." He shuffled his hands like he was balancing weights in front of himself. "It wasn't *on* Christmas. I didn't visit her until two days after."

She blinked at him. Well, that was much better. A couple of days after Christmas was clearly *much bloody better*. Wait. That was where he had been when she'd arrived at an empty town house? Instead of being home to greet his new wife. He had been in bed with his mistress. Her pathetic heart gave a pathetic flop on the floor. Pathetic, pathetic, *pathetic.*

"Gigi... please say something. Are you still upset—"

"Mr. Jennings, your family has arrived and is waiting out front for you," Pemberton's droll voice cut into the study.

Georgiana smoothed her skirts. "We should go. We do not want to keep the rest of the party waiting." She fell into step behind the butler, not glancing back at her husband. Dear Lord, how was she to hide the impact of this—this *bomb* her grenadier of a husband had just dropped—while attending their first supper party as husband and wife? This was going to be torture.

He hurried to catch up to her, falling into stride. "You still do not seem well, Gigi."

She looked straight ahead. "Let us not discuss in front of the servants," she said softly, tightly. "After the supper party."

But there was only one thing she wanted to do after the supper party. And that was to curl up in her bed and cry.

Her husband had slept with someone else.

And as effective as a grenade, it destroyed her.

40

Georgiana

GEORGIANA HAD SOMEHOW MADE it through the carriage ride without raising any suspicions, even despite the fact that she hadn't spoken a word. If she opened her mouth, all that would come out was a sob. She had to hold herself together until this supper party was over.

Fortunately, they had been ushered inside and quickly led to the drawing room to greet their hosts, so Georgiana was able to avoid the questioning glances Felicity was sending her way. Apparently, it had been the shadows of the conveyance that had hidden the pain she'd thought she'd masked. She wasn't fooling her sister-in-law.

They paused before their hosts and Lady Rutledge, radiant in a vibrant berry-red gown, raven-black hair adorned with matching red-berries, greeted them all, Georgiana included, like old friends. Lady Bentley excused herself, murmuring she had seen the dowager Duchess of Ironcrest, and the men wandered off to the sideboard. Fitz gave her a last searching glance and accidentally walked into a gentleman, as he wasn't watching where he was walking. Georgiana hated that he was so bloody endearing. Stupid, stupid man.

Lady Rutledge gripped Georgiana's hands, tearing Georgiana's gaze from her husband's stumbling form.

The woman's friendly green eyes sparkled. "It is so lovely to meet you, Mrs. Jennings. Lady Felicity has told me so much about you. Your sister-in-law sings your praises."

Georgiana's cheeks heated, and she shot a glance at her grinning sister-in-law.

"I may have included in our acceptance that you were the perfect addition to our family. That you fit right in with the Jennings chaos."

Lady Rutledge's grin turned wicked. "I *love* chaos."

Georgiana glanced between the two women, a bemused smile tilting her lips. "Goodness, there are two of you?" This was perfect. She could use two Felicitys to distract herself tonight.

Lady Rutledge and Felicity broke out in chuckles.

"Unfortunately, I was never able to master the art of a proper young miss like Lady Felicity. I am pure chaos, out-loud and proud. Bless my husband for putting up with me." She glanced at the sideboard, smiling fondly at her perfectly starched husband—well, perfectly starched but for his wayward brown curls. Goodness, they gave Fitz's a run for their money.

Georgiana's heart tugged, glancing between the two. A love-match. Clear as day.

"I do not think Lord Rutledge would use that phrasing. I'm fairly certain he quite likes your chaos." Felicity shot Lady Rutledge a knowing look. "At least if what I saw when I stumbled upon you two at the Marsden's ball last season was any indication." She waggled her eyebrows.

Lady Rutledge broke out in a sly grin, not an ounce of embarrassment in her expression. She let out a little sigh. "That was a spectacular ball."

"Yes, the *ball* was spectacular," Felicity said dryly.

Lady Rutledge giggled and shot Georgiana a wink. Georgiana couldn't prevent her smile. This woman was a spitfire, and Georgiana liked her immensely.

"I have to say, I am so glad to see Mr. Jennings has found such a lovely bride. And by lovely, I mean just as spirited as Lady Felicity here. Your husband is the kindest of gentlemen. A rare gem in our world. You two make quite the dashing pair."

Georgiana's stomach sloshed uneasily, and her smile turned strained. "Thank you, Lady Rutledge."

Felicity's concerned brows made it clear her upset was showing.

Georgiana hastily changed the subject. "I had wanted to ask you about the foundling home your husband runs. Do they have visiting hours? I would love to visit with the children. I think it is absolutely lovely that your husband and his partners visit them during the Christmastide."

Felicity bounced animatedly before she caught herself and settled for vibrating with excitement instead. "Oh, what a lovely idea! Perhaps we could visit them in the next day or so and have a snowball fight!"

Lady Rutledge brought her gloved hand to cover her mouth, stifling her laughter. "Egads, Lady Felicity. Have I mentioned I adore you and your fire? You and the children will surely get along splendidly." Lady Rutledge turned to Georgiana. "I think that is a fabulous idea. The gentlemen do their best to be active with the home, and the staff there are lovely, but it is not the same as having a loving family."

"I can imagine it can feel lonely," Georgiana murmured. She knew all too well what it meant to be lonely. Unwanted. "Even as much as I am sure they appreciate the home taking them in." This was something small she could do, and perhaps it would help her own lonely heart. What was left of it in the wreckage of her husband's grenade.

"We do our best to set them up for a life of success, finding them positions and apprenticeships. Hopefully, one day, they will be in a position to have the family they were not blessed with."

Another idea struck Georgiana. "Do you happen to have any young women who could serve as a lady's maid? I am in need of one, and I would love to offer the position to one of your girls if it fits."

Lady Rutledge tapped her lip and tilted her head. "I will have to speak with our matron who runs the home. We just might." Her lips curved softly, her green eyes gentling. "That is exceedingly thoughtful of you, Mrs. Jennings."

Her gaze shot over Georgiana's shoulder. "Ah, I see we are ready for supper! I must find the Duke of Ironcrest to escort me in." She leaned toward Georgiana and Felicity. "Perhaps make Lord Rutledge a mite jealous. He gets all growly when I get close to the Duke. Some old spat or some such between the two of them." She sent them a wink and left them in a swirl of saucy skirts.

Georgiana huffed out a laugh, watching as the woman disappeared into the crowd. "She is a vixen, is she not?"

Felicity took Georgiana's arm, and they meandered toward the supper room. "That she is. A woman after my own heart. Us hoydens have to stick together."

Wasn't that the truth? If she didn't have her husband, at least she'd have her hoydens.

She had miraculously managed to get through dinner without crying or casting up her accounts, mainly because she had barely touched her food. But Felicity's increasingly worried glances made it clear she wasn't fooling anyone. Which was how Georgiana currently found herself cornered in Lady Rutledge's drawing room, where the guests had reconvened, subjected to her sister-in-law's interrogation.

"What is wrong?" Felicity asked, fierce and beautiful as ever in her champagne silk gown.

Georgiana opened her mouth, but Felicity shot up an eyebrow.

"Don't try to say nothing. You are always smiling, chatty, and bright eyed. You're like an adorable little bushy-tailed bunny. And now?" Felicity paused, studying Georgiana. "Now you look like a carriage ran over your poor little bunny-self. Bunny roadkill."

"That's not very flattering," Georgiana muttered.

Her sister-in-law let out a hushed snort. "You're beautiful roadkill, if that helps at all."

Georgiana's lips twitched.

"Life! She lives!" Felicity's smile quickly faded, and her eyes grew serious. "But seriously, G, what is going on? I knew from the moment we stepped out of the carriage something was wrong, but this is the first moment we've had any privacy."

Georgiana's heart gave a weak flop at the pet name Felicity had just made for her. Apparently, the thing was still in there. She could have sworn she left it on her husband's study floor. She glanced at said husband. He stood with another scholar, deep in conversation, his brow set in concentration. Her husband had been correct. The Rutledge's supper parties were different. There were more men in trade and of business than there were other aristocrats. There were many academics, some who made Fitz's awkwardness appear tame. Even as he destroyed her, seeing him converse so freely, speak so assuredly, it made her deeply happy. For him.

"G?" Felicity prodded.

She glanced down at her ivory gloves and fidgeted with the button on her wrist. "I can't speak of it right now," she murmured.

She wasn't sure if she wanted to speak of it at all. She could hear her mother's voice in her head, what her mother would say to her in this situation: *This is the way of things, Georgiana. Just be glad you are the wife and not the mistress. You are the one with security, with power, with the potential to birth the heir to an earldom.*

"Perhaps you could call tomorrow?" Georgiana finally asked. Even if she decided against letting Felicity in on her troubles—which was how she was presently leaning. Fitz struggled enough feeling close to them. Georgiana didn't want to be the cause of any more distance—she would enjoy her sister-in-law's company.

She caught Felicity's gaze, and she saw so much concern there, her eyes blurred. Shite. No. She would not cry here. She cleared her throat and glanced around, looking for distraction.

Felicity reached forward and squeezed Georgiana's hand. "That sounds perfect. And since you look like you need cheering up, I thought you'd like to know that Lord Wessex couldn't make it tonight because one of my snowballs hit him so hard in the tallywags, he needed to stay home and ice himself. Ironic, since I hit him with a ball of ice."

Georgiana's eyebrows shot up. "No," she breathed.

Felicity discreetly patted herself on her shoulder and smiled. "Perhaps this will give me a few days of fidelity!"

Georgiana barely contained her snort. "You are wicked, Fliss. Absolutely wicked, and it is utterly fantastic."

Her sister-in-law sent a discreet wink her way. Something caught Felicity's attention, and her entire demeanor changed. A soft, polite smile curved her lips, and her gaze lowered to the floor.

Georgiana turned and promptly sucked in a breath. Lord Dunmore and the Duke of Ironcrest walked shoulder-to-shoulder through the guests directly toward them. The two men cut quite a pair. Both taller than average, they towered over almost everyone they passed. Where the Duke was broad, with the breadth of a blacksmith, Lord Dunmore was lean, all sharp angles. Both had jet-black hair—the Duke's cropped short, and Dunmore's longer than fashion dictated. They oozed arrogance, confidence, insouciance. It was all Georgiana could do not to take a step back. They were predators. Predators that made one want to be their prey.

The men stopped before them. The Duke's lips were set in a firm line, the scar that ran down the side of his face, eye to cheek, stark against his pale skin. Lord Dunmore's lips, on the other hand, curled up in a sardonic half-smile. It was an indecipherable smile. He could be seducing you. Or he could be laughing at you.

There was nothing kind in the smile. No softness, no warmth, no lop-sided bashfulness. And to Georgiana, it was entirely lacking.

"Lady Felicity, Mrs. Jennings," Lord Dunmore drawled.

Georgiana quickly lowered her gaze and dropped into a curtsy with Felicity at her side, returning the men's greeting. This was the first time she'd seen either rogue since she had propositioned the Duke. The night she had wound up betrothed to Fitz. And with the way the Duke eyed her now, his gray gaze nearly tangible, he hadn't forgotten.

Felicity peered at the men beneath her lashes. "I hope you are having an agreeable evening, Your Grace, my lord," she said softly.

"It just became much more agreeable," Lord Dunmore said, his smile widening. "We saw a pair of beautiful ladies standing alone without refreshment, and we knew we must rectify the situation immediately."

"Wine, ladies?" the Duke asked, his voice deep, rich...emotionless. He gently proffered a glass to Georgiana while Lord Dunmore held out one to Felicity.

Georgiana smiled and murmured her thanks, taking the glass from the Duke. His fingers grazed over hers, and he paused, holding onto that contact. Her gaze shot to his, and she sucked in a breath. He didn't smile, his lips didn't move, but somehow his expression turned wolfish. She swore she saw victory in his eyes. And it would have been. Before.

"How lucky we are to have such upstanding gentlemen looking out for us," Felicity said, smiling sweetly at the men. Nothing but perfectly polite.

It was shocking to see the woman who had just been swearing, discussing throwing snowballs at her fiancé's ballocks, turn into a soft-spoken, demure young miss. One would think she was made up of sugar and flowers and kittens. Not snowballs and headlocks and curses.

"I noticed Lord Wessex is absent. I had thought he intended to attend," Lord Dunmore said offhand.

"Unfortunately, he is indisposed and could no longer make it," Felicity said.

"I am sure he is," the Duke said under his breath.

Lord Dunmore's lips quirked behind his tumbler.

Felicity's smile turned brittle, and Georgiana took a discreet step closer to her sister-in-law, her shoulder leaning into Felicity's. Silent support. Lord Wessex's gallivanting was no secret. This wasn't the first time it had been mentioned this evening, and Georgiana doubted it'd be the last. Lord, how did the woman stand it? Georgiana was barely holding herself together after finding out about Fitz and his mistress. And this poor woman had to bear it nearly every time a new gossip column was published.

"Well, I have to say his loss is our gain, my lady," Lord Dunmore said. "It should be a sin to leave ladies such as yourselves neglected like this."

"Oh?" Felicity blinked innocently at Lord Dunmore. "And let me venture a guess, we would be in much better care in your hands?"

Georgiana bit back a grin at the subtle barb, knowing for a fact Felicity believed the exact opposite of her statement.

Lord Dunmore grinned, green eyes glittering with challenge. He cocked an arrogant brow. "There are ways of finding out the answer to that question." He studied Felicity. "I have always wondered, Lady Felicity, if you are truly as prim and proper as you appear to be."

Apparently, the man hadn't missed Felicity's slight.

Felicity gave a small, faux gasp, covering her mouth with a gloved hand. "Lord Dunmore, I pride myself for my adherence to decorum."

Georgiana nearly spit out her wine.

Lord Dunmore's grin grew. He looked like he very much wanted to test that fact. Felicity's amber eyes twinkled beneath her lashes, clearly having fun. The woman deserved some fun. And attention. Given her situation with her wastrel fiancé.

Felicity's gaze caught on something, and then she turned to the gentlemen, smiling cheekily. "Well, unfortunately, I am going to have to disappoint you gentlemen, and we'll never be able to investigate those intriguing statements. Lord Bentley is requesting my presence." She dipped a graceful curtsy, champagne skirts fluttering like silk waves. She lifted her wine. "Thank you for the refreshment, Your Grace, my lord. I will leave you in Mrs. Jennings's capable hands."

And now Georgiana was left alone. Two wolves. One hen. A moment like this, prior to her marriage, would have been an opportunity. An opportunity the men clearly thought was still on the table. And was it? The wine burned in her stomach. Most definitely not. But was Fitz planning to continue with his mistress indefinitely? Would Georgiana be able to stomach *that*?

"Congratulations on your recent nuptials," Lord Dunmore said, lifting his tumbler of amber liquid in a small toast.

Georgiana's gaze darted to her husband, who appeared completely oblivious to her whereabouts. Her heart slid down in her chest. "Thank you," she murmured. Congratulations felt awfully hollow at the moment.

"Tsk, tsk," Lord Dunmore said, his gaze narrowing on her. "It can't be easy, marrying a strange man, thrown into a new life you didn't ask for."

She shifted under the intensity of his stare but forced a smile. She shouldn't dwell on her husband; her husband, who preferred his mistress to her. She had two strapping men giving her attention, and she would bask in that for the moment.

"It has had its difficulties, but I am not one to back down from a challenge."

"Yes, not a simpering miss. You've always struck me as a woman with confidence. Knows what she wants," Lord Dunmore said, sharing a look with the Duke.

The Duke studied her over his whisky. "It is quite unforgivable on your husband's part, leaving his stunning new wife all on her lonesome."

She glanced at her husband again, and this time their gazes clashed. But he hastily looked away and leaned toward his companion. She blinked. He didn't even *care* that the two biggest rogues in England were moving in on her like hounds on a foxhunt? She almost stomped her foot. Perhaps if she blatantly flirted with them, he'd develop a modicum of interest in her. She would take a page out of Lady Rutledge's book. Perhaps she could make her own husband growly.

She drew her gloved finger over her low-cut bodice and shrugged. "How can I complain with one man leaving me unattended when I find myself with the attention of two gentlemen such as yourselves?"

"If you are feeling...neglected Mrs. Jennings," the Duke said. "Dunmore and I would gladly step in and correct that. You won't doubt for a moment our appreciation of you."

Why did Georgiana suddenly feel like the meat between a rake sandwich? She glanced between the two men.

Lord Dunmore's lips curled wider, a smile that could have been the devil's own. "Imagine what such appreciation would feel like, the attention of not just one, but two men. All on you, love."

Oh. She *was* the meat between a rake sandwich. Where before that would have thrilled her, now it—well, she still did like the idea of it. But only if the two men were both Fitz. Which only made her feel doubly heartbroken. Two Fitzes to sleep with his mistress. *Gah*. She couldn't do this. Provoking jealousy was not for her. Not for retaliation. Not for malice.

"I have no doubt I would feel thoroughly appreciated," she murmured. "But for right now, I am not in search of any outside appreciation." She smiled apologetically at Lord Dunmore and the Duke before letting her gaze stray briefly to Fitz again.

Once again, their gazes clashed, but he quickly turned and put his back to her. Ouch. She tried to swallow, but it was near impossible. Apparently, the jealousy tactic wouldn't have worked on her husband, anyway.

"If you ever change your mind..." the Duke murmured.

"The offer stands," Lord Dunmore finished.

They bowed and took their leave.

Georgiana was ready to do the same. Leave. She couldn't force her lips upward in a pathetic excuse for a smile any longer, couldn't hold back the tears constantly threatening to break free. Her head throbbed from holding them back. She just wanted to go home. Hide away in her room until she fell asleep and for a few blissful hours could forget this day.

Because just now, the melancholy was too heavy, too thick, too choking to fight off. It wasn't the first time Georgiana had been gripped in melancholy's unrelenting clutches. A lonely existence made it inevitable. Sometimes Georgiana could free herself; sometimes she didn't succumb. But the aching pressure in her chest, closing over her like a blanket covered in stone, was too much. She'd let it consume her tonight. One thing she always reminded herself of: tomorrow was a new day. She'd fight again tomorrow, for her marriage, for her future. But for tonight, she would let melancholy win.

She had to hold on to the hope that there was something to fight for. Because if there wasn't—this was the first time in Georgiana's life she thought she truly might break.

41

Fitz had mucked up his marriage No—he had fucked up his marriage.

The only problem was, he wasn't sure what had upset his wife. But he *knew* he had messed up. One moment they were tangled together in the snow, Fitz feeling as light as the fluffy powder, and the next she was in his study, cold as ice, nothing but a beautiful, frigid exterior. His wife had quite literally disappeared inside herself. And it wasn't the first time since they'd arrived in London that she had appeared downcast.

Georgiana had given him one-word—and more often no-word—responses all night. She had complained of a megrim at the Rutledge's supper party, so they had left early, and as soon as they arrived home, she'd fled straight to her room. He had chased after her—damn, the woman was fast for being so small—and had been greeted by a door shutting in his face.

Which had given him pause, because he had done something similar to her the other night. Perhaps that was it? She clearly hadn't liked seeing his ex-mistress visit their home, but he had explained that to her. Perhaps he hadn't explained well.

Fitz burst past the Jennings's family's butler without a word and went straight for the stairs of his old home, taking them two at a time. He had made sure his housekeeper, Mrs. Hutchinson, was informed of Georgiana's illness, ordered her to whip up a tonic for his wife, and to be at the ready for anything Georgiana needed. Once he had been assured his wife was settled and sleeping, he'd ordered his carriage and made for his family's townhome. He needed his brother. Felix would know what to do. He always knew what to do. He'd been heading the Jennings family since he was only four-and-twenty.

Lord, and at the Rutledge supper party? His hand shot to his chest, digging into the thick fabric of his wool coat. The Duke and Dunmore had closed in on her, and she'd smiled—*smiled*—at them. He let out a growl. Her smiles weren't for them, damn it. She belonged to him. She was *his*. He had been moments from throwing her over his shoulder and storming out of there, scandal be damned. He paused at the top of the stairwell and blinked. What was happening to him? Clearly, love made him bloody loopy.

Fitz shook his head and strode down the family wing of bedrooms in the home he had grown up in and stopped before his father's old chambers. Now his brother's. He sucked in a breath. And pounded on the door.

"Felix! Wake up. I need to speak with you. Now!"

Thumps and muffled sounds came from behind the thick oak door. Fitz bounced back and forth on his feet, fingers tapping rapidly over his thigh. Then, blessedly, the door cracked open.

A flushed, disordered Felix popped his head through the small opening. "This had better be important, Fitz," he gritted out.

Fitz's eyes welled, burning like the devil. Shite. Shite, shite, shite. Not tears. *Hold yourself together, mate.* "I think I have r-ruined my marriage." His stupid, cracking voice betrayed him.

Felix's demeanor changed instantly, his brow furrowing, eyes sharpening. The head of the household was ready to fix things for his family. "What has happened? What have you done?"

"I-I don't know. But I *know* I did something."

"Who's out there?" a deep voice called from inside Felix's chamber. "Did you invite a friend, handsome?"

Fuck. It would appear Fitz had interrupted his brother during something…important.

"I'm sorry, Felix. I-I will come back later. I shouldn't have—I'm sorry." Fitz turned on his heel, but Felix's fist latched onto his coat. Fitz's body jerked backward, and he stumbled to a halt in front of his brother again.

"Just let me grab my banyan, and we'll go down to my study. Don't worry, Fitzy. We'll sort this out."

Fitz turned and nodded at his brother's back disappearing into the bedchamber.

Felix's muffled voice rumbled through the small opening of the door, "I'm sorry, Benedict. My brother has called, and I need to address this. We'll have to pick this back up another time. Please see yourself out."

A clearly upset whine echoed into the hallway, and Fitz winced. But then Felix was popping back through, covered in a silk onyx banyan lined with thick, black velvet, and wasted no time leading them to his study.

Felix pushed Fitz into one of the two leather armchairs and made his way to his sideboard. "All right, Fitz. Start from the beginning. When did you first notice she was upset with you?"

Fitz pressed his fingertips to his temple, squeezing, and frowned. "Urm. I'm not sure exactly. There were possibly earlier signs, but one night she visited my rooms, and I shut the door in her face." He winced. He chewed his lip, wracking his brain. His eyebrows lifted, and he met his brother's gaze. "Or... I did abandon her...urm...left her bent over my desk."

All expression melted off Felix's face from where he leaned against the sideboard, and he blinked dumbly at Fitz. His mouth worked and eventually managed a disbelieving, "Bent over your desk? As in—"

"She asked me to spank her," Fitz argued. "I panicked." As any highly anxious chap would.

"Sodding hell, Fitz. Hand meets flesh. It's not that difficult."

Fitz glared daggers at his brother. "It is not simple for all of us. Regardless, I thought we had moved past that, but I know when she saw me today paying Adelaide in my study—"

"Adelaide?" Felix sputtered, nearly tossing his freshly poured whisky all over the floor. "Adelaide was in your home? Adelaide, your ex-mistress? Was in the home you share with your wife?"

"Yes... Earlier this evening before the supper party. I realize now I probably shouldn't have had her come to the house."

Felix shot him a *yes, you have that fucking right* look.

"I told Georgiana that!" Fitz said defensively. "I told her I wouldn't have Adelaide come to the house anymore."

Felix's eyes went wide, and he inclined his head in disbelief at Fitz. He threw back his whisky and closed his eyes. "Let me see if I have this straight. You want a happy marriage with your wife?"

Fitz nodded.

"So, you invited your mistress over to the home you share with said wife to have sex with her? And then told said wife, you would only tup your mistress outside the home from now on. Am I following?"

"No," Fitz said, shaking his head and scowling at his brother. "Adelaide is my *ex*-mistress. I didn't tup her and don't intend to. In my townhome or out of it. The only woman I want is my wife."

"Then what the bloody hell were you paying her for? What did you two do in your study?"

"She was dropping off some…items I requested. You see, I reached out to her for help." He lifted his hands beseechingly. "I needed some help in the bedroom because of some proclivities Georgiana has that I know nothing about. So, I went to Adelaide for tutelage."

Felix's eyes bugged.

Fitz shifted in his seat and wiped his sweaty palms on his trousers. "I…went to Adelaide. And she's been helpful," he rushed on.

His brother couldn't stop shaking his head. "Adelaide."

"Yes…" Fitz thought, perhaps—based on his brother's reaction—this might be where he had erred, at least the most damning err. He was sure he had erred quite a bit.

"Why? Why would you go to your mistress for help with bedding your wife?" He closed his eyes and pinched his nose. Realization dawned on Felix's face. "No. She is not the reason you left on Christmas, is she?"

Fitz nodded, shrinking into his shoulders, and Felix groaned.

"Please tell me you didn't actually practice with her."

"No! Of course not," Fitz growled. Why did no one understand what he was saying? "I went to her for *information*. I only want Georgiana. I don't want Adelaide. I couldn't even touch her when I was there. When I tried to choke her—"

"You *what?*"

Fitz hadn't thought his brother's voice could go that high. He blew out a breath. "She was teaching me hand placement," he said patiently. "Not literal harm. And not-sexual, purely instructional. And the feel of her skin?" He shuddered. "It was all wrong."

"I need more bloody whisky." Felix turned, slamming bottles and glasses around. "Want one?"

Before Fitz could even answer in the affirmative, a whisky was in his hand.

"So, do you think that is where I went wrong? I shouldn't have gone to Adelaide for help?"

His brother flopped down in the chair opposite him and deflated on a breath in the seat. "Partly. No wife, especially one who looks at her husband with hearts in her eyes like Georgiana does with you, wants their husband having contact with a mistress, with an ex-lover."

Fitz preened. She looked at him with hearts in her eyes? His elation immediately crumbled. He was sure after this muddle, there would be no hearts. Just daggers. And his brother's next words were daggers as well.

"And by God, Fitzy. You left her on Christmas for your mistress. Sex or not. That's a hard blow to swallow."

Fuck. How had he bungled this so badly? It had seemed like such a logical idea at the time. Who better to teach one about sex than someone who practices it all the time?

Felix threw back a large swallow of amber liquid and studied Fitz. "But it's more than that. I think I might be starting to make sense of your fucked up logic. Let me see if this time I have it correct. Your wife wants to do"—he waved a hand—"*something* in the bedroom that you have no experience with. So, you went to your mistress for help—on Christmas. She then showed up at your house with...items—whatever those may be—and your wife stumbled upon you paying her for said paraphernalia."

Fitz thought it over. That sounded about right. He nodded. "But I explained everything to Georgiana, and it seemed to only make things worse."

Felix winced. "Do you remember what you said? If not exact, very close wording? Because based on what you've told me so far, I have a feeling what you said isn't what you thought you said."

"Mmm, perhaps." He screwed up his face. "I said I didn't hire Adelaide for what she assumed. That it was for tutelage. That Adelaide had been teaching me certain things in the bedroom that I knew Georgiana was interested in. That I was doing it for Georgiana."

Felix's jaw dropped open. Wide open. Hit-the-floor open. "You-you-you-youuuu."

Fitz had broken his brother.

Felix cursed. "Heaven, help you, brother. You're lucky she didn't murder you on the spot. Do you not hear how that sounds? First"—he held up a finger—"you told her you would only visit your mistress elsewhere, implying you're obviously shagging her. And second"—he threw up another finger—"it sounds like you proceeded to tell your wife you've been *fucking* your mistress as practice. To then go home and fuck Georgiana with your new *techniques*." His shoulders sagged.

So did Fitz's. Fuck. Hearing it back. It did sound damning. That is not what he had meant at all. Why did the words never word properly for Fitz?

"Why didn't you just come to me if you had questions, Fitzy?"

Fitz's brows pinched. He had thought that was obvious. "Well, because you don't tup women."

His brother let out a strangled sound. "But I am well-versed in *sex*. It is not as though proclivities are reserved for tuppings between men and women. Honestly, there's quite a bit of overlap, two cocks instead of one, though some women are looking for that"—he eyed Fitz questioningly, and Fitz shook his head quickly—"different hole and more preparation—or same hole if that's what she's going for?"

Fitz's eyebrows shot up.

"Clearly not," Felix said with an exasperated laugh. "Now, if you asked me to help you locate the clitoris, I wouldn't be your chap, granted from what I've heard, most men can't seem to find it, regardless." He batted that away with a flick of his hand. "Anyhow, if there was something that pertained specifically to women, I could have pointed you in the right direction. Which would have been far, *far* away from your ex-mistress, I might add."

Fitz groaned and dropped his head in his hands. Only for his forehead to smack into his whisky glass. *Fuck*. He didn't even care. He just accepted the pain. "You know of the Duke of Ironcrest's proclivities?"

"Yes..."

"That is what she wants."

Silence greeted him.

He glanced up to meet a thoroughly surprised Felix, eyebrows having disappeared beneath the amber wave of hair falling over his brow.

"Sweet, Georgiana? The one who pretended to gallop around our entry after winning the tree competition?"

Fitz dipped his chin.

"Well, I'd never," Felix said, pursing his lips thoughtfully. "Some spanking is one thing, but that... Well, regardless, I wish you had come to me, Fitzy. That is definitely an area I could have helped you with. And I still can if you have any questions. I'm your big brother. You can always come to me."

Fitz nodded again, his throat suddenly suspiciously thick.

"But first let us see if we can rectify this situation with your wife. Where is Georgiana now? Is she still at your townhouse?"

"In her chambers with a megrim. She has barely spoken to me all evening. And"—he sucked in a choked breath—"God, Felix. She was crying."

"All right. Not great. But she hasn't left, so that is a good sign."

Fitz's heart rate picked up, took flight, the entire organ completely abandoning him. Georgiana *leaving* him? Everything tightened, everything constricted. No. He couldn't bear it. Why were the walls so much closer now? They were closing in on him.

"Fitzy," Felix said gently. "Look at me."

Fitz slowly met his brother's comforting amber gaze.

"You can fix this. You have some serious explaining to do. And given your word choice thus far, perhaps we should go over what you are going to say together. But your heart is in the right place. *This can be fixed.*"

"I should probably write it down," Fitz said, his tone defeated. "I should probably just hand her a letter and avoid talking altogether."

Fitz paused. Perhaps that was the way to go. Perhaps he could start with a written explanation—one his brother read over and approved first—and then he could surprise his wife. Surprise her with exactly what he had intended all along. Show her this was all a misunderstanding.

"Where'd you disappear to, Fitz?"

He looked at his brother. "I just had an idea."

Felix eyed him warily. "A *good* idea?"

"I believe so. I actually have two ideas, though one will take a bit more time." He frowned down at his trousers. He wasn't entirely sure where to even start with the second thing.

He glanced back at his brother to be met with a look that clearly said, *come on now, while the tea is still hot.*

Fitz drew in a breath. "So, this is what I had in mind…"

42

Georgiana

"GOODNESS, GEORGIANA, YOUR EYES are all swollen." Georgiana's mother grimaced, the creases exaggerated on her heavily powered face. "And they're *red*. You look as though you haven't slept in days." Georgiana's mother snapped her fingers at the maid who had just delivered their tea service, the inordinate number of gold embellishments on her plum gown jangling with the movement. "Get a cold compress for your mistress with haste."

Georgiana let out a slow breath, willing herself calm. She focused on the faded, pink, floral pattern of the paper-hangings in the drawing room in which they sat. God, they were bloody ugly. No doubt they were original to the home. While her husband had given no thought to redecorating, she most definitely had plans for it.

She glanced over at her maid and whispered, "Thank you, Jane. That would be much appreciated." Even though her words said thank you, it was an apology more than anything. Because in her mother's quest to appear as aristocratic as possible, she was incessantly rude to servants.

Jane smiled, and Georgiana didn't fail to notice the sympathy in the curve of the young woman's lips. Whether it was because her maid knew Georgiana had been up all night a sobbing mess or because of Georgiana's intolerable mother, she didn't know.

She turned to her mother, who sat next to her on the rose-colored settee in the very pink, very floral drawing room. "I am just a trifle tired, Mother. We had Lady Rutledge's supper party last night. Perhaps I had overindulged in wine." Or perhaps the amount of crying she had done had left her swollen, red, and tear streaked.

But she had her little watering pot wallowing session. Now she was ready to speak to her husband. To figure out what this meant for them, for the kind of future they would have. Her heart sank like a poorly thrown skipping stone. *Thunk.* Because she had woken up to find her husband gone.

God, she hoped he hadn't visited his mistress last night. Had she inadvertently pushed him to the woman? She had quite clearly given him the cold shoulder. Had told him she hadn't wanted him to visit her that night. So, had he visited a different woman instead? A warmer, more willing woman. Her heart cracked.

Her mother set down her cup of tea, her lips pursed. "Yes, well, you must take care, Georgiana. It is of utmost import you appeal to your husband. How do you expect to produce the next heir to the earldom if your husband isn't interested in what you have to *offer?*"

Georgiana decided she'd much rather eat another spiced biscuit in silence than reply to *that.*

"Ignore your mother, Georgiana," her father said from where he sat across from them in an armchair upholstered in yet another shade of pink. He lounged, one leg crossed, foot resting on his knee. The picture of nonchalance.

He let out a low chuckle. Because what her mother had just said—which was slightly mortifying having repeatedly brought up in front of one's father—was apparently *so* funny. But that was his habitual demeanor—laugh amiably and smile.

"She is just overeager to have an earl as a grandson. I've tried to explain to her it is very unlikely, as eventually Lord Bentley will settle down. But you know how your mother loves to dream."

Georgiana tried for a smile, but when that seemed a lost cause, she went for another biscuit.

Her mother swatted at her arm. "Enough biscuits, Georgiana. Your husband won't look twice at you if you continue indulging so excessively in sweets. You have never been the slimmest to begin with."

Georgiana's mouth pinched, but she traded her biscuit for a cup of tea. *Do not dump your scalding hot tea on the infuriating woman. You are not five.* But sometimes she wished she could act like she was.

"Despite that fact..." her father continued, ignoring her mother's little outburst. "You have done very well for yourself, Georgiana."

She looked up from her tea, eyebrows inching up, and met her father's identical green gaze. He stared at her as if he really saw her, for perhaps the first time in her life.

"Mr. Jennings may not be titled. But it is no secret the Jennings are highly regarded in society. I am proud of you."

Her mouth worked. He was...proud of her? She didn't think her father had ever been proud of her before. But somehow, in this weird twist of fate where she accidentally ended up married to a stranger, she had made him proud. Her heart floated back up in her chest, humming happily.

And she hated that fact.

Because it shouldn't make her happy that this man was proud of her. She didn't need his validation to know her worth. Perhaps when she was younger, she would have given anything to hear those words. But she had learned long ago not to hope for them. And now? She hated that she still wanted them. That she was still that lonely girl grasping for attention.

"Th-thank you, Father."

She downed the rest of her tea, hoping the steaming liquid would help clear the thickness building in her throat. Help clear the confusion caused by the little girl she used to be, dancing in joy, and the grown woman she had become, chastising herself for that very reaction. It was not as though Thomas Hartley had been a poor father, exactly. He never said anything cruel, never laid a hand on her. He just had never found any use for her at all. Which was its own kind of hurt. But apparently, she had finally done something to deserve his regard.

He smiled at her. But it was like every other smile he had ever given her. Skin-deep. Surface only. The warmth thrumming in her heart weakened.

"I have been in negotiations with the Earl about garnering his support of Hartley Textiles. Unfortunately, he was hard-pressed against agreeing to anything as part of the marriage contract—especially considering our hands were tied with you ruining yourself. I had hoped the joining of our families would go a long way in furthering negotiations."

The thrumming stopped altogether. Snuffed out. Smothered. Dead.

"If you could do your part and convince your husband of the benefits of the earldom throwing its support behind us, perhaps his brother will see reason. Securing the Earl's backing would greatly enhance our ability to attract more members of the ton to our textiles."

And there it was. He wasn't proud of her. The businessman in him saw a use for her. That was all.

"I don't even know what to say," she said tightly.

"Oh, do not worry about that." Her father gave a careless wave. "We can discuss exactly the points you should bring up with your husband. I will make sure you are thoroughly prepared."

That had not been what she meant by her statement at all. She didn't know what to say to his bloody outrageous request.

"And it's not as though what you say will matter all that much," her mother added flippantly. "The best way to persuade him will to be to put your *charm* to good use. I am sure with your blunderbus of a husband, it will be no task at all."

Georgiana blinked. It was all she could ever do with this woman. Because what in the bloody hell? Not only had her mother just told her to seduce her husband for their family's gain, but the woman also just insulted Georgiana's husband in his very own home. The audacity. The *nerve*.

Fury built inside her, a keg filling with gunpowder. The story Felicity had shared of Fitz's past came flying to the surface. A match dropped on her fury. Her husband didn't deserve such disrespect. How dare them! He was *not* a blunderbus. He was nervous and struggled a bit socially, but he was a good man.

Lord, she had to hope he was a good man. That this current muddle was just a temporary setback, one with an explanation.

But the thing was, Georgiana knew beyond all doubt that even if things turned out to be dire, she'd champion her husband, regardless.

She loved him too much not to.

43

FITZ PAUSED OUTSIDE HIS townhome's drawing room. He had just returned from his very important errand. The one that set his surprise for his wife into motion. In searching for said wife, Pemberton had informed Fitz that her parents had called unexpectedly. Which was quite unfortunate. Because Fitz knew he wasn't in good graces with his wife right now. And he would much prefer seeing her, apologizing to her, without them present.

"I have been in negotiations with the Earl about garnering his support of Hartley Textiles. Unfortunately, he was hard-pressed against agreeing to anything as part of the marriage contract—especially considering our hands were tied with you ruining yourself. I had hoped the joining of our families would go a long way in furthering negotiations."

Fitz froze at Mr. Hartley's deep baritone.

"If you could do your part and convince your husband of the benefits of the earldom throwing its support behind us, perhaps his brother will see reason. Securing the Earl's backing would greatly enhance our ability to attract more members of the ton to our textiles."

His lungs stopped working. Ice burned through his body like a searing cold flame. His hand shot out to the wall, and he leaned all his weight against it, all strength deserting him. *If she could do her part.* His past and his present swirled together in a nausea-inducing storm. It couldn't be true. It couldn't be happening a second time. That the entire ruination, the scene in his study at the ball, had all been a ruse, a part of their plan. To get to his brother. Again.

"I don't even know what to say." Georgiana's voice floated into the hallway.

Say more than that, Gigi. Please say that I'm mistaken. Please, love. His heart tacked itself onto a target, ready and waiting for his wife to shoot the arrow that would destroy him.

"Oh, do not worry about that," Mr. Hartley said. "We can discuss exactly the points you should bring up with your husband. I will make sure you are thoroughly prepared."

"And it's not as though what you say will matter all that much," Mrs. Hartley added. "The best way to persuade him will to be to put your *charm* to good use. I am sure with your blunderbus of a husband, it will be no task at all."

His other hand fell on his chest. It appeared Mrs. Hartley shot an arrow of her own. Because, while he did not know the woman well, really not at all, her words were salt in a wound that had never fully healed.

"I must ask you to leave." His wife's voice was soft, barely audible out in the hallway. But the softness did nothing to hide the scathing disgust laced in it.

Mrs. Hartley laughed, hesitant and confused. "Pardon, Georgiana?"

"Out!"

Fitz jumped back from the wall and blinked at the furious demand from his small, ever-smiling wife.

"The both of you. Will. Leave. Immediately. I will not tolerate such affronts toward my husband in his own home. I will not *use* my husband for your purposes. *You* will not use my husband for your purposes. I have been in that position enough to know that no one deserves that treatment, let alone my husband."

An unbearable burning welled behind Fitz's eyes, and his chest ached as his heart expanded to rib-cracking proportions. He stumbled backwards, relief clogging his throat. *Thank the bloody gods.* He turned and hurried to his study. How did he get so lucky with her?

Lord, he needed to fix things between them. He *had* to. Because Georgiana? She was the best thing that had ever accidentally happened to him. For once, the stars had aligned and blessed him with a blonde-haired, green-eyed avenging angel. And he needed her to know how much that meant to him. How much she meant to him.

Fitz settled down at his desk, pulling out the note in the pocket of his coat. He had been intending to apologize to her. He flattened the slightly crumpled draft of his apology. He hadn't wanted to muck it up with his misuse of words, so he had written his main points—with Felix's approval. But now he had a better idea. He would pen her a letter and have Pemberton deliver it to her. Then he'd finish the apology in person when she joined him later that night.

Currently, he needed to concentrate on a much more pressing matter. He had significant studying ahead of him. Because tonight—he was going to gift Georgiana with the man of her dreams.

44

Georgiana

GEORGIANA GLANCED DOWN AT her lap, at the letter that lay open in her hand. The one from her husband that their butler had delivered to her earlier that day. She sniffled, reading it again for what seemed the hundredth time. It wasn't the easiest to make out in the dim light of the carriage, but she'd read it so many times she'd memorized most of the words.

My Dearest Georgiana,

I believe my inability to human properly has caused me to make a muck of things. Gigi, love, I need you to know: I have not had any sort of intimate relationship with my ex-mistress since you and I became betrothed. And I do not want there to be. The only woman I want, in my bed, in my life, in my heart, is you. As you know, my skill set resides in translating someone else's written word. I quite clearly am inept at speaking English for myself. Now, I hope to explain properly this time, with carefully chosen words that actually articulate what I mean:

While in Kent, I overheard a conversation you had with my sister. One about your desire of the Duke of Ironcrest and his proclivities. I am woefully uneducated in this area—I was unsure what these proclivities would even consist of. But I wanted to be able to offer those to you, whatever they may be. And this is where I erred, erred in the most egregious of fashions.

I went to my ex-mistress for guidance, <u>purely</u> for information. There was nothing untoward, no touching, no physical lessons. She informed me of the Duke's interests and secured pamphlets for me—so that I could familiarize myself with such acts. That is what I was paying her for in my study, for said reading material.

I realize now it was utterly dim-witted of me to go to her, and I should have sought guidance elsewhere—literally anywhere else. I want you to know, I most assuredly won't be seeing her ever again for <u>any</u> reason.

I promise I will make this up to you. For as long as it takes. And I would like to start with tonight. I have a surprise for you, one which I hope will show you how dedicated I am to you, solely you, and your desires. I want to be the one to fulfill them for you. Just please bear with me as I stumble along the way. In the box accompanying this note is a black mask. You will need to wear this mask and present the small card tucked in this letter to gain entry. A carriage will be waiting for you at 9 o'clock to escort you to your surprise.

I desperately hope you will take it. Do not fret over much about what to wear. If things go as I plan them to, you shan't be wearing it for long.

A thousand apologies,
Your hair-brained husband,
Fitz

She dabbed the back of her glove at the corner of her eyes. This letter? It filled her with an overwhelming hope. For her marriage. For her future with Fitz. Her eyes slid shut, and her head sank into the squabs of the rumbling carriage. He hadn't been unfaithful. He had no desire to be unfaithful. Her husband was simply a fool. An adorable, always-saying-the-wrong-thing fool.

She still was unsure exactly what all this meant—besides the fact that her husband clearly had *not* slept with his mistress. He made it seem as though he wanted to explore her desires with her. But when she had brought one up—one which she thought was relatively tame—he had fled.

Hopefully, whatever this surprise would be, it would also allow for discussion. One where the meaning of her husband's words were thoroughly deciphered. Goodness, he was as inscrutable as a hieroglyphic. She needed a bloody Rosetta Stone to understand him.

The carriage jolted to a stop, and then a moment later the door swung open, the dim light of the lantern hanging on the building outside filling the conveyance. A white-gloved hand appeared, and she took the servant's hand and stepped down to the cobblestones. She glanced around. Darkness greeted her on either side of the alleyway, and the hairs on the back of her neck prickled. The lantern in front of her was the only light in the whole of the narrow cobblestone street. She stepped to the door, and the footman hurried forward, knocking on the door for her, then sliding away.

The door opened, and a large man, hair shorn down to his scalp, who looked like he might have a career as a pugilist, eyed her. She lifted her chin and extended the card, proud that her hand didn't tremble, even despite the hard, scrutinizing stare the beastly man was giving her. She couldn't imagine Fitz would send her anywhere unsafe. But goodness, he could make some incredible mistakes. The man nodded, and with a hefty step, moved backward, exposing a finely dressed servant in a black tailcoat and bright gold breeches and waistcoat. The footman beckoned her forward and took her card, glancing at it briefly.

"Please follow me, my lady. Your room is ready for you."

The servant led Georgiana into what was apparently her assigned room. She stepped past the man and paused in the small area just after the door. A giant four-poster bed resided directly in the center of the room, the deep-red velvet curtains tied back with black tassels. There was no headboard, just a generous amount of space surrounding the bed, which looked as though it could be accessed from any of the four sides.

"Please undress, and your *amante* will be right with you, my lady. There is a robe in the armoire for you. Refreshments and a light repast, including chilled champagne and spiced biscuits"—he gestured to a small table in the corner decorated with an assortment of nibbles—"are set up for you just there. And there is a fully stocked dressing table. Help yourself to whatever you need to prepare yourself. Any of the items you use are yours to keep after today. They are all new, never before used. If you will require assistance removing your garments or with your coiffure, I can send in a lady's maid."

Georgiana blinked at the man, eyes wide. "I can manage. Thank you." She somehow formed the words through her bewilderment. *Any of the items are yours to keep.* Whatever did that mean?

He bowed and left the room, closing the door behind him.

Her head was spinning. She was clearly at a brothel. And a *very* nice one, if the state of the room was any indication. She supposed she now saw what her husband meant when he said not to worry over much about what she chose to wear. Since apparently, she was to remove it immediately. She hastily shrugged out of her dress, a simple one that buttoned down the front—thankful she'd forgone a corset—and slipped into the charcoal silk robe. She hummed happily; it was delectably soft.

She grabbed a glass of champagne and a biscuit and began exploring the room. The walls were wood paneled with a rich walnut, oak, the entire back wall laden with shelves chock full of items. Georgiana walked forward, slowly perusing the shelves. Birch rods, riding crops, cat-o'-nine-tails. Her eyes widened. Paddles, feathers, rope. She paused before an assortment of fabrics, scarves of thin-silk, others made of thicker, sturdier materials, leather, but all for the same purpose—restraints, blindfolds, gags. Her heart rate kicked up. She glanced back at the bed and couldn't believe how she had missed the loops and knobs decorating the frame. Limitless places for things to be tied. Her breath hitched. Fitz truly was going to give her anything she desired.

She downed her champagne, the bubbles tickling down her throat, the tart, crisp liquid sending a shiver down her spine. She leisurely made her way to a small table, nibbling on her biscuit, and her eyes widened. The table was covered with an assortment of...intriguing...items: connected beads, dildos in various shapes and sizes, clamps, melted wax, a bowl of ice—

"Well, isn't this a surprise," a deep, familiar voice murmured behind her.

She spun, and her eyes threatened to pop right out of her head.

Because there before her—

Was none other than the Duke of Ironcrest.

Georgiana was frozen, as frozen as the chunks of ice in the bowl next to her. The Duke stepped into the room, his face expressionless, lips flat, dark eyes unreadable, scar stark.

What was happening? Why was he here? Where was Fitz? Her mind reeled. She couldn't make sense of this. And then quick as the snap of a whip, her mind flew to her husband's letter.

I have a surprise for you.

I overheard...your desire of the Duke.

I will show you how dedicated I am...to your desires.

Oh my God.

"You are here to sleep with me?" she asked weakly.

His eyes slid down her, slow, sensual, scorching. "It appears so."

Georgiana could barely form words. Everything went slack: her jaw, her shoulders, her muscles. *Thump.* She glanced down. At her half-eaten biscuit. How was she even still standing? Her husband had arranged for her to sleep with the Duke?

And just like that, she snapped straight, something sharp and searing hot flying through her veins, coursing into her chest where it went up in flames. The absolute *imbecile!* She had half the mind to sleep with the Duke just to teach Fitz a bloody lesson. She wasn't going to, but *arghhh!* The man was cracked in the head. And she was going to crack it further when she walloped him. How could he ever think this was what she wanted, that this was a *gift?*

She bared her teeth and growled. And promptly took a step backward.

Because the Duke's lids lowered on her growl, and his mouth curled up in a predatory smile. Well, what would be considered a smile for the Duke. His lips tilted in the general direction they were supposed to if one was to smile. Up-*ish.*

Focus, Georgiana. That smile was the last of Georgiana's worries.

Because the Duke was advancing.

Shite.

45

Shite.

Fitz froze in the doorway of the room he'd been assigned at Madame Beaumont's. Because the naked woman laying within the sapphire, canopied bed was *not* his wife. She popped up on her elbows and cocked her head, her light-brown hair fluttering. She studied him with large, curious, dark eyes. Clearly, she knew he wasn't in the right room as well. Heat crawled up his neck and slapped over his cheeks.

"P-p-pardon. My ap-pologies." He stumbled backwards and slammed the door shut.

He let his head fall to the door with a *thud*.

You bloody idiot, Fitz.

He *would* go to a brothel and accidentally walk into the wrong room. He had been assigned room 2A, and that room had clearly not been 2A.

He stepped back, gaze homing in on the plaque.

2A.

Fitz frowned. He shuffled about in his coat pocket and retrieved his card that had his room assignment. Room 2A. Well, that didn't make a lick of sense.

Letting out a weighty sigh, he spun on his heel and made his way to Madame Beaumont's office. Why could nothing ever go smoothly for Fitz? He couldn't even apologize to his wife without incident. He hurried down the stairs, nearly skating to the bottom, and strode to the double doors at the end of the hallway.

Madam Beaumont's office was a large, dark-wood paneled room with rich, burgundy velvet upholstered furniture, and a desk that would rival the one in his brother's study. Which was where the Madame sat, quill in hand. Her head sprang up before he even made it through her doors, her deep-rose rouged lips splitting into a smile. She nonchalantly flicked back one of her loose ebony waves and put down her quill.

She rested her elbows on her desk, studying him, chin resting on her hands. "Mr. Jennings, how can I assist you? Is there something not to your liking with your rooms?"

"Yes, the woman."

Her head jerked back, and she blinked at him. "You...are not pleased with your wife."

He frowned. "Urm, no. What I mean to say is the woman in my room is not my wife."

Her slim, black brows furrowed, and she sifted through some paperwork on her desk. "Room 2A, was it not?"

"Yes, that is the room I was assigned."

She pulled out a paper and scanned it, tapping her lip. Her eyes widened, and her mouth dropped in a small "O". She glanced at him. "Oh, dear."

Fitz's pulse sped up. "What happened?"

Her brows pinched, and she grimaced. "It appears there was a slight mix-up. It appears your assignment was accidentally switched with someone else."

His assignment was switched? Did that mean...

"I promise you, sir, this has *never* happened before. I have just hired a new assistant, and it appears they will not be long for employ here. This is completely unacceptable. I assure you we will make this up to you. Tonight is free of charge, along with another visit as recompense."

He waved her apology off. He just needed to know what this meant and where his wife was. "What do you mean, my room was switched?"

"It means you and another gentleman were assigned each other's rooms."

Fitz's eyebrows shot off his head. *Another man* was going to his wife's room right now? Another man was going to walk in and see his wife—possibly naked? He started backpedaling out of the office, his heart drumming a chaotic rhythm in his chest.

"What room?" he barked out.

"Room 3B." She glanced down. "It appears your assignment was exchanged with the Duke of Ironcrest."

His heart fell out of his chest. *What?* He took off at a run.

Dear God, he had just sent his wife to a brothel and presented her with everything she had ever desired on a silver ducal platter.

Fuck, fuck, *fuck!*

His chest heaved as he made the climb to the third floor, but he barely noticed. He didn't need air, every part of him too focused on getting to his wife. Before he was too late. HE bared his teeth. If the bastard touched her, Fitz would cut the man's bloody hands off. He snarled. He'd disembowel the man and he would revel in it.

And after that, he was having *words* with the Madame. Because this was completely unacceptable. Inexcusable.

He slid to a stop and slapped a hand on the wall next to the plaque. 3B.

He threw open the door.

46

Georgiana

CRASH!

The door ricocheted off the wall—right back into her husband. Georgiana winced. But the door was already hurtling back into the wall again with a thundering bang, Fitz's palm outstretched. Georgiana's eyelids stretched round, her hand frozen on the Duke's chest. Fitz took a step forward, his chest heaving, gaze darting between her and the Duke. It settled on her palm, and his eyes went black.

Oh dear. Her husband was murderous. And Georgiana should not be melting into a puddle of lust at the sight. But a fanatical Fitz? Curls wild, nostrils flaring, jaw sharp and clenched, hands balled into fists? She sucked in a shuddering breath.

"I would ask you to step away from my wife. Immediately," Fitz ground out, his eyes not leaving Georgiana.

The Duke cocked his head, gaze slowly moving between Georgiana and Fitz. His eyebrows lifted slightly, bored, bemused. He stepped back, and her palm slid off his chest. Fitz growled, and the Duke let out a soft chuckle. There was a warning in that chuckle.

Apparently, it didn't faze her husband.

"It appears there was a mix-up," Fitz said, his voice low and lethal. "Your assignment is in room 2A."

Oh, buon Dio. That voice? Georgiana fanned herself. Perhaps she could convince him to do some role-play where he was her captor. Because she desperately wanted him to talk to her in *that* voice.

Fitz's gaze finally moved from Georgiana to the Duke. They locked gazes, neither moving. Her husband wasn't as tall and not nearly as broad and muscled as the Duke, but right now? If Georgiana was a wagering woman, her coin would be on her husband. Her husband reminded her of the little mongoose she had seen at a menagerie once. It was said a mongoose could take down a King Cobra. So, a Duke should be no task at all.

Either the Duke agreed or had something of a conscience hiding inside his dark exterior, because he took another step back. "Your wife was just telling me she didn't want to sleep with me." He paused, the only sound in the room Fitz's rough breathing. "Not the most flattering thing I've ever heard."

The Duke slowly backed away as Fitz approached Georgiana, neither taking their eyes off each other, as though at any moment one would lunge for the other.

The Duke stepped into the doorway and tipped an imaginary topper. "Best of luck to you two." Then he was gone, the door swinging shut behind him.

The tension holding her husband's body went limp, and he rushed the rest of the way to her, crushing her into his chest. His arms squeezed the breath right from her, his nose burying into her hair.

"God, I pushed you right into the arms of-of another man, the man you've always wanted," his mumbled words drifted to her ears.

She nudged at his stomach where her hands were trapped, and he reluctantly loosened his hold. She searched his volatile amber eyes. "So you didn't set up a rendezvous with me and the Duke, then?"

"No, *no*." He shook his head emphatically, his rich, brown curls flopping. "I-I... Is that what you want?" His chin jerked back, and his eyes went wide, panic or hurt or fear—maybe all three—swirling like a tempest there. The room went silent, her husband's ragged breathing stalling.

"No, it's not what I want, Fitz," she said gently. She slid her hands up and down his chest soothingly. "And what on earth did you mean, 'the man I've always wanted'?"

He swallowed, his Adam's apple bobbing, and looked away. "I over-heard you speaking with Felicity when we were in Kent. The day we went out for those bloody trees." He met her gaze. "You had said you had been waiting for the Duke that night I accidentally compromised you. That he, and the things he partook in"—he waved his arm around the bedroom—"were what you desired. The Duke is everything you could ever ask for in a man. And I'm—"

"No," she said sharply, fisting his cravat. "No, Fitz. You have that completely wrong. That man who just left has *nothing* I desire. He and I may share an interest in certain proclivities. But there is only one man I desire. One man I desire to do those things with." She slid her hand up and gripped his chin. "And that man is you."

Instead of the relief she was expecting, her husband stared at her like she had five heads. "You want me?" He circled his hand in front of him. "This whole mess?" His forehead wrinkled, and his expression oozed skepticism. "Are you sure? Because I'm fairly certain I just made a complete hash of things this past sennight. I have been the biggest idiot. Repeatedly. I have been just piling on the idiocy left and right, building the largest tower of idiocy ever known to man."

She breathed out a chuckle. "You have been a bit idiotic," she agreed. "But you're my idiot," she said tenderly, smiling up at him.

His forehead dropped against hers. "I want to be your idiot," he whispered.

Her chest swelled. With hope. With love.

"I'm so sorry, Gigi," he murmured. "I never intended to hurt you, to make you feel as though you are not the only woman in this entire world I want. Because there is no one else for me. You are my person, Gigi. I can feel it deep in my bones. I never thought that person existed, not for someone like me."

He drew in a slow breath. "I'm different, and I've accepted that, learned to live with who I am. But then you came into my life and quite literally knocked me off my feet. I felt things, things I can't even put into words. For a while, I thought perhaps I was having some indigestion. But now I know what it is. I've finally found someone I fit with. When you're in my arms, God, I feel like I belong, like I've found my place in this world. And I'm terrified—terrified I will do something incredibly Fitz-like and ruin this, lose this, lose you."

Georgiana swore her heart was at risk of taking flight, light and un-tethered like one of those grand balloons.

"You won't lose me, Fitz," she whispered, the emotion tightening her throat, not allowing for anything more.

Her hands slid up his chest to his shoulders, under the lapels of his coat. She pushed slightly, and he helped her slide the coat off.

"Even when I had believed the worst," she finally said. "I wasn't going anywhere." She met his heady amber irises. "I was crushed"—her voice faltered, her heart lurching at the memory of when she feared the worst—"but I was determined to see if we could work through it."

His hands came up to cradle her face; warm, reassuring, safe. "I'm so bloody sorry, Gigi."

But those rich mahogany eyes swam with fear.

"You won't lose me," she reiterated, injecting strength into her tone.

Her husband needed this. Needed to know she was wholeheartedly committed to him, to them. Unwavering. Because standing in front of her right now? She thought might be the young man who had been tossed over for his brother. But Fitzwilliam Jennings deserved to know he was the one someone chose. He deserved the world, to be someone's world. And he was her world.

"We'll work through every bumble you come up with, Fitz. I promise. With plenty of conversation and clarifying questions until we are certain we are both on the same page. I don't care how many pages it takes to get us there, I'd read an entire book, if that is what it took."

Georgiana had fought much of her life with nothing but a flicker of hope fueling her. Now that she had something truly worth fighting for? There was nothing in this world that could ever take it from her.

Georgiana's husband sighed against her lips and pressed a soft kiss to them.

Finally, she had answers. Finally, they seemed to be making their way out of this muddle. There was one thing that still confused her, however. Her husband had just stormed into this room, snarling and spitting like an enraged mongoose. He looked poised to kill the Duke for possibly touching her, for *her* touching the Duke. *Urghh, bloody delicious.*

But at the Rutledge supper party when he quite clearly saw her talking—flirting—with the Duke and Lord Dunmore...he had turned his back. As though he didn't care.

"You've gone quiet," he murmured.

She leaned back and caught his amber gaze. "I...It is just... at the Rutledge's," she said, voicing her doubts. "I had been speaking with the Duke and Lord Dunmore..."

His jaw clenched.

"You hadn't seemed to care that I was blatantly flirting with them. Not in the least bit jealous. You turned your back like it meant nothing to you."

He watched her, saying nothing for a long time. And then finally, "I turned my back because I was so unbelievable consumed with jealousy, I feared I'd make a scene." His words were pure gravel, repressed possessiveness thick in his tone. "There was a very real risk I would toss you over my shoulder; consequences be damned."

"Oh," she said breathlessly. She was getting quite warm again.

"You did it on purpose," he said softly, eyes darkening.

The hairs on the back of her neck prickled at his tone. She didn't think he required an answer, but she nodded anyway. "I wanted your attention back on me. I wanted you to want me. Not that woman back in your study. I wanted you to know other men found me desirable." She swallowed. "I wanted you to feel like you were lucky to have me," she whispered.

For once in her life, she wanted to feel as though she, Georgiana, was what someone wanted. No. Not someone. Just Fitz.

His arms tightened around her, and his eyes cleared, earnest pools of burned amber. "I am the luckiest man on this earth, having you as my wife." He gripped her chin and squeezed gently. "I've thought that many times since we married. Trust me, Gigi. I want you. I want you so badly I don't even know what to do with it." He released her and stepped away.

Georgiana shivered at the loss of heat. She needed it back. She reached for him.

"Though perhaps..." He cocked his head at her. "One of the things you desire is punishment, yes?"

Her arm dropped, and she blinked at the random question but dipped her chin in a nod.

Her husband took a bracing breath and then his hand went to his cravat, pulling at it until it loosened and came undone. He stretched his neck from side to side, the corded muscles flexing, then softening as he pulled it loose and dropped it to the floor.

He locked gazes with her. "Then get on your kn-knees, micetta cattiva. And show me how sorry you are for that little display at the Rutledge's."

She sucked in a breath. Her gaze darted around the chamber as though she would find the man who had absconded with her husband. Because her brain could not process that the man who had just uttered those wicked, demanding—albeit slightly wavering—words, the one who had just called her a *bad kitty,* was Fitz.

"Knees, Gigi. Now."

There was nothing hesitant or wavering that time.

She dropped to the floor in front of her husband, the silk of her robe settling around her. Heart in her throat, pulse racing through her veins, she waited. Waited for her husband to bring one of her private fantasies to life.

His knuckles dusted over her cheekbone, trailing down her jaw before a finger settled under her chin. "I've been reading. Studying. For you." His voice was dark, dangerous. "It's been...enlightening. Do you want to be d-degraded, *micetta?* Is that on your list as well?"

Georgiana shivered at his velvet tone; she wanted to wrap herself in that voice, bathe in it. She dipped her chin slowly. God, she wanted him to stutter horrible things to her. She knew that probably wasn't common. But she wanted to be used, punished, disparaged. It was that dark, sinful secret inside of her.

His hand left her and joined his other at his placket, making quick work of the buttons. He took out his half-hard cock and stroked slowly, teasingly. Her lips parted, and her gaze shot to his. But for no longer than a breath. She couldn't help it. Her stare fell back to where his hand worked himself, where he grew thicker with every stroke. She licked her lips. She wanted it.

He chuckled, deep and strangled. "Desperate for it, are you, micetta? If you keep looking at it like that, this is going to end e-embarrassingly quick."

Her eyes snapped back to his face, and she leaned forward, nodding eagerly. She rested her hands on his thighs, squeezing.

"Desperate, Fitz," she whispered. "I need you so badly."

He sucked in a breath through bared teeth, his cock twitching in his hand. "Well, what are you waiting for, then? Suck my cock like the needy whore you are."

She froze.

He froze.

Both equally shocked by his words.

But as frozen as they were, between her thighs went up in flames, went liquid. *Oh, my fucking heaven.*

"Oh God. Was that too much? A-Apologies, Gigi. I d-don't even know where that came from. It just flew out."

"No!" She leaned forward, hands clawing up to clench his hips. "It was perfect, Fitz. More of that. Please, say any filthy, demeaning thing to me. *Please.*"

And like the needy whore she was, she batted his hand away, gripped his base, and wrapped her lips around the head of him. She needed him *now.* To show him what his words did to her. She flicked her tongue over him, a burst of salty flavor overwhelming her senses. The overwhelming flavor of lust. Her eyes closed, and she hummed, flattening her tongue and sliding down his length. She worked over him, the slickness from her mouth sliding him deeper with each pass.

His low groan filled the room, and she glanced up. Head tilted back, eyes shut tight, neck stretched and taut; he was the picture of pleasure.

She slid up so just the head of him rested in her mouth and gave a strong suck. His breath hitched, and so did his hips. She took that cue, and with a slow breath, relaxed her jaw, and sank down on him, taking him almost to the back of her throat. His gaze flew to hers, a rough grunt rumbling from deep in his chest.

And then his hips gave an especially forceful jerk. His cock hit the back of her throat, and she gagged. An array of curses, some English, some Italian, flew from Fitz's mouth; then his hand shot to her hair, pulling her off him. His face contorted as though in pain. And then he relaxed and let out a breath, slowly opening his eyes.

His lips curved, sheepish, bashful. And her heart fluttered like a leaf in the wind. The things this man did to her.

"You almost unmanned me with that one, micetta."

She wanted to unman him. She wanted him mindless, out-of-his-head with lust because of her. Her fingertips dug into his thighs, her gaze darting between his eyes and his cock.

He released her, chuckling. "So needy for my cock. What a good little wife."

She moaned, rubbing her wet lips over the head of him, but not taking him back inside. Instead, she traced down him, the tip of her tongue trailing down the underside and then back up. His entire body trembled, his breaths shuddering and jagged. God, the sound of him, the feel of him, the taste of him. She knew she was wanton because she loved the taste of man. It lit her core on fire, the taste of Fitz, the taste of sex.

Heaven, help her, she wanted everything he had to give her. She wanted to be covered in him—

She stilled. *That thought has merit.*

"Come on me," she rushed out breathlessly.

"P-Pardon," he squeaked.

Georgiana smiled softly. She'd shocked the stuttering right back into her husband. She sat back on her knees and shrugged out of her robe, the silk cascading over her skin like the softest of caresses. Her husband's gaze shot to her breasts, and his chest heaved. She bit her lip. Perhaps she would have a bit of fun with this. She trailed the back of her fingers over her thighs and up her stomach until she reached her breasts. She cupped them, her thumbs sliding over her nipples, sending a spark straight to her core. A soft moan fled her lips.

"*Cazzo,*" he swore. Breaths exploded from Fitz, his entire body rigid, as rigid as certain delicious parts of him.

His eyes locked on her hands. She squeezed harder. She liked a rough hand.

"Touch yourself, Fitz." She pinched her nipples and gasped. "*P-please,*" she begged.

His hand flew to his cock. "Fuck, cazzo, *fuck.*" He groaned. "What am I to do with you, Gigi?" His breath stuttered, his hand stroking faster over his erection.

"Come on my tits, hopefully," she managed between pants.

He huffed out a laugh that ended on a strangled groan.

God, she ached between her thighs. This was pure torture. Her eyes locked on his cock, glistening from the mettle that had leaked from him, because of how badly he wanted her. She wanted—needed—him inside her. Her core clenched, and she rolled her nipples in her fingers. Heat coiled tight, the pulsing growing to dangerous heights. She squeezed her thighs, and her body shuddered. Bloody hell, she thought she might be able to come like this.

"Fuck, Gigi. I can't—" With a guttural moan, Fitz curled over her, his free hand landing on her shoulder, gripping her nape in a hold so tight she felt it like a shock to her core.

Her skin was met with the warmth of his release, coating her breasts, her fingers. She let out a soft cry, her body trembling at the feel of him on her skin. At the feel of being marked by him. Claimed.

He dropped to his knees in front of her, chest heaving, and buried his face in her neck. After a few struggling breaths, he pulled back, his gaze scouring over her. His lids, already heavy and languid, lowered further.

"Exquisite," he whispered, his voice nothing but an out-of-breath rasp. "Look at you dripping in my cum."

She whimpered. Blast and damn, was it possible for this anxious, awkward man to be any more of a surprise?

He slid his fingers through his seed, gathering it and swirling it around the pebbled peak of her nipple. She inhaled sharply, arching into his touch, a sharp pang arcing to her core with every pass of slick fingertips.

"You love it, don't you? Love being covered in me. Being well-used by me." He coated more cum on his fingers. "Show me how much."

Oh, God. Yes, apparently, he could be more of a surprise.

He brought his fingers to her mouth and slowly spread himself over her lips.

"Assaggiami," he commanded.

Taste me.

She licked them, sucked his fingers into her mouth. A muffled cry left her at the taste of him, her tongue tracing around his finger.

He groaned. And in a flurry of movement, his arms snaked around her, then he shot up, and Georgiana found herself thrown onto the massive four-poster bed.

Fitz crawled after her, gaze black, heady—hungry—from where he watched her beneath heavy lids. He aggressively pushed open her thighs and gave her mind no time to process what was happening. He dove straight between her thighs, his fingers sinking inside her. A sound of pure lust, pure appreciation, rumbled from him, and he buried his face further.

Her breath stuttered, her hips canting. Her body didn't know what way was up. Her core tightened, an overwhelming pressure building to staggering heights. The pounding of her heart in her chest echoed between her thighs, where his tongue was flat and pulsing against her clitoris.

"God, I can feel you throbbing against my tongue, Gigi. Così disperata per me." He gave a tortuously soft lick to her swollen flesh and then pierced her with his blackened amber gaze. "You love being covered in my cum? Rub me into your skin, Gigi. Cover those glorious breasts with my seed. Mine."

She stopped breathing. Where had this sinful man come from? This devil who turned her into a puddle of wanton woman. She reached up and rubbed him over her chest, into her skin, moaning as she cupped and clenched her breasts, rolling her thumbs in a slick glide over her aching nipples.

"More, Gigi. Show me how you like those tits touched, how rough, how hard. Show me how good my cum feels coating your nipples."

Georgiana was going to explode. The coiling pressure was going to combust just from the words flying from his tongue.

He dropped back between her thighs, his fingers and mouth working in tandem. She moaned, noises that were nothing but feral, ragged, broken, ripping from her throat. She almost couldn't believe they came from her. But she could still taste him on her tongue, feel his seed on her skin, feel his lips, his tongue, his fingers between her legs. It set her afire.

"Oh, Go-od. God. Fitz. I...I..." She was incoherent, that was what she was. She was gone, brainless, nothing but molten liquid lust.

And then he sank his fingers deep, curling and pressing in a devastating rhythm. His tongue flattened against her clitoris, and the tight, swirling pressure inside her broke, shattered. She cried out, half-sob, half-moan, her body shaking violently against the bed linens. Pleasure shot through her, pulse after pulse surging through her body all the way to her toes. Her hands tightened on her breasts involuntarily as her muscles clenched tight, her back arching off the bed, sending more jolts of bliss reeling through her.

She shuddered and fell limp on the bed, breath bursting from her. Her eyes slid shut, entirely replete, satiated, small aftershocks quivering through her limbs. Slowly she came to, the languid haze of post-orgasmic bliss settling in.

The breath shot from her. She was unceremoniously yanked to the edge of the bed and pulled into her husband's lap.

The blunt head of her husband's cock notched at her entrance.

His *hard* cock.

47

FITZ PULLED GEORGIANA INTO his lap, her legs straddling his from where he sat on the edge of the bed. Gripping her hips, he brought her down, lining himself up at her entrance. God, he could feel the heat of her, how she throbbed for him, aftershocks of her release still fluttering her intimate muscles. Muscles he wanted to be surrounded by.

Her eyes flew wide. "You-you. Isn't it supposed to deflate after?"

He laughed, deep and rich with want, shaking his head. "Jennings family trait. I only need a few minutes between bouts. And after tasting you? Seconds." And to prove his point, he thrust at the same time he dragged her hips down and sank to the hilt.

The breath fled her lips on a shocked exhale and ended on a moan that melded with his. Bliss. Heaven. Home. That was what it was to be inside her.

Her lips skimmed over his cheek until she found his mouth and then she was sipping at him, nipping at him, his greedy little wife.

Gigi rocked and ground against him, rode him without hesitation, without a hint of uncertainty. She took what she wanted, unabashedly.

She let out a low, guttural groan, her hips picking up speed as she clearly found a perfect spot, a perfect rhythm. Fuck, fuck, *fuck*. Whatever she had just done had the head of his cock rubbing against a spot inside her that had lust pulsing out of control to his cock. God, it was like she was ribbed, and she rocked herself on that spot, again and again and—*fuck*—again. This was going to be over—for her and for him—if he didn't take control. And he wasn't ready for it to be over.

He tightened his grip on her hips and pushed her back. She whined, her pelvis thrusting forward, desperate to get back to that glorious spot.

But what his wife didn't know was that he had been doing a *lot* of reading since he received those pamphlets. And it had been eye-opening. There was this tactic of staving off orgasm—repeatedly—which sounded like pure torture. But apparently, the constant denial led to overwhelmingly intense orgasms. And he wanted nothing but overwhelming orgasms for his wife. She deserved nothing less.

He slowed his thrusts, giving her only a semblance of what she wanted. She writhed in his lap, desperately seeking, trying to increase the pace, to control the angle. But he denied her the pressure she craved, the impact she needed. Only to give her a tease. A hard thrust. Retreat. A grind of hips, rubbing over her clitoris. Retreat. Another thrust. Retreat.

She growled at him, her fingers digging so hard into his sides he could feel her nails through his linen shirt. His free hand flew to her jaw, and he yanked her to face him, his grip biting. She stilled, panting against him, warm puffs of champagne-and-spice-tinted breath.

He tsk'd at her at the same time he inwardly groaned. Because it was delectable when his kitten let out her claws. Her eyes bore into him, black as the night outside. He squeezed, and she gasped, head dropping back, supplicant. He petted her jaw softly. It still felt new, being rough with her. He liked it—no, loved it—but he needed to break it up with soft touches.

"You don't growl, micetta," he murmured, tracing the pad of his thumb over her bottom lip. "The only thing you do for me is purr. Understood?"

The prettiest whimper fled her lips, and his eyes rolled back. God, this was bad. She was bad. Because the way she turned to putty in his hands when he bossed her around, dictated to her like the only purpose she served was to *serve him,* it was heady, consumed him with an addicting lust. And he wanted more, needed more to attain that high again.

It had always been easy to let lust take over him during amorous encounters; it was one of the few times Fitz came out of his shell, his nerves and anxiety pushed away by something stronger and more potent. But this level of lust? He thought it very possible he could be that sinister, wicked man she wanted. And he would revel in being that man for her.

His hand dropped to her breast, squeezing, rolling his thumb over her nipple. He needed a taste. Would not survive without one. He lifted her by the hips until his mouth landed nearly level with her nipples. And he finally went in for a sample of what he craved. He hummed, trailing his tongue over the rough, peaked tip. It was heady, the taste of her skin, the taste of him on her skin. The taste that she was his. His cock twitched inside her, and she gasped.

He sucked her into his mouth, and she cried out, her hips moving frantically over him. His hand went to her arse, stilling her with a forceful squeeze. He was in control here. He leaned back on his free hand for leverage. And while his mouth attacked her breasts, tongue and teeth licking and grazing, he held her immobile in a bruising grip as he thrust his hips into her. He drove hard, the sound of slapping skin, his grunts and heavy breaths, her choked cries, filling the room.

He moved to her other breast, rolling his tongue over her, flicking the tip of her nipple. She pushed her chest closer to him and, God, what a way to die. Suffocation by his wife's breasts. He dug his fingertips into the plush flesh of her bottom. Pleasure raced through him, demanding and unstoppable. His cock was moments from bursting.

He needed her to get there first, wouldn't accept anything less. He sucked her nipple into his mouth and gently bit down. She shuddered, her muscles fluttering lightly. He bit down harder and slammed her down on him as he thrust up into her. A sharp cry burst from her, and her back arched. Her cunt clamped down on him, and he was done. That perfect, pretty part of her squeezed the orgasm straight from him.

He thrust into her once more and held, burying his face into her breasts and groaned his release. His body convulsed, hers still trembling and jerking from her own release. And then he fell back on the bed, limp, her slumping against him, just as boneless. Boneless together, nothing but a tangle of limbs. Nothing but one.

Georgiana rolled off him, eyes shut, features relaxed in what he hoped was what she had found a very blissful encounter. Her eyes peeped open and tracked over him, and she promptly burst out laughing.

"What?" He smiled bemusedly at her. He wasn't so sure laughter after a bout of lovemaking was a good thing. But he was Fitzwilliam Jennings, after all.

"Y-you're still f-fully clothed, Fitz." She broke down in another fit of giggles. "Goodness, y-you're still w-wearing your boots."

His face split in a grin and a chuckle rumbled in his chest. God, she was right. He hadn't even shucked off his boots in the heat of the moment.

His very naked wife crawled over to his feet and tugged off his boots, her delectable arse wiggling in front of him. Absolutely glorious. He reached forward and gave it a soft swat.

She froze, then turned to look at him, her lids heavy. "Careful, husband. You might end up thoroughly shagged again, still fully clothed."

He let out a soft snort. "Is that supposed to be a threat? Because I have to say, all that does is make me want to spank you more."

She walked on hands and knees back over him, leaning down and pressing a kiss to his lips. "Perhaps that was what I was after all along."

He gave her another playful swat, and she fell to her side, snuggling into him with a giggle. This he could do. The playful swat. But he wasn't sure how hard to do it when in the middle of a shag. One thing he had learned in his reading was that there were *very* different levels of roughness. Some people desired serious pain. He didn't know where his wife fell. He so desperately didn't want to do anything wrong with her. He wanted everything to be perfect for her.

"You are in your head," she murmured. She must have noticed his quiet, his stillness.

"I just... I am very new to all of this. I have no idea what I'm doing."

She dusted her lips over his shoulder and across the protruding bone of his collarbone, then pushed up and studied him. "First off, you are doing *extremely* well. But I don't expect you to be some sort of proclivity expert, Fitz. We will figure it out as we go along." She gently ran her finger through the curling amber hair that lightly covered his chest.

"Why did you go to your mistress?" she asked into the silence. "Why did you not just come to me? They are my desires, after all. Who better to tell you what they are, what I want you to do to me?"

He grimaced, letting his head sink into the pillow. He stared into the crimson canopy. "When you say it like that, I feel like a complete arse and utter cod's head. I just…"

"You just?" She tugged at his chin, pulling his gaze to hers.

"I knew you favored the Duke, Gigi. I thought if I were to disappoint you in bed, not deliver what he could, I would push you toward him. I thought if I fumbled as I tried to give you what you desire—and I know I will fumble—I would risk losing you, would risk earning your disgust."

"Fitz—"

He shook his head. "I'm not done. Let me finish." He winced. That had come out boorish. "A-apologies."

She rubbed his chest soothingly, her eyes gentle. "You're fine, husband. Keep going."

He blew out a breath. "It wouldn't be the first time I was found lacking." His throat grew thick. "Nor the first time I was passed over for a different man," he managed.

His stare locked on his fingers, plucking at the bed linens. He couldn't bring himself to look at her. Not when he was so exposed. Vulnerable. He knew he was safe with Georgiana. Knew she wouldn't hurt him. But some wounds were just too deep, forever to be left flayed open.

48

Georgiana

GEORGIANA MADE A SOFT, crooning noise and leaned over to brush her lips against her husband's. Pain was tight on his face, glossy in his eyes, thick in every word. She hated it. Hated what that evil woman had done to him.

She gently grasped his chin and pulled his gaze to hers. "I do not want any other man but you. And you are so far from lacking, Fitz. You are *everything*. I never even deigned to think about what I actually wanted in a husband. I wasn't ever destined to have a choice. From the moment my mother realized my looks and my family's fortune might snag her a title, I was pushed in front of every destitute lord she could find.

"The only reason I went after the Duke was because I was so utterly alone, so utterly miserable. I wanted to feel—anything at all. It was purely to escape. But, Fitz, I cannot put into words how happy I am that it was you—you and *not* the Duke—who stumbled into that room that night."

She studied him. How could she help him understand?

"If I had thought to even consider what I might want in a husband, in a man"—she traced a finger down his nose—"it would be one who has freckles"—she ran the pad of her fingertip over his cheeks—"who blushes the most adorable crimson"—she traced his lips—"who gifts me the most heart-stopping of smiles.

"Who has a large, pure heart," she murmured, flattening her hand over that very pure heart. "Who is surprisingly competitive. Who laughs when I make inappropriate, juvenile jests. Who drinks whisky with me while we converse casually in front of the fire. Who I can enjoy a companionable silence with while I cozy up with a book and he works on his translations."

She dropped her voice to a whisper. "Who says the most delicious things to me in Italian with that filthy tongue of his."

His eyebrows shot into his amber curls, and she grinned.

"Y-you know what I've been saying to you in Italian?"

She nodded, biting her lip to hold back her amusement. "Sono fluente, caro."

"*What?*" he yelped.

Her giggles broke free. "Oh, goodness. You should see your face." She traced over his blush, the warmth akin to happiness on her fingertips. "I am part Italian. My mother is from Northern Italy."

His mouth worked for a moment. "How did I not know this about you?" he said weakly. "Lord, I am the world's worst husband. I hadn't known you had a brother. I didn't know you were Italian. I—"

She put a finger to his lips. "Shhh. Fitz, we haven't known each other very long. I am sure there are many more things we will discover. And frankly, I look forward to each and every one." She tucked in her chin and glanced at him from beneath her lashes. "I may have kept that particular fact from you because I loved the filthy words so much, I didn't want you to stop."

His shock faded, and he broke out in a toothy grin. "Piccola furfantella."

She smiled back at him. Yes, she was his little minx.

He curled up until his lips pressed against hers, smiling lips greeting smiling lips. "God, how I love you," he murmured against her mouth.

She stilled.

He stilled.

He collapsed back to the bed, panic lighting up his wide amber eyes.

"You—You love me?" she asked, her words mere breath.

He nodded slowly, the panic fading into heady, raging emotion. "So very much," he said hoarsely. "I know it hasn't been very long. I know it's probably too soon, but—"

Her eyes burned, and with a squeak, she dove on top of him, peppering kisses all over his adorably freckled face. "I." Kiss. "Love." Kiss. "You." Kiss. "Too." *Kiss kiss kiss.* "So bloody much." She punctuated the final statement with a kiss on the tip of his nose.

He beamed up at her, his chest shaking from stifled laughter.

"What?"

"I feel thoroughly assaulted," he said, amber eyes sparkling. "In the best way, of course."

She collapsed next to him with a grin, and he pulled her into his side. She searched until she found his hand and weaved their fingers together.

Georgiana studied their interlocked hands. "From now on, we will always come to each other with our problems?" she murmured softly.

"Yes. Always, Gigi. And I need you to know I will never, *ever* hurt you. If I ever say something that makes it seem as though I have, promise me you'll pester me with questions until we can get it sorted out. I guarantee it is just me mucking up my words."

"I promise."

He turned toward her and kissed her forehead.

"I love you, Gigi." His words coasted over her forehead, the warm puff of his breath skimming over her skin.

"I love you, Fitz." She and her heart snuggled in as close as they could get to her husband. A perfect fit. Albeit a sticky perfect fit. Speaking of…

"Where on earth did those wicked demands come from?" She tilted her head back and caught her husband's gaze. She arched a brow and lowered her voice. "*Look at you dripping in my cum.*" She shivered at the memory, her next words coming out husky, sultry. "*Assaggiami.*"

He groaned and buried his face in her neck, the heat of his blush warming her skin. "I had no idea how much that would affect me," came his muffled response. His body trembled against hers. He lifted his head, his gaze piercing in its intensity. "Seeing you covered in me?" His voice was like coarse stone, rough, a rasp, as he traced his fingers over her chest where the remnants of his seed remained. "Feeling myself on your skin, tasting myself on your skin?" He shuddered again. "Cazzo, love. It does dark things to me, dangerous things."

Georgiana thought she might understand. Considering the dark, dangerous thing pressing into her hip.

But then he abruptly pushed up to sitting, eyes wide. "Bugger me. I should have gotten you a cloth to clean yourself with. I mean, I would have cleaned you, of course. I wouldn't make you. How inconsiderate, utterly selfish of me. One moment, and I'll—"

She gripped his wrist and stopped him, her lips twitching. "Easy, Fitz. Come back down here with me." She pulled him back to her, and he collapsed at her side. "Lie with me. We can clean—order a bath if they offer that—later. For now, I want to bask in this moment a little longer." She pressed a soft kiss to his lips and whispered, "And quite frankly, I love being covered in you. It makes me feel owned by you. Utterly yours."

He groaned, and Georgiana found herself buried beneath thirteen stone of highly aroused male.

"Well, micetta, allow me to demonstrate just how thoroughly you belong to me."

49

Georgiana

GEORGIANA'S EYES FLUTTERED OPEN slowly, and she blinked away the sleep blurring her vision, her peach-hued bedchamber gradually coming into focus. And what did she see when her vision finally cleared? The most beautiful view. A bleary-eyed Fitzwilliam, staring back at her.

"Good morning, husband."

Fitz blushed to the tips of his ears, the color nearly identical to the color of the curtains surrounding her four-poster bed. "Good morning, wife."

She grinned and rolled to her side, her hand lazily drifting up his taut stomach, over his chest, to fluff lightly in his dusting of amber chest hair. "Truly, Fitz, you are blushing? Last night, you fucked me multiple times at a brothel and told me to suck your cock like a needy whore." *Mmmm.* The filthy things her awkward husband said. It did it for her. She squeezed her thighs together, her eyes fluttering shut. "It was utter perfection. *And* you came on my breasts." She shivered.

Ugh, and that third time? She wasn't sure if it had been their admissions of love, or her husband was just ravenous for her. But her muscles were still sore from the thorough pounding he'd given her afterwards. She winced at the tender throbbing on her arse. It might be a bit uncomfortable to sit today. Her husband had finally let go of his reservations and spanked her like she'd wanted. *Hard.*

She tilted her head, studying him, his blush still deep, but with the way his eyes had darkened she thought it might also be from arousal.

"You, my little crimson crustacean, were utterly *depraved*. Yet, we wake up this morning and you are blushing and bashful?" She traced her finger down his adorably freckled nose.

"Crimson crustacean?" His eyebrows lifted, his lips tilting up in the sweetest boyish half-smile.

She shrugged her shoulder not buried in the mattress. He was her lobster. He'd just have to deal with that.

"This is me, Gigi," he said hesitantly. He let out an exhale, his breath a soft puff dancing over her cheeks. "I am awkward and an idiot. I may have brief flashes of confidence, especially in the heat of the moment when I can battle away my nerves, but at my core, I am always this man. This man will always resurface." He looked away, gnawing on his bottom lip.

She frowned, and her heart squeezed. That word—idiot—and others like it, were so flippantly thrown around, and while her husband may sometimes act foolish, he wasn't an idiot. But he truly believed he was. That there was something wrong with him. When he was perfect.

She gripped his chin and forced him to look at her. "You are *not* an idiot, Fitzwilliam Jennings. Having difficulties with social interactions does not make you an idiot. Stumbling over your words does not make you an idiot. We all have strengths and weaknesses. I love you, Fitz. You.

Weaknesses and all. All versions. Whichever one shows up, bumbling or bold."

She pressed a soft kiss to his lips, making a mental note to remove that word—and all others like it—from her vocabulary. She would continue to assure him for the rest of their days that he was everything she could ever want. That he was the opposite of lacking. That, without a doubt, no one could ever compare to him.

"I love you, too, Gigi."

Her body sighed in a warm, happy thrum. She was finally where she belonged.

A muffled bellow reverberated through the door. "Georgiana!"

Georgiana's chin jerked back, and her gaze flew to the door. The door that burst open, a swirl of light-gray wool coat barging in.

"Felicity!" Fitz squeaked, his face, ears, neck, and chest blooming a deep red.

Georgiana smiled fondly. Her poor lobster.

Felicity paused, her gaze bouncing between the two of them. Her amber brows inched up her forehead. Her stare landed on Georgiana, and she crossed her arms. "We are supposed to leave for the foundling home in thirty minutes." That tone had been nothing short of accusatory.

Shite. Was it really that late already? Clenching the bed linens to her chest, she scurried over her sputtering husband to grab his pocket watch on the nightstand. Half past ten. Double shite.

"Have y-you never heard of kn-knocking! Is there no b-bloody privacy in this g-godforsaken family?" Fitz's incredulous stammering echoed through the chamber.

Felicity waved him off. "There is no such thing as privacy in this family. You know that, Fitzy."

Georgiana giggled at her slack-jawed husband.

"W-what if we had—What if"—he flapped his hands frantical-ly—"What if we had *been*..." He glared at his sister.

She tilted her head at a cheeky angle. "What if you had been... making the beast with the two backs? Dancing the blanket hornpipe? Joining giblets? Doing the featherbed jig?"

"Basket making?" Georgiana threw in.

Fitz threw her a crimson glare that screamed traitor.

"If you were busy in Georgiana's mutton?" Felicity asked.

Georgiana choked. Fitz wheezed. She broke into uncontrollable laughter.

Fitz reached for his pillow and pulled it over his face. A muffled, "Kill me, just kill me, put me out of my misery," drifted from the white cushion he was currently trying to suffocate himself with.

Georgiana drew in a deep breath, waving a hand in front of her face. "Dear *God*, Felicity. That was—I have no words."

Felicity was wearing a face-splitting grin. She took a small bow. "You're welcome for your daily dose of entertainment. Honestly, I hadn't thought there would be any issue barging into Georgiana's chamber. Given we *have plans*. And I figured if you two were shagging, you'd be in Fitzy's room." She shrugged.

"Give us a moment, Fliss. To make ourselves decent," Georgiana said.

Felicity winked and left.

Georgiana turned to her pillow covered husband. "Fitz? Caro? Are you well?"

A strangled groan was his reply.

She gently pulled the pillow from his face. To be met with her hus-band's eyes squeezed shut tight, mouth in a down-turned grimace.

"That really wasn't all that bad. She could have walked in on the...actual act. Even I might not be able to look at her after something like that."

He slowly opened one eye and peered at her. "You're going to *the* foundling home?"

She nodded. She knew what Fitz was referring to. *The* foundling home. As in the *Duke's* foundling home. She had pried a bit more from her husband last night about his worries and insecurities. She hoped he understood her visiting the foundling home had nothing to do with the Duke. But they were walking on a fragile new foundation.

He rolled his lips in, his eyes studying the peach canopy of her bed. "Would it be all right if I joined you?" His words were slow and laden with uncertainty. He glanced at her. "I don't want to intrude. If this is sister-bonding between you and Flick. Or if—"

"I would love for you to come!" She pounced on him, caging him in between her arms. And the little bumbling rascal's gaze dropped straight to her bare breasts. She rolled her eyes. What a rogue. "Eyes up here, love."

His gaze shot up, and he smiled sheepishly at her. "Apologies. You have lovely tits, micetta."

She chuckled. This man. Her heart was fit to bursting with how much she loved him.

"I think it would be lovely if you joined us. Felicity wants to have a snowball fight. And I am sure the boys would love to have a man to visit with. Perhaps you can even teach them some Italian."

He frowned, his gaze turning inward. "That's interesting."

Her eyebrows lifted, and she stared at him in bemusement. Interpreting her husband was a constant puzzle. "Interesting?"

He nodded and met her gaze again. "Perhaps I can make a habit of it. Visiting the foundling home to teach them Italian." He shrugged. "It might be useful for them in some capacity."

"That is a fabulous idea, caro," she murmured. Her husband—so genuine, so kind. She pressed a kiss to his lips and jumped from the bed. "Now, let us make haste!"

50

Georgiana

GEORGIANA AND FELICITY MEANDERED over to the drawing room that had been converted to a small library for the children of the Second Chance Foundling Home. They paused in the doorway, and Georgiana leaned against the door frame. Little boys with mops of disorderly hair were crammed onto settees and lying on their bellies on the floor, chins propped in hands, all giving her husband their full attention. Fitz sat in a well-worn leather armchair conversing with the boys, that lop-sided grin that never failed to make her knees weak spread over his face.

"Look at him," Felicity mused. "Not even a hint of his nervousness or apprehension in sight. He's always loved children. Both my brothers, really. I don't think Fitzy ever really dared to hope he'd have a family one day. I know it's something that deeply plagues Fifi." She shot a glance at Georgiana, scanning her from head to toe. "Considering how I found you and Fitzy this morning, it seems he'll have no problem securing that dream."

315

A fit of giggles floated out to them.

"How do you say, 'you smell like a toad'?" one boy asked.

"Smell like a toad?" another small voice said incredulously. "That's a blasted stupid one. What does a toad even smell like? A better one would be bum sniffer."

"Ya!" a chorus of voices said. "How do you say bum sniffer!"

"Or fart sniffer!" another voice chimed in.

Fitz glanced around at the gaggle of boys, his lips twitching. "I'm not sure I'm supposed to be teaching you how to say *those* things." He leaned forward. "But if you promise not to tell." He dropped his voice so Georgiana could no longer hear, and the boys broke out into cheers as her husband clearly just taught them how to say "fart sniffer" in Italian.

She shared a grin with Felicity, both women rolling their eyes. *Boys*.

Goodness, the pressure in her chest could barely be contained. It had to be detrimental to one's health to have their heart thumping like a tot with a drum so often. But that was what her husband did to her. He made her utterly, incredibly, unequivocally happy. Somehow, through boundless blunders, they had found their way. And Georgiana didn't have a single doubt that she and her husband, the lonely girl and the awkward boy, had found their happily ever after with each other.

"You will stay over New Year's Eve?" Felicity interrupted Georgiana's sickeningly sentimental thoughts. "I know your town house is a brief ride away. And obviously as newlyweds who have finally found their way"—she bounced her eyebrows—"I am sure you have other things on your mind. But it's always so lovely having the whole family wake up together in the New Year."

Georgiana reached out and squeezed Felicity's hand. "We will be there. And we will stay over. After twenty years, I finally have a family. I'm not ringing in the new year without them."

Felicity beamed at her. She gave Georgiana a squeeze in return. "I'm overjoyed for you and Fitzy, G. It appears your hopes and dreams did come true."

They had. But her sister-in-law's smile was a little too big, her eyes a little too flat, her grip on Georgiana's hand a little too tight.

"You seem awfully sad, Fliss, for someone declaring such joy."

Felicity swallowed and looked away, dropping Georgiana's hand to fiddle with her skirts. She eventually met Georgiana's gaze again, and when she spoke, her voice was strained. "I am nothing but happy for you two. I swear it. But I cannot stop the rush of sadness that follows in the wake of that joy. Because what you two have…" She gestured between Georgiana and where Fitz and the children were in the drawing room. "Hopes and dreams," she finally managed to whisper.

Hopes and dreams her sister-in-law had, just like Georgiana. Hopes and dreams that were not to be for Felicity.

"Perhaps if you spoke to Lord Wessex? Or perhaps if you spoke to your mother? She must be able to sway Felix's mind."

"Perhaps," Felicity murmured. But her words were as unconvincing as the dullness in her amber eyes. She shook her head, her eyes clearing, a wide grin back on her face. "All right. Let us corral these boys. It is time for a snowball fight!"

51

Epilogue - Fitz

April 1817, four months later

Kent, England

FITZ WATCHED ON in bemusement as his sister flopped back on the settee in his family's library.

Felicity let out a long groan. "Do we *have* to go back to London? I feel as though my lungs have just started working properly again now that I've been able to breathe *clean* air instead of that dreadful smog."

"We have the Chesterfield ball," Felix reminded her. "Plus, you always enjoy their functions. For some reason, the wildest things seem to occur at their balls." He frowned thoughtfully. "Haven't the slightest idea why."

Felicity propped herself up on one elbow, her lips pursing. "That's true. Lord and Lady Chesterfield are quite the riot. Their high spirits must seep into the food and drink somehow."

"No wonder I always end up foxed," Fitz added with a chuckle.

The room went quiet, and Felicity cocked her head at him. "You—foxed? You've never been even a trifle disguised at a function."

"No, I know." His smile faded as he was met with three pairs of blank expressions. "It was a jest...because they infuse everything with high *spirits*."

Felix groaned, shaking his head. "Fitz, if you have to explain it..."

Fitz opened his mouth and paused. He had thought his pun quite obvious. His brows scrunched. Perhaps not? Georgiana's giggle distracted him from his tumult, and he turned to look at his lovely wife curled into his side.

Her eyes danced, and she reached out to interlace their fingers. "I wouldn't have you any other way, love."

The right side of his mouth kicked up. How had he gotten so bloody lucky with her?

"Have you heard their love story, Georgiana? The Chesterfields'?" Felicity asked, a wicked grin spreading across her face.

Georgiana leaned forward, practically bouncing on the seat cushion. "No! I *must* know."

Felicity dropped her voice, her eyes wide with dramatics. "The marquess accidentally married her when he—"

"Mr. Jennings, you have a caller," their family butler announced. He cleared his throat, eyes shifting to the side. "Mrs. Smith is with the—urm—caller in the front entry."

Fitz frowned. What on earth—

Oh. Oh! Fitz shot to his feet. It was here! He jolted for the door—

Thud—

Thwack.

Fuck, fuck, *fuck.* He palmed his face, which had just collided with the plush rug, his aching knee having thankfully taken the brunt of the fall. Why was he always falling and colliding with things?

"*Ohmygod!* Fitz!" Georgiana screeched, dropping to his side. "Are you all right?"

He popped back up, rubbing his smarting knee. He shot his wife, who was now in a pile of burgundy skirts on the floor, a wide smile. "Pine"—he cleared his throat—"*Fine.* Everything's fine." He stumbled backward toward the door to the hall. "Foot got stuck in the settee leg. No worries. Ferfectly pine!" He spun on his heel and hurried out of the room.

"I don't think I've ever seen Fitzy so excited," Felix's baffled voice followed him out into the hallway.

Fitz chuckled. It was the truth. Excitement had his limbs jittery, his heart kicking against his chest. It was here!

Georgiana's surprise. *Finally.*

Well, part two of her surprise. The brothel surprise—which had almost ended in disaster—turned out to be a gift that kept on giving. A sly grin spread across his face, and his cheeks heated. They had been back at Madame Beaumont's *many* times since their first visit. His green-eyed angel of a wife had thoroughly corrupted him.

He picked up his pace and jogged the rest of the way to the entry. He frowned, his gaze landing on his housekeeper, who appeared to be desperately flailing as she tried to contain a blur in her arms. "Oh, thank goodness. Mr. Jennings. I cannot contain this little rapscallion!"

She held out the culprit—a round-bellied, wrinkly, tail-wagging, Bloodhound puppy.

Fitz relieved Mrs. Smith of the black and brown wriggling thing—only to almost drop the rascal! His arms scrambled to keep purchase on the puppy as it tried to disappear right under his arm and leap for its death. Saving it just in time, he hugged the thing to his chest—and was promptly attacked by a small, rough tongue. And razor-sharp teeth!

"Bugger!" Fitz yelped, his voice embarrassingly high.

Who knew puppy teeth would be so bloody sharp? He pulled the scamp back, a piece of his cravat—now shredded—in its teeth. Goodness, the little devil was out of control.

"Isn't it supposed to be in the basket?" He kneeled where a large wicker basket with a soft blanket inside rested on the entry's marble floor. He carefully stuffed the squirming puppy into the basket—only for it to hop right up on the edge—and promptly topple the entire basket over.

It scampered down the entry, small paws slipping and sliding over the slick marble floor. One of its paws caught on its long droopy ears, and it face-planted—and tumbled arse-over-head. Apparently, Fitz and Bloodhound puppies had a lot in common.

"That's why," Mrs. Smith's amused voice floated to him as Fitz hurried after the puppy and scooped it into his arms.

He held it out in front of him, its little tongue hanging out of its wrinkly, tan face. The pup was black as night except for four brown, blurry, flailing paws and a tan face that darkened to black just around the muzzle. Fitz had to admit, he was a cute little scamp.

He strode back to the basket and plopped the offending pup back inside. "Stay," he demanded in a firm, low voice. That was how one got a dog to listen, wasn't it?

The puppy looked up at him with big, bright brown eyes. "Yip!" And then it hopped right out again. Or tried to. The walls of the basket were much too high, so the little pot-bellied pup got stuck on his belly, and the entire basket flipped over on top of him.

Fitz blinked at the basket. Perhaps he would leave the training to his wife.

The basket scurried across the floor as the puppy blindly attempted to scamper down the hall, even waylaid by a basket cage. Fitz snickered. He might be able to see why his wife liked these little whelps so much.

Mrs. Smith chuckled. "What a wild little thing."

Fitz rescued the puppy from its basket bastille, a grin splitting his face. Yes, a wild little thing. Perfect for his wild little wife. He scooped up the puppy and held him tight to his chest again.

"I will forgo the basket, Mrs. Smith."

He strode back to the library, stifling laughter as a little tongue, wet nose, and horribly tickly whiskers launched an assault on him.

Fitz stepped into the room, his whole body shaking with the force of his chuckles. "You stop that!" he said between laughs. He looked up, three pairs of overlarge eyes staring back at him, frozen.

His laughter faded, and he smiled softly at his wife. "Surpris—"

A high-pitched squeal pierced the air, slicing straight into his eardrum. His chin jerked back. *Egads*. He hadn't realized his wife could make such a noise. Apparently, the puppy loved it, because its squirming took on an impressive new vigor.

In a blink, the puppy was whisked away from him, his wife twirling with the wriggly thing in a flurry of burgundy skirts, lavishing affectionate kisses on its nose.

"Why hullo there, sweet darling," she cooed. "Are you not just the most handsome little pudgy-poo I've ever seen?" She snuggled the puppy to her bosom, and the puppy yipped, snuggling in happily.

Fitz couldn't blame the thing. His wife's bosom was a lovely place to be.

Felicity's squeaky coos blended with his wife's. "Oh, my bloody God! Fifi, come here! This little tyke is the cutest thing I have ever seen in my entire life. I could just *die*."

Georgiana giggled, handing the puppy over to Felicity, who hastened over to Felix, and held the wriggly pup up to their brother's face, where it promptly greeted him with an abundance of puppy kisses. His deep chuckle echoed through the library. Blast and damn, Fitz's face ached like the devil from smiling.

A small, yet solid form hurled itself at him. *Oomph*. Arms squeezed around his waist, and he glanced down, meeting his wife's sparkling green gaze.

"You like him?"

"I love love love *love* him, Fitz. Thank you. He is perfect." She turned in his arms, her back pressing flat to his front, and they both took in the scene before them. The pup tripping and stumbling across the library floor as it tried to drag a pillow double its size by a tassel, Felix and Felicity crawling after the puppy on all fours.

The puppy was perfect. Seeing his family with the puppy, he found it hard to believe they'd never gotten one before now. But luckily for them, Georgiana was finding new ways to bring joy to the Jennings one great idea at a time. From chopping down trees to procuring puppies.

His wife shook against him on her inhale, followed by a small sniffle.

He spun her, searching her watery gaze. "Gigi? Micetta?"

"I am happy. I swear it. Goodness, the little thing is adorable, and I cannot wait to shower him in love. But it also just"—she shrugged, eyes welling—"Bernie," she managed hoarsely.

Fitz's heart ached for her, and he so desperately wished he could ease her hurt. "I'm sorry, Gigi." He squeezed her tight and pressed a hard kiss into her hair. "I love you," he whispered.

She pushed against his chest, leaning back and staring up at him, a stray sniffle escaping her. "I love you too, darling."

The puppy came bounding over and launched itself at Gigi's skirts, grabbing a mouthful and shaking the victim fabric in its little black muzzle. Small yips and growls blended with Georgiana's giggles.

Fitz blinked. What a ferocious little alligator.

And true to form, his fearless wife scooped the tiny alligator right up, snuggling him close to her chest.

Fitz tightened his arms around the two of them. He couldn't imagine feeling happier than he did in this moment.

52

Epilogue - Georgiana

A few days later
Chesterfield Ball
London, England

GEORGIANA SIDLED UP next to the Duke of Ironcrest where he stood like a stone gargoyle with his back against the wall of the Chesterfield ballroom. He slowly perused her figure from head to toe, his dark gaze molten. Perfect. This would do splendidly. She nearly giggled. His expression was unreadable, his scar stark against his cheek, but he seemed...curious.

"Mrs. Jennings," he murmured, looking back out at the ballroom. "Have you reconsidered my and Lord Dunmore's offer?"

She flicked open her fan and covered her mouth. "Apologies, Your Grace, but my answer remains firmly in the negative." She scanned the crowd, searching for a head of disorderly amber curls. "Plus, I happen to know you already have an assignation with Lady Camoys tonight." She winked at the Duke, and he blinked. He clearly had no idea what to do with her.

"But considering our...history," she continued. "I was hoping you could stand there with your ducal smolder on full display. You know—the one where you look as though you're going to devour a woman without even touching her."

His black brows lifted incrementally.

"I am aiming to make Mr. Jennings jealous," she said in a hushed voice. "Like back at the brothel, if you recall. You, in particular, will—let us say—light a fire in him." She nearly moaned, thinking back to that night.

Since that night, they'd been exploring each other's desires quite thoroughly. No seeking outside help—just communication and experimentation. Though she couldn't deny the pamphlets he'd gotten from his ex-mistress had been enlightening, even for Georgiana. Which was saying something.

She fluttered her fan and leaned closer to the Duke. "It is a game we play, you see. I am sure you understand the appeal of punishment."

That was one of the first discoveries they'd made together. After Georgiana nearly expired in a pile of lust when Fitz had burst into the brothel in a fit of jealous rage, she knew she needed more of *that*. More of angry mongoose Fitz. Feral Fitz. Possessive *I'm going to punish you* Fitz. And her adorable, bumbling husband? He liked to punish her. Something about the jealousy made his stumbling disappear, something primal took over him. And once he learned her limits—which were essentially non-existent—he lost all reservations.

The Duke's eyebrows were nearly at the hairline of his short, cropped locks. "You would like to use me in some sort of sex game with your husband?"

"Yes, exactly!" She bounced on her toes. "I knew you would understand. And, of course, it would be unkind of me to ask you to do so without recompense."

He tilted his head, his lips twitching ever so slightly. His eyes didn't seem as dark as usual. Was she *amusing* the Iron Duke?

"Recompense..." he questioned.

"I may have shared a few tricks with Lady Camoys." A saucy smile curved her lips. As she had said, she had learned some *very* interesting things in those pamphlets. "I think you'll be quite pleased."

His eyes widened in pure shock. He shook his head, sliding his expressionless mask back in place. "You surprise me, Mrs. Jennings. It would appear I missed quite the opportunity when you propositioned me last year."

"That you did," she said with a cheeky smile. "Oh! He's heading this way now. Hurry, seduce me!"

She blinked up at him, channeling every ounce of innocent, impressionable maiden. His lips twitched again, and he nearly—nearly!—broke into a smile. She fluttered her eyelashes and shot him her best *come now, make haste* look.

He cleared his throat and reached for her gloved hand, his thumb brushing over her knuckles as he bowed over it. "You are an absolute spitfire, Mrs. Jennings," he murmured huskily, his lips coasting over the back of hand.

She tittered, her gaze darting to Fitz. Who was mutinous. Yes! She met the Duke's gaze, and he ever so slightly tilted his head in question.

"Perfect," she whispered. "You are an utter angel."

He straightened, his furrowed eyebrows the height of disbelief.

"Fine, you are an utter devil. Thank you, Your Grace."

A hand fisted the back of her skirts, giving it a powerful tug that nearly had her stumbling. Georgiana sucked in a breath and then nearly squealed in delight.

"Your Grace," Fitz practically growled.

"Mr. Jennings," the Duke drawled. "I have been keeping your lovely wife company. We have been having the most...delectable of conversations."

Fitz's lips flattened. "Thank you for being so solicitous, but I will take it from here." His words were as stiff as his bow to the Duke.

Her husband's hand flexed on her back, and she didn't even have time to curtsy her farewell before he was already discreetly guiding her down the wall toward the exit of the ballroom.

"You will pay for that little show, wife," he murmured, lethally soft.

She practically vibrated with anticipation.

She really, really, *really* hoped she would.

GEORGIANA'S BACK COLLIDED with the wall in the dimly lit chamber, the first empty room at the Chesterfields' that she and Fitz had found. Her husband stood feet in front of her, his chest rising and falling rapidly, breath bursting from him. His cheekbones were tinted with a flush, his amber eyes pure fire. He clenched and unclenched his fists. She shivered.

"The Duke, Gigi?" He whispered the question, the promise of retribution sharp in his gravelly voice.

She dipped her chin, looking at him from beneath her lashes. "It was nothing, Mr. Jennings. I swear it."

"He. Touched. You." His palm slammed against the wall next to her head.

Oh, heavens. The vibration of the wall reverberated straight through to her core. They'd played this game before. But never with the Duke. She was going to be fucked so hard for this. She couldn't wait.

"He was merely being p-polite." Her words stumbled as his teeth grazed the shell of her ear.

His free hand slid up her body, skipping over the spots that craved his touch the most. She tried to arch into his hand when he reached her breast, but he denied her. He skipped on past until his hand settled around her throat, his thumb pushing up her chin, so she was forced to meet his penetrating gaze. His amber irises churned dangerously, like a glass of swirling whisky.

"There is only one man who touches you."

Her heart rattled in her chest, her pants echoing harshly in the quiet room.

"Who is that man, Gigi?"

Lord, she was supposed to be able to form words right now?

His hand flexed on her neck, and her knees went weak. "You answer me when I ask you a question," he demanded.

"Y-you. Mr. Jennings."

"Better," he praised, and she preened. His lips brushed over hers, his thumb gently caressing the edge of her jaw.

This man. He knew the exact right balance of punishment and praise. At first, he'd told her it was because he was nervous he was being too hard with her. He needed to offset it with softness. She'd eagerly informed him she loved the combination. He'd grown more bold, more confident. Her husband was nothing if not a quick study. And nothing made her heart swell—and her core pulse—more than a self-assured Fitz.

Her lips tingled with want. He hadn't granted her more than that one soft brush of his lips. And she was dying. She licked her aching lips, and his gaze dipped. But he denied her. He stepped back, her body going cold. She whimpered.

His hands went to his cravat, tugging, loosening the fabric. His bored gaze scanned her from head to toe, his mouth turned down, contempt arching his brows.

"You were flirting with him." He pulled his cravat free. "In full view of the *ton*. Like a fucking harlot."

She sagged against the wall. *Yum.*

He squeezed his hands into fists and let out a slow breath. She nearly smiled. He still struggled with the degradation. The things he said were delicious, the most sumptuous of desserts, but she thought he might still surprise himself each time something so cruel fled his lips.

"Is that what you are? A harlot, wife?" He stepped toward her, closing the distance. His features tightened, his gaze so sharp it was cutting.

She shook her head adamantly, her coiffure jostling dangerously.

His hands shot to her waist, and he spun her, pinning her chest flat against the wall. She turned, her cheek sliding along the smooth wall covering, trying to meet his gaze. He yanked her arms together behind her back, and cloth slid against her wrists, then cinched tight. Her body trembled, anticipation roaring through her ears, coursing through her veins.

His nose traced a path up her neck to her ear, and he gave a quick, hard tug as he knotted his cravat. "I think you lie, wife. I think you love nothing more than a thick cock down your throat." His tongue replaced his nose, trailing over the column of her neck. "Filling you." He ground his stone-hard erection against her, sending streaks of heat between her thighs. "Flooding you with cum." He growled viciously. "Mine, and mine alone."

Yes, please.

A sharp tug at her wrists had her stumbling backwards, her husband's hand curling around the back of her neck to guide her—control her. He squeezed, and the ability to stand nearly deserted her. Her gaze jumped to various pieces of furniture in the darkened chamber, finally landing on the large piece her husband was leading her to. Her eyes widened.

"Fitz," she hissed. "This is Lord Chesterfield's *study*." They couldn't do this in the man's study. It was one thing in a drawing room or broom cupboard—everyone did that. But in a man's private domain? If they were discovered...the ramifications could be horrendous.

His chuckle was dark and evil and hair-raising. He pushed her up against the lord's desk.

"That it is, love." He bent her over the desk, pressing her stomach flat against the hard surface. Rustling of skirts melded with his low rasp, "And I'm not going to just fuck you in his study, I'm going to fuck you on his desk."

She groaned, and her traitorous hips pushed back against him, seeking the press of his cock. Her heart rate kicked up, beating hard against the wood surface below her. Another discovery they had made was her husband loved the thrill of having sex in public. The risk of getting caught had always held a thrill for Georgiana, but Fitz?

Let's just say their visit to the theater had proven just how wild for it he was. He'd made her sit in the front row of his family's private box, and promptly disappeared beneath her skirts while she was left clinging to the balcony rail, desperately trying not to let her face show all the wicked things her husband's tongue had been doing to her. *He* had been hidden behind the solid balcony wall—her face not so much. Later, he informed her it had been punishment for her doing the same thing to him in his study when Felix had interrupted them.

The blunt head of his swollen cock slid between her thighs. Her muscles went instantly tight. If he wasn't in her in the next five seconds, she was going to die.

He bent over her, leaning his heavy weight on her. "I knew you were a whore," he whispered in her ear, his cock slipping easily back and forth over her, his head rubbing perfectly against where she was most sensitive. "Look at how wet you are for me. Do you ache for me, love?"

She whimpered in assent. Her fingers flexed where they were trapped between their bodies. She wanted to touch him desperately, and the denial sent lust spiraling through her. He lifted off her, his hands going to her hips. And then, like the torturous bastard he was, he sank inside her slowly. Inch by slow bloody inch. He retreated just as lazily, his thick length teasing her, her intimate muscles clenching on him, greedily trying to pull him back to her. But the devilish man continued with his slow, sensual strokes, overwhelming her with a slow, sensual stretch.

"God, you're lovely," he said, his voice hoarse. "Non credo che mi abituerò mai a quanto sia delizioso vedere il mio cazzo affondare nella tua bella fica."

I don't think I'll ever get used to how delicious it is to see my cock sinking inside your pretty cunt.

Georgiana's eyes rolled back in her head. She loved how he sometimes reverted to Italian. Filthy words were so much more potent with an accent. But the love and reverence in his voice had the need for closeness, for touch, for embrace barreling through her.

"Fitz," she whined. "I can't—I need—"

Her wrists were freed before she even finished saying the words. He pulled out of her, and she was spun and lifted onto the desk in a breath. Her legs wrapped around his hips, and he drove back inside her, his arms pulling her close, his nose sliding against hers. He knew. He always knew exactly what she needed. The compatibility they had in the bedroom almost seemed surreal. But perhaps that was what happened when you were in love.

His hips slammed into hers, his hands gripping her arse so hard it was sure to leave a bruise. He practically lifted her off the desk. Her hands fell to his biceps, straining under the effort, and her belly went molten, the pleasure in her core weaving tight.

Fitz's lips crashed into hers in a feverish kiss. His tongue delved inside, mimicking his thrusts, and her hands shot to his head, disappearing into his soft amber curls. She held him to her, matching him thrust for thrust, a battle of tongues, a battle that was building to a tumultuous pitch.

The pressure in her core surged, and her thighs scrambled around him, practically climbing him like a tree as she sought that perfect angle. She was *so close*. The pleasure was hovering just out of reach, simmering, but not boiling over. All it would take would be his cock hitting her in that spot, his hips grinding against her pulsing core. She lodged her heel in his lower back, using his arse for leverage and—she moaned—there was the angle.

He groaned into her mouth, and his hips took on a frantic pace, drilling into her. She was lost. Lost to an unfathomable void, pleasure filling her limbs from fingertips to the tips of her toes, her entire body vibrating. Her skin lit on blissful fire, and she cried out against his lips. His arms wrapped tight around her, his hips delving into her, delivering stroke after stroke of ecstasy. An ecstasy that convulsed through her like the pull of an unstoppable tide, ripping pleasure from her. His mouth fell to her neck, and he bit down, his hoarse yell buried in her skin. And God, did she love him being buried in her, his pleasure, his body, his love.

Her forehead dropped limply against his shoulder, and he sagged against her, the desk the only thing holding them up at this point.

"Well, that was all right," he murmured into her neck, gooseflesh popping up over her skin.

She huffed out a laugh, and he pulled back to look at her, his lop-sided smile in place. She tapped her lip thoughtfully. "Would most definitely shag again."

His smile turned wicked. He grabbed her wrist and dragged her hand to his already hardening cock. "That can be arranged."

Georgiana giggled. She'd created a monster.

She stroked him slowly and whispered over his lips, "I love you, Fitzwilliam Jennings."

He groaned. "I love you too, Georgiana Jennings," he managed, his voice strangled.

And then she proceeded to show him just how much. A second time.

53

Epilogue - Felicity

One day earlier...

LADY FELICITY JENNINGS'S world had just been destroyed.

She blinked dumbly at her mother. "I beg your pardon. I must have misheard..."

Mother reached out, gently taking Felicity's hand in her own, her delicate features twisting into a grimace that shouldn't have been pretty—yet it was, for her mother was a diamond, an incomparable. Just as Felicity was. She was her mother's mirror image in every way, save the shade of her hair. Instead of Mother's soft, rosy hue, Felicity blazed a fiery amber—not just in color, but in spirit as well.

"Felicity, darling. It did not mean that your father and I didn't love each other. We did."

And while the sincerity shining in her mother's eyes confirmed the words were true, the soul-crushing shock of Mama's earlier admittance drowned out all sense.

"That's a load of horse-shite."

"Felicity," her mother warned.

"No!" Felicity jumped off her mother's bed and whirled to face her. "You and Father were the perfect marriage. You were a rare, genuine love that is nearly impossible to find in our world. From the day I was old enough to dream of such things, I dreamed of a life like you and Papa had. Love and affection and *fidelity*. Good lord. Happiness, home, family. And you just told me that it was all *a lie*. I am the biggest bloody fool."

"Felicity... Just because we had lovers outside our marriage, does not mean we did not have a happy marriage, one that you would be happy with. Your father was my best friend. You and Lord Wessex could have what your father and I had."

Felicity snorted, and her mother's lips pressed in a flat white line. Mama's eyes fluttered shut, and Felicity could almost hear her mother's silent prayers for patience.

"You enjoy Lord Wessex's company—"

Felicity opened her mouth to argue, but Mother shot her a glare.

"Do not deny it. Why would you invite him to partake in your snow-ball fights and tomfoolery if it were otherwise?"

"So, I could throw balls of ice at his ballocks," Felicity grumbled.

Her mother's lips twitched. "Dear, I know you detest his caterwauling. And perhaps your father and I are to blame in all of this. We thought we were protecting you, keeping his mistress and my affair with Mr. Campbell—"

"*The stable master?*" Felicity gaped at her mother.

Mother ignored her. "But I see now it has only left you with unrealistic expectations."

The stable-master-swiving woman could say that again. Dear heavens. Mr. Campbell? That big ole Scotsman? Good Lord. She had no words. No thoughts. Her brain had deserted her.

As did her heart. Felicity rubbed her chest where the slab of muscle used to be. All the memories she held on tight to, that she closed her eyes and relived when she was dearly missing her papa, who had passed six years ago, were tainted now. The family gathered in the library playing charades. Christmastide season full of ugly waistcoat competitions and snapdragon. Picnics on their family estate in Kent, everyone sprawled out on blankets, eating pastries until they were sick to their stomach. Dinners where the not-very-rare food fight would break out. All tainted. By lies.

"Friendship in a marriage is much more important than love," her mother continued. "You and Lord Wessex get along swimmingly. That is a great start for a marriage. You can find love elsewhere, darling."

So, that was that. This conversation had started with Felicity pleading—desperately pleading—to her mother to convince Felix to allow her to back out of the betrothal contract with Lord Wessex. Her brother was adamant she marry the stupid mutton monger. And as Earl and a man—Felicity's lips curled—her brother had all the bloody sway. Felicity loved her brother. But sometimes she wanted to push him into the Thames.

She thought her mother would understand. How could her mother deny Felicity the future Mama and Papa had shared? Any mother would only want that, would want the best, for their child.

But apparently a fiancé who slept with all of London was actually exactly the future Mother thought was best for Felicity. Because that philandering fiancé was a fun chap.

Felicity supposed her only option was to speak with her fiancé then. So, they might come to a mutual understanding of what their future would look like.

Hullo, Colborn. So, I know you're fond of mixing giblets. I have a proposition for you, and I think you'll quite like it. You continue on in your merry mixing of giblets way, and I'll mix my own giblets in a separate bowl. But we'll be friends. Perhaps we might even regale each other with tales of our escapades! Capital idea, I know.

She nearly laughed.

What a bloody farce.

Thank you so much for reading *Compromised for Christmas*!

Up next is Felicity's story—releasing January 14th, 2025. Felicity has had enough. Enough of spoiled, unfaithful ducal heirs. Enough of having her pleas for escape dismissed. Now, she's taking control—with a plan that promises freedom, revenge, and the life she deserves. Her target? The Duke himself.

Want more Fitz and Gigi? You can get an exclusive BONUS epilogue that takes place seven years from now by signing up for my newsletter: https://lizzieckoz.com/compromised-for-christmas-bonus-epilogue/

Historical Notes

Ready for some fun historical facts? Let's dive right in with...dildos! Dildos have been around for a *very* long time. The earliest dildos date back to around 30,000 years ago. And many of the ones that have survived are especially ornate. There have been double-ended dildos dating back 13,000+ years ago. People have liked getting freaky since the beginning of time.

Georgiana's dildo in *Compromised for Christmas* is inspired by an ivory carved dildo from the Victorian era. If you want to see the inspiration just google: Victorian-Era Dildo Carved From Elephant Tusk. Pretty amiright? .

Besides ivory, they were made of many different types of materials—wood, siltstone, glass, silver, gold. There was even an Ancient Greek comedy *Lysistrata* where women withheld sex from men as a means to force them to negotiate peace, and then used dildos made out of leather to satisfy themselves during the protest.

They might not have vibrated yet (which was invented by physician John Mortimer Granville in the late 1870s/1880s) but some of them still had...urm...interesting features. In a French sex manual published in the 17th century, it says dildos were made hollow and filled with liquids like warm milk to simulate ejaculation.

But the research and evidence on dildos is hard to find. Fortunately, we have determined dildo historians digging up the dirty facts for us. The reason for its scarcity comes down to the age-old sex is a sin and pleasure is shameful. Throughout history there have been bans on sexual implements and erotic literature (including the piece mentioned in Fitz and Gigi's story: *Fanny Hill: Memoirs of a Woman of Pleasure* by John Cleland. Cleland was actually arrested shortly after its publication). So, dildos were kept hidden away...or destroyed.

John Wilmot, Earl of Rochester, imported dildos into England for his sex club in 1670. And they were all destroyed. Lord Wilmont also wrote the poem *Signior Dildo* which depicts various ladies of high standing engaging in sexual encounters with phallic objects instead of men. And while Wilmont seemed to be a lover of the dildo, the majority of men feared exactly what Wilmont wrote about—that dildos would replace them. Which only encouraged the ban on them. I'm rolling my eyes SO hard right now. Naturally they'd try to ban them instead of...learning how to use their own willies better.

And this brings me to the next topic I want to discuss. How accessible were these things?

Now, sexual censorship and oppression (especially during the Victorian era) did it's damnedest to try and eradicate this. But before women were as confined in sexual purity culture as they were in their corsets, there were quite a few ways women learned about pleasure. In fact, the more society sought to punish sexual gratification, the more many people seemed to rebel against it.

Lewd publications sold in huge numbers. There were smut connoisseurs with private collections. Yes, sadly, we are not the first ones to have collections of smutty books. There was a porn (though it wasn't called porn back then) network that distributed these things throughout England!

And guess who their biggest customers were? SCHOOLS. FEMALE SCHOOLS. And I quote (from Robert Morrisons *The Regency Years*) "According to the Society for the Suppression of Vice, their biggest customers were schools, and chiefly those for females, into which they would contrive to introduce these articles by means of servants."

So, yes, there were plenty of ways for women to stumble upon information about pleasure. I am sure aristocratic families held tight to their daughters and did their best to stop this from happening. But when there's a will there's a way.

This has grown longer than expected, so I'll wrap it up here. I hope you enjoyed these tidbits of scandalous history. Thank you for coming along for the ride!

Xoxo,

Lizzie

Acknowledgements

THANK YOU

First, I want to thank you, my wonderful readers, for taking a chance on a debut author. I wanted to create a feel-good book for you to cozy up with during the holidays, and I hope it brought you a few laughs and a happy heart.

This book was actually one I never planned to write—I originally wrote Felicity's book first with the intention of it being a standalone. But the Jennings cast demanded to each have their own tales. They are a unique and vibrant bunch, representing neurodivergence and LGBTQ+ identities, with a family dynamic I like to imagine could be found behind the closed doors of certain aristocratic homes.

To Caroline my critique partner. Thank you for reading the endless manuscripts, passages, and questions I throw at you. Finding someone to trust with you unpolished words isn't easy, and I couldn't ask for anyone better to help me shape something so personal and vulnerable.

To my historical romance discord group. Thank you for helping me hash out my ideas and historical conundrums— like our very long discussion about whether or not doorknobs existed in Regency homes. (They did, though mostly in newer or wealthier houses!)

To Gloria. For reviewing my Italian to ensure Fitz's filthy words were accurate and I didn't accidentally make him say *"you have the prettiest potato, kitten"* or something equally absurd. (Find her on IG: @gloria_s_happily_ever_afters)

To Christy. For keeping me sane throughout the ups and downs of the author biz, for always making me crave Subway for dinner, and for being my literal twin in so many ways it's scary. Our daily chats and plans for the future keep me motivated, and it's thrilling that we're beginning our journeys together at the same time.

To my husband. Thank you for your unwavering support—for taking days off work when possible to help me meet deadlines, for watching our son for entire weekends so I could use those days to work, for picking up my slack around the house, and for always being my biggest fan and champion.

Thank you for being here. Thank you for reading my work. Thank you, a million times over, <3

—Lizzie

About the author

Lizzie C Koz is a writer of fast-paced stories full of heat that will have you fanning yourself, and humor that will have you spitting out your wine.

She lives in New England in a fixer-upper with her husband, toddler, and Golden Retriever. When she's not writing, she's likely trying to convince her husband to tackle yet another DIY project around the house.

Lizzie loves nothing more than falling into a romance book as an outlet, especially when she was struggling through postpartum with her son. Now, she hopes to provide that same escape and small slice of joy to others.

You can find Lizzie at her website: https://lizzieckoz.com/

Instagram: @lizzieckoz

Facebook Author Page: Author Lizzie C Koz

Facebook Reader Group: The Swoonworthy Scoundrels Society